"Am I distracting you?" Krista asked.

"Ya think?" He vowed to keep his eyes on the road, but Alex's mind was mired in the past. "To set the record straight, I didn't break things off until after you accepted the job."

"You had to realize I wanted to keep seeing you until I moved," Krista said.

"What would have been the point?"

"We were having a good time together."

"The good times had to end, sooner or later."

"It would have been nice if it was later," she said.

Were they really having this conversation? Alex didn't know any other woman who talked so bluntly. Was that one of the reasons he'd been attracted to her?

"More time together would have changed nothing," he said. "You still would have moved to Europe and I still would have stayed here. What's over is over."

"What if it's not over? What would you say if I propositioned you now?" Krista asked, in the same low voice she once used when they were in bed together.

Just like that, remembered sensations assailed Alex. The smooth texture of her skin. The fresh smell of her hair. The sweet taste of her kiss.

Alex focused on another memory as he pulled the truck into the parking lot—the disappointment that Krista was leaving when things between them had barely begun.

"You won't proposition me," he said in an equally soft voice. "You won't be here long enough."

Dear Reader,

A few winters ago when the back-to-back blizzards that came to be known as Snowmageddon dumped record snowfall on the mid-Atlantic, I was stuck in South Florida.

I'd spotted a fantastic round-trip airfare and impulsively taken what I thought would be a short trip to visit family and friends. Then the snow hit, wreaking havoc and closing airports. My original return flight was canceled. So were two of my rebooked flights. Instead of staying in Florida for five days, I was there for twelve.

From that personal experience, the idea for *The Christmas Gift* was born. In my story, Krista Novak is snowbound in the Pennsylvania hometown she hasn't visited in eight years. Flights that are repeatedly canceled because of snow force her to come to terms with the pain in her past and the man she left behind.

I won't give away the meaning behind the title of the book but I will tell you what my gift was when I was stranded in Florida. While my husband shoveled a total of thirty-seven inches of snow from our driveway and sidewalks, I got to sunbathe at the beach.

Until next time,

Darlene Gardner

P.S. Visit me on the web at www.darlenegardner.com.

The Christmas Gift
Darlene Gardner

Harlequin®

TORONTO NEW YORK LONDON
AMSTERDAM PARIS SYDNEY HAMBURG
STOCKHOLM ATHENS TOKYO MILAN MADRID
PRAGUE WARSAW BUDAPEST AUCKLAND

Recycling programs
for this product may
not exist in your area.

ISBN-13: 978-0-373-71745-3

THE CHRISTMAS GIFT

Copyright © 2011 by Darlene Hrobak Gardner

www.Harlequin.com

Printed in U.S.A.

ABOUT THE AUTHOR

While working as a newspaper sportswriter, Darlene Gardner realized she'd rather make up quotes than rely on an athlete to say something interesting. So she quit her job and concentrated on a fiction career that landed her at Harlequin/Silhouette Books, where she wrote for the Temptation, Duets and Intimate Moments lines before finding a home at Superromance. Please visit Darlene on the web at www.darlenegardner.com.

Books by Darlene Gardner

HARLEQUIN SUPERROMANCE

*Return to Indigo Springs

To my husband, Kurt,
for telling me to have fun in Florida
and not complaining about digging
out of the Snowpocalypse.

CHAPTER ONE

IF NOT FOR THE CALL from the hospital, nothing could have induced Krista Novak to return to this tiny slice of Pennsylvania she'd left behind eight years ago.

With eyes gritty from eighteen hours of traveling, Krista stared out the backseat window of the taxi cab at the modest neighborhood of mostly ranch houses.

Winter had robbed the trees of their leaves and frosted the barren ground and cars parked in the street. From almost every home shone Christmas lights, some hung haphazardly, others arranged in neat, colorful patterns.

"Which house?" the taxi driver asked, two of the few words he'd spoken since picking up Krista outside baggage claim at the Harrisburg airport. Not that he'd been silent. He'd hummed along to "White Christmas," "Chestnuts Roasting on an Open Fire" and Alvin and the Chipmunks.

"The tacky place with Santa and his reindeer on the roof and the Christmas animals in the yard," Krista mumbled.

She didn't bother to add he couldn't miss it. If there were life forms in outer space, they'd be blinded by the blaze from the lighted yard decorations and the tiny multicolored lights that covered every inch of her parents' house.

"I love it!" The driver, who was probably in his late

sixties, wore a red knit cap similar to the one outlined in lights on the candy-cane cat. "That animated dancing penguin is my favorite!"

The penguin was new, as were the seals that were tossing a wrapped gift back and forth. Krista had seen most of the other animals many, many times before. Her family had been collecting them for years.

"Are you kidding me?" Krista asked. "Don't you think the display is excessive?"

The driver pulled up to the curb, turned his head and peered at her. In the darkened cab at nearly seven o'clock in the evening, it should have been hard to see his face. The glow from the yard illuminated his widened eyes. "Hell, no! It's three days before Christmas, lady."

Krista felt herself bristle. Not for the first time, she wished she'd thought to call ahead and reserve a rental car. This close to Christmas, none of the rental agencies at the airport had anything available until possibly tomorrow.

"I'm not as into the season as the rest of my family," Krista said.

The decorations had probably gone up the day after Thanksgiving. Yard art, Krista's grandmother called it. It used to take Krista's father two full days to create the monument to the season. Krista's heart clutched. This was somebody else's handiwork. Since the accident, her father couldn't so much as string lights.

Krista banished the harsh reality from her mind. She couldn't think about her father now, not when her mother was the one who was ill, not even to note that he hadn't bothered to call and tell her about it.

She let herself out of the cab and came face-to-beak

with a flamingo wearing earmuffs. Swallowing a sigh, she met the driver at the trunk of the taxi.

"Home for Christmas, eh?" the driver said.

"Yeah." Krista didn't elaborate. She certainly wouldn't tell him she hadn't been home in eight years. Krista wouldn't be here at all if her mother's phone call hadn't woken her up last night in Prague.

Her mother's voice had sounded thin, reedy and very far away. "Krista, I'm in the hospital."

Krista had bolted to a sitting position, coming jarringly awake. Her heart had thumped so hard it felt like the bed in her one-bedroom flat was shaking. "What's wrong?"

"I was, um, bleeding," her mother said.

A memory of Krista's father lying bent and broken flashed in Krista's mind. She imagined her mother tumbling down a flight of stairs, slipping on a patch of ice, accidentally gashing herself with a cooking knife.

"Are you all right?" Krista heard the panic in her own voice and tried to tamp it down. "Was it an accident?"

"No, no. Nothing like that," her mother said. "It was, um, internal."

Internal bleeding!

"Do you need me to come home?" Krista asked.

Her mother hadn't hesitated. "Oh, yes, dear. That would be wonderful."

A nurse had entered her mother's hospital room then, cutting their conversation short. As soon as Krista hung up the phone, she'd booted up her computer and booked a flight to Pennsylvania that left at six that morning. Then she'd contacted one of the friends she was supposed to meet in a few days' time for a skiing trip in the Swiss Alps to let her know what was going on.

The cab driver swung Krista's suitcase from the trunk and told her how much the fare was.

"Could you wait for me? I need you to drive me to the hospital, too." Krista's mind was so fuzzy after a full day of traveling, she couldn't be sure if she'd mentioned it. Although it wasn't yet 7:00 p.m. in Pennsylvania, it was nearly 1:00 a.m. body time. "It'll only take me a few minutes to drop off this suitcase."

"The hospital?" the driver repeated, but Krista was already rolling the suitcase up a sidewalk lined with toy soldiers and past a hippo with a red bow tied around its neck.

Krista supposed she could have asked somebody, possibly her grandmother, to make the twenty-minute drive to the Harrisburg airport to pick her up when no rental cars were available. With her parents' house in Jarrell en route to the hospital, though, it seemed to make more sense to hire a cab. Especially because Krista had discovered her cell phone was dead as she dashed to make her second connecting flight in Philadelphia.

Once Krista dropped off her luggage, the cab driver should get her to the hospital in plenty of time for visiting hours. The last she'd checked on her mother's condition, during the layover that morning in Frankfurt, her mother was stable. Krista expected her family to be at the hospital although somebody was obviously home or the lights wouldn't be blazing.

Krista dragged her suitcase up the handicap ramp and stopped in front of a door partially obscured by an enormous wreath. The doorbell was doubling as a snowman's button nose. Should Krista ring it? What was the protocol when you were the prodigal daughter?

A blast of wind almost blew Krista over. She shivered, deciding she was being ridiculous. Drawing in a deep breath of pine-scented air, she pushed open the door and stepped onto the tiny tiled foyer that opened into the living room.

It was empty aside from a floor-to-ceiling Christmas tree wrapped in gold garland and cloaked by twinkling lights and ornaments. Holly and a strand of lit plastic Santa heads outlined the fireplace. About the only tasteful thing in the room was a gorgeous framed photo Krista had never seen before of a field of wildflowers under a clear blue sky.

The scents and sounds of Christmas past assaulted Krista: honey ham, freshly baked bread, apple cider, instrumental Christmas carols, voices drifting from the kitchen.

"Hello? I'm ho—" Krista stopped midshout. Pennsylvania hadn't been home in a very long time. "I'm here."

Nobody answered, which wasn't surprising considering the noise level. Krista pulled her suitcase into the living room and headed for the large kitchen at the back of the house, her high-heeled winter boots clicking on the hardwood.

She passed under the mistletoe hanging from the archway leading to the kitchen and stopped dead.

Krista's grandmother, considerably older and possibly even shorter than when Krista had last seen her, was at the stove stirring a pot of soup. Grandma had moved in with the family after she was widowed two decades ago to help care for Krista and her younger sister, Rayna, and never left.

Sitting on a chair at the butcher-block table over-seeing the entire operation was Krista's mother. For a moment, Krista couldn't speak.

"Mom!" she finally blurted out. "What are you doing out of the hospital?"

Both women turned at the sound of her voice. Grandma gaped at Krista as if she'd materialized out of thin air. Her mother smiled and clapped her hands.

"Krista! You came!" Her mother opened her arms but didn't get up. She looked wan, and a crocheted shawl covered her shoulders.

Krista crossed the room and bent down to embrace her mother, relief making her knees weak. Unshed tears burned the backs of her eyes. "Of course I came."

Her mother hugged Krista tight, enveloping her daughter in warmth. A few seconds passed before it dawned on Krista that her mother's grip was not that of a sick woman. She drew back, examining her mother more closely.

Aside from the paleness of her complexion, Krista's mother seemed much the same as she always had. A tall, big-boned woman with dark hair showing no trace of gray, Eleanor Novak had always filled up a room with her presence.

"I thought you were bleeding internally," Krista said.

"So that's how you got our Krista to come home, Ellie." Krista's grandmother addressed her daughter-in-law but hurried from the stove to Krista's side. At about five feet tall and one hundred pounds with hair that was completely white, Krista's grandmother had an elfish charm. She added to it by wearing a Rudolph-the-reindeer shirt.

"Hey, Grandma." Krista bent down to hug the older lady while trying to make sense of her comment.

"I missed you, sweet girl," Grandma said. "We all did."

Krista felt her eyes grow moist except things weren't adding up. She drew back from the hug and swung her gaze to her mother. "I don't understand. Why aren't you in the hospital?"

Her mother's eyes shifted.

"Ellie was discharged this morning," Grandma said. Great news, but Krista couldn't make sense of it. "We're having a celebration dinner. Now the only one missing will be Rayna."

Krista's sister had only been thirteen when Krista moved away. Krista wondered where Rayna was, but another question was more pressing.

"What about the internal bleeding, Mom?" Krista asked.

Her mother still wouldn't meet Krista's eyes. "It stopped a few days ago. The medication they have nowadays is amazing."

"Most people with bleeding ulcers recover fast," Grandma said. "The doctor told Ellie this morning she's already almost as good as new."

"This morning? But last night, you made it seem like you were really sick." Krista collapsed into one of the kitchen chairs. "How could you do that? I thought you were dying."

"Okay, so it wasn't my finest moment." Her mother did not sound sorry. "But it's been eight years, Krista. How else was I supposed to get you home for the holidays?"

"You could have asked," Krista said.

"I ask every year," her mother said. "You never come."

The radio tuned to the station that played all Christmas carols, all the time, was between songs. In the rare moment of silence, Krista heard the unmistakable sound of wheels rolling on hardwood. Krista's body tensed.

Her father maneuvered the wheelchair into the kitchen, a blanket thrown over his useless legs. Although he was only five years older than his wife's fifty-seven, what hair he had left was completely gray and visible wrinkles creased his face.

"Krista?" His thick gray brows drew together. "What are you doing here?"

Krista swallowed, aware those were the first words he'd spoken to her in years. The few times he'd answered the phone when she called, he immediately handed her off to her mother. She tried not to let it hurt that he didn't seem glad to see her. "I thought mom was sick."

"Ellie called Krista from the hospital and told her she was dying," her grandmother said.

"That's not so, Joe!" her mother cried. "I told her I was bleeding."

Krista's father set his mouth in a tight line. "You shouldn't have done that."

"Why not?" her mother demanded. "Don't you think it's past time our daughter came home?"

"Our daughter can—" her father began.

"Ho, ho, ho. Merry Christmas!" The greeting was loud enough to drown out all sound.

A stranger about her father's age came into the kitchen wearing a Santa hat, a fake white beard and red suspenders that were visible through his open overcoat. He was about five-nine with a wiry build, lessening the effect.

"Welcome home from the hospital, Eleanor," the stranger said to Krista's mother. "You look fantastic!"

"Thank you, Milo," Ellie said. "You look great, too. I never get tired of seeing you in that get-up."

"One of the fringe benefits of being a mall Santa." Milo snapped the suspenders, then turned his attention to Krista. "And who is this pretty young lady?"

"Our daughter Krista. She's the interpreter who lives in Europe," her mother said. "Krista, this is our next-door neighbor, Milo Costas."

Costas? Krista didn't remember anybody named Costas living next door. She only knew one person with that surname, an unusual one for central Pennsylvania. Was this a relation?

"Nice to meet you, Mr. Costas." Krista tried to convince herself she must be wrong. Not everybody named Costas was connected to each other.

"It's my pleasure, young lady." Milo Costas commented at the same time another male voice—a *familiar* male voice—called out, "Where is everybody?"

"In the kitchen," Krista's father yelled, his scowl vanishing.

Alex Costas strode into the kitchen, a bottle of red wine in his right hand, a bottle of sparkling apple cider in his left. A good five or six inches taller than Milo, Alex had thick black hair, an athlete's build and strong, classic features. The first time Krista had seen him, she'd sworn her heart had skipped a beat. Right now it sped up.

"Did you know there's a ca—" Alex's voice trailed off midquestion, his dark gaze swinging to Krista.

Attraction rocketed through Krista, as hot and intense as when they'd been in bed together eight years ago and she'd told him about accepting a job in the Czech Republic.

He'd driven her home and told her he thought it was best if they ended things cold turkey, and she hadn't seen him again until this moment. She took a deep breath and plastered on a smile.

"Hello, Alex," she said. "Fancy meeting you here."

ALEX COMPOSED HIS FEATURES to mask the jolt of sexual energy he felt. He'd known Krista would walk through her parents' door one day but he hadn't expected it to be today. Neither could he have predicted the way his body would react to her.

"Hello, Krista," he said.

Eleanor Novak tilted her head, her eyebrows drawing together. "You two know each other?"

Alex and his father owned a landscaping business and had been buying plants and supplies from Novaks' Nursery for years. They hadn't become close friends with the Novaks, however, until Krista had already left home.

"You could say that," Krista said. "We met before I moved to Europe."

Eleanor's gaze swung to Alex. She talked about Krista semiregularly, mostly to complain that her daughter never visited. "You never mentioned that, Alex!"

Alex's father was watching him with interest. Alex had never brought up Krista to him, either.

"Wasn't much to tell." Alex shifted his weight from foot to foot.

"Where did you meet her?" Eleanor asked.

Alex zeroed in on Krista's golden-brown eyes and

recalled he could never tell what she was thinking. He didn't see any way to dodge the question. "At the nursery."

"The nursery! Oh, wait! I remember that day!" Krista's grandmother had a wonderful memory, although Alex hoped it would fail her now. "The poinsettia incident!"

Nope. His elderly neighbor's memory was working just fine.

"Alex came into the nursery for the first time," Grandma Novak continued. "He was already working with his father in the landscaping business and wanted to buy two dozen poinsettias."

"I think it was one dozen," Alex murmured.

"No, two dozen." Grandma Novak smiled so sweetly, it felt like she'd agreed with him. "Anyway, Alex was wheeling the poinsettias to his pickup when the cart overturned."

"How does Krista enter into this?" Eleanor asked.

Krista's eyes were still locked on Alex. "I was dropping by to say hey to Grandma when it happened."

So she did remember.

Alex would never forget. Krista had been wearing black boots and a winter coat, much the same as the one she had on now, except the coat had been black instead of red. She'd flipped her long, brown windblown hair back from a face that was rosy from the cold. Then she'd spotted him and smiled.

That was when the wheels of Alex's cart had bumped over a curb and the plants had slid off.

"That's right, Krista," Grandma Novak said. "You'd just gotten back from college for winter break. Dirt and poinsettia leaves went everywhere."

Alex had insisted on cleaning up, and Krista had

helped. By the time they were through sweeping up the debris, Alex had Krista's phone number and a date for the next day.

"Why didn't I hear about this before?" Eleanor asked.

Because Krista thought her mother was too involved in her life. Funny that Alex could remember the reason after all these years.

"You can't know everything about everything, Ellie," Grandma Novak said with a laugh.

"I like to be kept informed," Eleanor muttered. "Alex, what were you about to tell us when you got here?"

The strange sight had completely slipped Alex's mind. He snapped his fingers. "There's a taxi driver outside singing Christmas carols."

"Oh, I forgot!" Krista jumped up from her chair. Her hair was several inches shorter but otherwise the physical changes were negligible. Years ago Krista had told him she considered her looks average. She thought her nose was too long and her mouth too wide. Alex disagreed. Taken alone, none of her features were exceptional; together they were dazzling. "I better go pay him."

Alex had to force himself not to turn and watch her hurry from the kitchen. He set down the bottles on the kitchen counter and shrugged out of his winter jacket while his father did the same.

"I'm surprised nobody mentioned Krista was coming home." Alex's father put into words what Alex was thinking.

"I didn't know it myself until she walked in," Joe said.

"So Krista surprised you?" Milo asked.

"Only because Ellie tricked her," Grandma Novak said.

"For heaven's sake! I didn't trick Krista!" Eleanor cried. "My own daughter has a right to know I was in the hospital."

"You shouldn't have told her you were dying," Joe said.

"I did nothing of the sort!" Eleanor denied. "You better watch what you say to me, Joe. If you stress me out, my ulcers will come back."

"I talked to your doctor," Joe retorted. "He said your ulcers were caused by bacteria."

"*Probably* caused by bacteria," Eleanor said. "Not definitely."

"I'm gonna hang up my coat," Alex announced before Joe came back with another zinger. It used to seem to Alex that the Novaks were on the brink of divorce until he realized they enjoyed arguing. They were actually the most devoted couple Alex knew. Eleanor acted as Joe's nurse. Joe had cried when Eleanor had been admitted to the hospital. "Dad, can I take your coat?"

Alex's father handed over his black overcoat, then slipped off his fake white beard and gave that to Alex, too. "Can't risk getting food in my valuables."

Alex smiled and headed for the coat closet in the foyer, one ear listening for Krista's return. He admitted to himself he was angling for a moment alone with her. He stepped back to make room when she came in the front door.

In her high-heeled boots, she was only a few inches shorter than him. For a moment, they stared at each other and it seemed to Alex that electricity rather than blood flowed through his veins.

He finally found his voice. "How have you been?"

"Fine." She cleared her throat, the sound a sexy purr. "Now that I've gotten over the shock of seeing you in my parents' kitchen."

"My dad and I are here a lot," Alex said. "We couldn't ask for better neighbors."

She tilted her head quizzically. "You live with your dad? In this neighborhood?"

When she knew him, Alex had been renting a one-bedroom apartment in downtown Jarrell above a hardware store. Back then, his father had lived in an equally small condo he'd purchased after Alex's mother died and he sold the house where Alex had grown up.

"I moved in when he bought the house next door," Alex said.

"Recently?" Krista asked.

"Three years ago," Alex said.

"Nobody told me," Krista muttered.

Nobody should have to tell her. If she visited her parents even semiregularly, she'd know who their neighbors were.

She unbuttoned her coat and slipped it off to reveal a long blue sweater worn over skinny black jeans tucked into her boots. The clothes were wrinkled from traveling, but the jeans outlined the shape of her lovely legs and the sweater hugged her breasts. He took the coat from her and missed the rod on his first attempt at hanging it up.

"How long are you home for?" he asked.

"Now that I know Mom's okay," she said, "just until the day after Christmas."

The news hit Alex like a snowball to the face. Holding back his reaction would have been impossible. "You're kidding me! That's only four days. You haven't been home in eight years!"

Krista's spine stiffened and her chin lifted. "I wasn't going to come at all. I made other plans."

"Are your plans more important than being with your family?" Alex had witnessed Eleanor's tears when she talked about how much she missed her daughter. "Look at the lengths your mother went to get you here."

"You're out of line," Krista said tightly.

"Why?" Alex shot back. "Because I'm telling you something you don't want to hear?"

She glared at him.

"Alex! Krista!" Eleanor's voice drowned out the Christmas carols drifting through the house. "Time for dinner."

Alex swept a hand in front of him, calling himself a fool for maneuvering to be alone with her. "After you."

With a toss of her head, Krista preceded him into the kitchen. He fought to keep his eyes from dipping to the sway of her hips, reminding himself that what had happened between them had been very brief and very long ago.

He'd been right to break things off the instant Krista told him she was moving to Europe, no matter how wrenching the decision had been.

A woman who could stay away from her family for eight years, returning home for a few days only because she thought her mother was gravely ill, was not the one for him.

KRISTA COULD BARELY taste the honey ham she was chewing, although she was sure it met her grandma's excellent standards. Her body was still on Prague time, where it was 2:00 a.m. That wasn't all.

The mother she thought was dying sat at one end of the long dining room table, her paralyzed father at the other. Grandma smiled and laughed like nothing had changed and the only man Krista had slept with after one date was seated next to her in silent disapproval.

Krista felt like she was caught in a snow globe after it had been shaken. Her vision seemed hazy and her equilibrium off. Her temper, though, was still broiling. How dare Alex judge her when he didn't know the whole story?

"Nobody's said why Rayna isn't here." Krista and her sister weren't close. Krista had made some overtures over the years and the miles, but Rayna seldom responded.

"She's working," Alex answered. He would have been easier to ignore if he didn't smell better than the food. "The dentist is open late for the next few days."

Did that mean Rayna already had her associate's degree in dental hygiene? Krista was relatively sure her sister was still taking classes at a community college near Harrisburg but could be wrong. Krista certainly wouldn't ask, not with Alex in the room.

"Why didn't you bring your girlfriend, Alex?" her father asked.

Krista refused to acknowledge her sense of disappointment. It didn't matter to her if Alex was involved with someone. Come to think of it, why wasn't he married? Even eight years ago, it had seemed to Krista he'd been in the market for a relationship with a future.

"Alex broke up with Cindy before Thanksgiving," Krista's mother answered before Alex could. "Don't you remember, Joe?"

"How am I supposed to remember all Alex's women?" Her father sat in his wheelchair instead of one of the dining room chairs, a constant reminder that he was paralyzed from the waist down. "Seems like he has a new girl every year."

Krista thought a year was a long time. She couldn't remember the last guy she'd dated for more than a few months.

"He's looking for the right woman so he can settle down and raise a family," Ellie said. "Aren't you, Alex?"

Grandma wagged a finger at her daughter-in-law. "Don't put Alex on the spot like that, Ellie. I'm sure he doesn't like it."

"I wouldn't keep coming over here if I minded." Alex smiled at her mother, but Krista noticed he hadn't answered the question. She wondered if both Krista and her mother had Alex pegged wrong. He was thirty-two, after all. Maybe he was a serial dater, like Krista.

"You can ask me about Charlie," her grandmother said.

Krista felt like someone had just shaken the snow globe harder. Who was Charlie?

"He's auditioning to be my new beau." Grandma addressed Krista, answering one of her unspoken questions but raising others. Auditioning? "Your grandpa's been gone a long time so I figured it was time I got myself one. You'll never guess where I met him."

"The senior citizen's center?" Krista guessed.

"The internet!" Grandma announced. "Alex set up one of those computer profiles for me."

Krista gaped at him, glad for an outlet for her residual displeasure. "You got my grandma into online dating?"

"Hey, don't look at me like that." Alex waved both his hands in the air. "Online dating was Grandma Novak's idea, not mine."

Alex called her grandmother Grandma Novak?

"In my day, we went on blind dates. That's how I met my wife," Milo Costas said. With his olive complexion, dark hair and angular features, he resembled a smaller, older version of his son. Milo's dark eyes fastened on Krista. "She died when Alex was nineteen."

Why hadn't Krista known that? She searched her memory but couldn't remember Alex mentioning his mother in the past. Then again, they'd probably known each other better in bed than out of it. "I'm sorry," Krista told Milo.

"Don't be sorry for me," Milo said. "I have my memories, my son and great next-door neighbors. It's a wonderful life."

Grandma laughed. "Milo works that line in every year. It's his favorite Christmas movie."

"It's his favorite movie, period," Alex said. "The dogs we had when I was growing up were named George and Bailey after the Jimmy Stewart character."

"That's right," Milo said. "I got your grandmother to stock it at the store, too. The holiday movies are big sellers."

Krista put down her fork, the better to concentrate on the conversation. "People buy movies at the nursery?"

"Not the nursery, the Christmas Shoppe," Milo said.

Krista blinked, trying to dispel the haze clouding her brain. "What Christmas shop?"

"The one your grandmother runs next door to the nursery," Milo said.

The fog Krista was trying to plow through got even

thicker. Beside her, she could almost hear Alex asking why she hadn't known about the store.

"We opened November first." Grandma seemed to sit taller in her seat. "Our specialty is lighted yard art."

Considering her grandmother's love of Christmas, the shop was a logical extension of the nursery business. Had Krista really been so out of touch that the new venture hadn't come up in conversation? She talked to her mother every month or so, although lately Krista made excuses to get off the phone when her mother started pressuring her to visit.

"Why don't you come see the shop tomorrow, Krista?" Grandma asked. "If you want, you can even help. We have a lot going on."

"Sure," Krista said through a tight-lipped smile. She would prefer avoiding the nursery altogether but would never admit that to her grandmother.

"Great!" Her grandmother clapped her hands. "I'm going to love having you home! I might not let you go back after the new year."

"If she stays that long," her father muttered.

"Of course she's staying!" Krista's mother exclaimed. "It's the holidays. There's no reason for Krista to hurry back to Europe."

Krista avoided looking at Alex. "Actually, there is. I'm supposed to meet friends in Switzerland the day after Christmas for a ski trip."

"You can't go back that soon!" Krista's mother insisted.

Krista steeled herself against her mother's protests. As soon as she was through with dinner, Krista intended to book her return flight. She wouldn't be in Pennsylvania at all if her mother hadn't manipulated her. "I already paid for the trip, Mom. The reservation's nonrefundable."

Krista's mother stuck out her lower lip. "What if I were still in the hospital?"

"You're not," Krista's father interjected. "Leave the girl alone, Ellie. If Krista has to go back, she has to go back."

Krista reached for her glass of water to wash down the tight feeling in her throat. Next to her, she was aware of Alex watching her silently.

So much had changed since Krista had left Pennsylvania, yet one thing remained constant—her mother didn't want her to leave, but her father couldn't wait to shove her out the door.

Krista didn't blame him, especially because she was the one who'd put him in the wheelchair.

CHAPTER TWO

KRISTA WOKE TO THE SOUND of silver bells.

As a child snuggled under her warm blankets, Krista used to listen for the bells until she fell asleep. They'd dangled from the wreaths that hung from her bedroom window, tinkling together with every gust of wind.

Krista's room had been her refuge while she was growing up. She'd never tired of the glow-in-the-dark yellow stars her father had put up on the ceiling, insisting that one day she'd travel to the moon. In her teens, she'd plastered the walls with posters of more realistic places to visit—Venice, Paris, Rome, London.

Now that bedroom was a home office, and Krista was sleeping on the sofa bed in the basement recreation room. So why had she still heard the bells?

They jingled again. Pushing the cloud of hair from her face, Krista sat up in bed. Something sleek and white leaped onto the chair opposite the sofa bed and stared at Krista from glistening green eyes. It was a cat with bells on its red collar. Since when did her family have a pet?

"Where did you come from?" Krista asked aloud.

With sinewy grace, the cat jumped down from the chair and disappeared, the bells tingling together in its wake. Krista was about to lie back down when she caught sight of the bedside alarm clock.

Nine o'clock!

She didn't even sleep that late in Prague, where it was already partway through the afternoon. Krista should have asked what time to be ready to leave for the Christmas shop and set an alarm.

She scrambled out of the sofa bed and hurried to her open suitcase. Since it was carry-on size, her wardrobe choices were limited. She yanked out dark slacks and a plain red sweater that was as Christmassy as her wardrobe got.

Ten minutes later, after using the bathroom in the basement that was adjacent to her sister's empty bedroom, Krista hurried up the stairs. The smell of brewing coffee assailed her before she reached the kitchen.

A young woman sat at the kitchen table, her hands wrapped around a coffee mug, her long blond hair parted in the middle and tucked behind her ears. A newspaper was spread in front of her but she didn't appear to be reading it.

If they'd been anywhere but inside the house, Krista might not recognize the woman as her sister, Rayna. The twenty-one-year-old's face was thinner and her hair much lighter than when Krista had last seen her.

Feeling her mouth curving into a smile, Krista started toward her sister. "Rayna! You're so grown up!"

Rayna lifted her large dark eyes from her coffee mug. Her lips were unsmiling, her body language distant. "I heard you were home."

Krista stopped midstride, her hands dropping to her sides. She blinked sudden moisture from her eyes, annoyed with herself. Only a fool would expect a warm welcome after so many years apart. "I got here last night but crashed early because of the time difference."

Rayna said nothing.

Krista cleared her throat. "I came because Mom called me and made it seem like she was really sick."

"A few days ago, she *was* really sick. Her skin was gray and she was so run-down she could barely stand." Rayna's eyes didn't waver from Krista's face. "Then she started vomiting blood. Nobody knew why when we got her to the emergency room."

Krista hugged herself, disturbed by the frightening scenario her sister was describing. "The doctors must have figured it out pretty quickly."

"Not until the endoscopy. Even after they put her on medicine, she was too weak to get out of bed. They kept her in the hospital for three days."

Some of the annoyance Krista had felt at her mother the day before faded. "I didn't know any of that."

"Yeah, well, it's not like you live around here," Rayna said.

Even though the statement was true, it felt like a criticism.

Rayna's eyes dipped to the newspaper. It was open to the sports page, the section Krista usually skipped. Was Rayna into sports? She hadn't been as a child. She didn't have a cat, either, although Krista's guess was that the one downstairs was hers.

"Where is Mom?" Krista asked.

Rayna didn't look up. "She and Grandma left early for the nursery."

Krista had missed her grandmother, just like she thought. She hadn't considered her mother would be working at the shop today, too.

"Shouldn't Mom be resting?" Krista asked.

"Sure should," Rayna mumbled, eyes still on the page.

The topic was too important to let her sister's lack

of response dissuade her. "Then why isn't she?" Krista persisted.

"Mom promised she'd take it easy," Rayna said.

"Will she?" Krista asked.

"Probably not."

"Maybe I can make sure she doesn't overdo it," Krista said, thinking aloud.

Rayna's eyes finally flickered upward. "Yeah. You do that."

Krista tried not to take offense. She couldn't expect her sister to instantly trust her. "Is Dad still here? Maybe I can hitch a ride with him."

"Dad doesn't drive, Krista," Rayna said dryly.

Krista should have expected that. Her parents had purchased a handicap-accessible van before Krista moved to Europe but it hadn't been equipped with hand brakes. Once again Krista wished she'd thought to reserve a rental car. "How will he get to work?"

"The Christmas Shoppe isn't his thing." Rayna waved an arm in a dismissive gesture. She wore a sterling silver bracelet with a heart-shaped charm dangling from it. Inside the charm was the name Trey. Was he Rayna's boyfriend?

"But the nursery's still open, right?" Krista asked. Her parents typically closed the business in January and February and reopened in March.

"They shut down early because of the Christmas Shoppe," Rayna said. "Good thing, too. We've had a lot of ice this month. It's hard for Dad when the weather's bad."

The first winter their father had been in a wheelchair, he'd struggled to get around. Krista hadn't expected him to become a wheelchair whiz since then, but it hadn't occurred to her that he'd be housebound.

"Where is Dad?" Krista asked.

"In his office," Rayna said. "But don't go in there. He doesn't like being disturbed."

So their father wasn't only housebound, he was also a recluse. Suddenly in need of sustenance, Krista moved across the kitchen to the coffeemaker and poured herself a cup. Rayna closed the newspaper and stood up. At thirteen, she'd been as tall as Krista and spindly. Now she topped Krista by a few inches and her figure verged on voluptuous.

"I've gotta get to work," Rayna said.

"So you got your degree?" Krista ventured.

"No." Rayna's head shook slightly as she regarded Krista. "I got a part-time office job at a dental practice while I finish school."

The implication was that Krista should have known that. In reality, Krista wasn't even sure how Rayna had escaped getting roped into going into business with their parents at the nursery. "That's great."

"Whatever." Rayna started to walk out of the kitchen.

"Rayna, wait," Krista called. Her sister stopped but didn't turn, making it even harder to ask for a favor. "Can you drop me at the shop on your way to work? Or someplace where I can rent a car?"

"The rental agency's too far away," Rayna said, "and work's in the opposite direction."

Before Krista could figure out where that left her, dogs started barking to the tune of "Jingle Bells." The doorbell.

"That'll be Alex," Rayna said.

"Alex?" Some of the coffee in Krista's cup sloshed onto her hand. If it hadn't been lukewarm, she would have gotten burned. "What's he doing here?"

"Grandma asked him to pick you up." Rayna walked the rest of the way out of the room, leaving Krista to answer the summons.

The irony didn't escape her that the man who'd criticized her last night was willing to give her a ride to the shop when her own sister was not.

THE FIVE MILES BETWEEN the Novaks' house and their business traversed a rolling stretch of rural road that led to the sprawling downtown of Jarrell.

Alex drove his company pickup past a diner, a dry cleaner, a hardware store and a bank branch clustered within a few blocks. Giant fake snowflakes decorated the light poles, which he thought provided a nice festive touch.

"Not much has changed around here, has it?" Krista asked.

Jarrell's population was less than five thousand but the town was only thirty minutes south of the city center of Harrisburg. Anything Alex needed, he could get without driving more than a half hour, including streams to fish, trails to hike and mountainous scenery to photograph.

"Some of us think that's a good thing," Alex said.

"I was never one of them," Krista said. "When I left, I felt like the town was smothering me."

"You said you'd suffocate if you didn't leave." Alex braked at a red light at the intersection where his favorite bakery was located. Sometimes in the mornings, he dropped in for a cinnamon-raisin bagel topped with cream cheese, one of the simple pleasures of life.

"I'm surprised you remember that," Krista said.

Alex could call the moment instantly to mind. They'd been lying naked in each other's arm, having just made love. Her cheeks had been flushed, her hair awry, her lips well-kissed. Alex had been about to surprise her with tickets to a concert at the Forum in Harrisburg, but he'd never gotten around to it. There wasn't any point. The concert had taken place the day after she left town.

"Probably because it's the opposite of how I feel about Jarrell," he said. "The clean air makes breathing easy for me."

"Lots of places have clean air," Krista said.

"Only one of them is home," Alex said, then felt frustrated at himself for getting in the last word. They weren't arguing. He liked living in Jarrell and she preferred Europe. End of story.

The light turned green and he stepped on the accelerator, but not before noticing she'd lost none of the vibrancy that had first attracted him to her. She filled up the truck with her presence, her skin glowing with health, her hair shiny clean. Dressed in the red coat, she looked even more alive.

"I'm surprised you agreed to drive me," Krista remarked.

"Happy to do it," Alex said.

"Oh, come on," she drawled. "Why don't you just admit Grandma twisted your arm?"

Alex's eyes left the road. She gazed back at him, her expression challenging. For a woman who should be suffering from jet lag, she was surprisingly lucid.

"You believe in speaking your mind, don't you?" Alex asked.

"You didn't mince words yesterday. Or just now, for that matter," she pointed out. "It's obvious you disapprove of me."

Alex focused in front of him, unwilling to be

drawn into an argument. "You were right last night. I shouldn't have criticized you."

"But you meant what you said?"

"I did," he confirmed. In his rearview mirror, Alex noticed a black SUV that was following too closely. The driver had a cell phone to his ear. "But I heard your mom at dinner. She doesn't need me to speak for her. She does a pretty good job herself."

Krista laughed, the last thing he expected.

"I guess my mother and I have something in common, after all," Krista said. "So while we're being outspoken and clearing the air, let's hear why you dumped me."

Alex abruptly turned to Krista, not able to determine from her expression if she were joking. "I didn't dump you! You moved to the Czech Republic."

"You dropped me like a hot potato two weeks before that." She gasped and pointed at the road. "Red light!"

They were approaching a traffic light that was turning from yellow to red, but Alex only had one choice because of the SUV on his bumper. He kept his foot steady on the gas and went through the intersection. Behind them, the SUV came to a screeching stop.

"You ran that red light!" Krista said.

"It was safer than stopping." Alex counted himself lucky he didn't hear a police siren. How could he explain missing the red light when he'd driven this route thousands of times?

"Am I distracting you?" she asked.

"Ya think?" He vowed to keep his eyes on the road, but his mind was mired in the past. "To set the record straight, I didn't break things off until after you accepted the job."

"You had to realize I would have liked to keep seeing you in those two weeks before I moved," Krista said.

"What would have been the point?" he asked.

"We were having a good time together."

"The good times had to end, sooner or later."

"It would have been nice if it was later," she said.

Were they really having this conversation? Alex didn't know any other woman who talked so bluntly. Was that one of the reasons he'd been attracted to her?

"More time together would have changed nothing," he stated. "You still would have moved to Europe and I still would have stayed here."

"I suppose," she said, a sigh in her voice. "But it's not like we had a commitment."

The few weeks they'd known each other had been enough time for Alex to suspect he wanted more from Krista than sex. Her surprise announcement that she was leaving had forced him to conclude he hadn't known her at all.

"Why didn't you mention you were considering moving to Europe?" Alex posed the question he should have asked back then.

"I wasn't," Krista said. "The job offer came from out of the blue, and I accepted on the spot."

Alex hadn't seen it coming. One day, he was dating a woman with a semester left at a college less than three hours away in Philadelphia. The next, she was moving across the Atlantic Ocean.

Looking back on it, Alex had envisioned the same future for Krista that her mother had. She was a business major at the University of Pennsylvania and her parents owned a nursery. It seemed a given that she'd eventually join the family business, perhaps because that was the choice Alex made.

No, he hadn't known Krista well at all.

"You sound like you have no regrets," he said.

"Not about moving," Krista replied. "But if I had it to do over again, I'd wait a lot longer before telling you I was taking the job."

The last mile before they reached the nursery was on a fairly steep road with a narrow shoulder. Krista didn't sound as if she were teasing, but Alex couldn't risk a glance at her to find out.

"We still would have had an expiration date," he said.

Krista agreed. "But think of the fun we could have had in the meantime."

Alex would rather not. "What's over is over."

The paved parking lot that served both Novaks' Nursery and the adjoining Christmas Shoppe came into view, half-filled with cars even though it was barely past ten o'clock. Alex switched on his turn signal and slowed down.

"What if it's not over? What would you say if I propositioned you now?" Krista asked in the same low voice she once used when they were in bed together. Just like that, sensations assailed him. He could recall the smooth texture of her skin. The fresh smell of her hair. The sweet taste of her kiss.

Alex focused on another memory as he pulled the truck into the parking lot, found a space and shut off the ignition—the disappointment that Krista was leaving when things between them had barely begun.

"You won't proposition me," he said in an equally soft voice. "You won't be here long enough."

KRISTA COULDN'T IMAGINE what had possessed her to say those suggestive things to Alex.

Sure, the abrupt way he'd cut things off with her eight years ago had stung. And, yes, he'd crept into her thoughts over the years. He remained the one and only man who'd ended a relationship before she had.

Maybe that was why whatever was between them didn't feel as though it were over.

She pulled on the fur-lined black leather gloves she'd taken off during the drive and prepared to be gracious. With only a few days remaining before she left Jarrell, Krista wouldn't be spending much time— if any—with Alex.

"Thank you for the ride," she said.

He dipped his dark head in a formal little bow. "Like I said, it was my pleasure."

No wonder she'd fallen for him, Krista thought. She'd always been a sucker for guys with good manners.

"See you around," she said and got out of the pickup.

Almost immediately she heard the driver's door open and shut. Alex strode around the pickup, joining her on the path leading to the nursery.

"You don't need to walk me to the door," Krista said.

"I'm not." Alex's breath was visible in the frosty air. "I'm working at the shop today, too."

She noticed that he was carrying a black athletic bag over his shoulder. "Doing what?"

"You'll see soon enough," he said.

"A mystery," Krista said. "You know how much I love them."

Years ago they'd discovered they shared a passion

for true-crime books and classic whodunits. They both considered Alfred Hitchcock to be a genius.

Up ahead, the blooms that added color to the nursery yard in the spring and summer were gone. A few empty crates and leafless trees in burlap bags added to the barren feel. A few steps farther, however, the atmosphere underwent a dramatic change.

A charming wood sign hung suspended from a post. It was painted red and featured a winking elf and white lettering that spelled out Novaks' Christmas Shoppe.

Past the sign was a covered entranceway lined with poinsettias that transported Krista back to her first sighting of Alex. He hadn't been the only one who was gobsmacked. If Alex hadn't overturned the cart, she would have found another reason to talk to him.

He looked even better now than he had then. With his height and broad shoulders, he still cut an impressive figure. But he'd let the black hair that went so well with his olive complexion and dark-as-night eyes grow a little longer. His hair curled at the ends, a soft touch that made his lean face appear even more masculine.

Alex placed his hand at the small of her back. She nearly jumped, even though there was a coat and a sweater between his hand and her skin.

Who was she kidding? She was still as sexually attracted to Alex as she'd been as a twenty-one-year-old. Her candid talk when she'd propositioned him in the car had been more than just talk.

"Your family decided not to use the nursery's retail space," Alex said, then indicated the expansive structure that was just past it. "The Christmas Shoppe is in the old storage building."

The revelation drove all other thoughts from Krista's mind. Though sizeable, the storage building was dank and dark. It had been her least favorite place whenever she worked at the nursery, which was saying something.

"Both your mom and grandma are proud of the job they've done with the place," Alex said.

Was he warning her not to hurt their feelings by making a tactless remark? As though she'd do such a thing. Krista schooled her features while he opened the door to the strains of the Christmas song about grandma getting run over by a reindeer.

Alex chuckled, and Krista felt the warmth of his breath on her neck as she preceded him into the shop. "Grandma Novak plays that song at least a couple times a day," he said.

Krista stopped dead. She'd expected the place to be lit up like a candelabra. She hadn't anticipated the place to be tasteful. The ceiling was gold, the walls red. Gaily bedecked artificial trees competed for space with shelves neatly packed with colorful ornaments and holiday decorations.

"Krista! Alex!" Grandma Novak must have been watching for them. She rushed to their side, wearing a long red skirt and a matching jacket trimmed with white fur. "What do you think of the store, Krista?"

"It's fantastic," Krista said truthfully. "Really impressive."

"Grandma Novak drew up the plans herself." Alex sounded like a proud grandson. "She knew exactly how she wanted it."

"Today I'm not Grandma Novak." She pushed her glasses up her nose. "I'm Grandma Claus."

"You look the part," Krista said. "Love the outfit."

"I've sold four of these getups this week." Grandma

lowered her voice. "You wouldn't believe the kinds of things customers buy. Get a load of this."

She led them to the end of a nearby aisle and picked up one of an identical stack of boxes. It contained a mechanical Santa holding together the edges of a fur-trimmed red cape. Grandma pressed a button, and Santa gyrated to the tune of "Santa, Baby." He opened the cape wide. Underneath he wore nothing but green boxer shorts adorned with twinkling Christmas lights.

"It's a flashing Santa!" Grandma exclaimed. "It's a bestseller!"

A deep, inviting laugh bubbled up from Alex that Krista felt reverberate down to her toes.

"Are you going to buy one of those for Charlie?" Alex asked in a teasing voice.

"No! Never!" Grandma exclaimed. "But I can't think about Charlie. Not when Burton's stopping by the store."

"Burton?" Krista said. "I thought you were interested in Charlie?"

"I am." Grandma threw up her hands. "But what was I supposed to say to Burton when he saw my profile and asked to meet me?"

"No," Krista suggested. Her grandmother really did not have the hang of online dating.

"On that note," Alex said, "I'm gonna change."

Change into what? Krista wondered. Before she could ask the question, she got distracted watching Alex leave them with his sexy, hip-rolling walk. The attraction was still going strong, she admitted.

Her grandmother grabbed Krista by the hand. "I'll give you a quick tour before I put you to work."

Talking so fast her words nearly ran into each other, Grandma showed Krista sections of the store that contained lighted yard art, personalized ornaments, collectibles and Nativity scenes. The biggest surprise was the ball crawl tucked away in a far corner, its pit filled with green and red balls.

"What a good idea!" Krista exclaimed. "If you get children into the store, you'll make sales to their parents."

"It was Alex's idea," Grandma said. "He got us to make up flyers and post them around town. I don't know what we'd do without him."

Even when Alex was out of sight, Krista thought, someone brought him to mind.

"We're starting the children's activities soon," Grandma said. "Do me a favor and try to convince your mother to run the ball crawl. We've got a chair over there."

Krista's mother was at the cashier's desk, fur-trimmed reindeer antlers sticking from her head. She didn't have much color in her face aside from the splotches of rouge on her cheeks, but her eyes were bright.

"Darling, you made it!" her mother cried. "We can use the extra hands today. I've got a feeling our Santa Claus is going to be very popular."

She indicated a point over Krista's shoulder. The tall man in the red suit heading their way was lean and muscular instead of soft and round. His posture and manner of walking were familiar. Krista squinted to see past the white beard.

"Is that Alex?" Krista asked.

"Isn't he a dear?" Grandma replied. "Milo was already booked at the mall so Alex said he'd step in."

"After you begged him," her mother said.

"I didn't beg. I bribed him with Christmas cookies."

Her grandmother went to meet Alex, who was already gathering a small group of children in his wake. Taking him by the arm, she led him to a thronelike chair that hadn't been on Krista's tour of the shop. The children talked excitedly and jostled for better positions in the line that was forming.

"Time for me to switch places with your grandmother. I'm on crowd control." Krista's mother emerged from behind the cash register, preparing to enter the fray.

Krista laid a hand on her mother's arm, waylaying her. "Let's trade jobs, Mom. If you run the ball crawl, you'll be able to sit down."

"I don't need to sit down."

"Yes, you do," Krista said firmly. "You just got out of the hospital, and you promised Rayna you'd take it easy."

"That snitch!" Her mother crossed her arms over her chest, gnawing thoughtfully at her lower lip as she openly surveyed Krista. "If I let you manage the line, you can't do it looking like that."

Krista sighed and stuck out her hand. "I'll put on the antler ears."

"I've got a better idea." Krista's mother crossed to a nearby display, plucked a package from the shelf and held it up. The illustration on the front showed a curvaceous model wearing green tights and a short red dress. "You can be Santa's elf. Won't that be fun?"

CHAPTER THREE

THE BABY WAITING IN LINE to see Santa Claus was seriously lacking in Christmas spirit.

No more than six months old, she was an adorable little thing with wisps of dark hair and big brown eyes that dominated her face. She'd be cuter if her fists weren't clenched and her wails weren't loud enough to drown out the holiday music.

"That baby has an excellent set of lungs." The speaker was a beautiful blonde in an eye-catching burgundy coat who Krista had noticed browsing the store aisles.

"Good stamina, too," Krista said.

The little girl refused to be soothed no matter how much her mother cooed to her and bounced her. With a start, Krista recognized the mother as an acquaintance from high school. Once upon a time, before Krista had lost touch with everybody in Jarrell, she and Tracy Timmons had served on the high-school-yearbook committee together.

"I'm sorry." Tracy apologized to the children in line and their waiting parents, not for the first time. "I'd leave but my little boy is next."

Her son was a serious child of about four years old who kept his eyes straight ahead, probably for fear Tracy would pluck him out of line before he got his turn with Santa Claus. He rushed forward the instant the child ahead of him was through.

"Don't move 'til I get a picture." Tracy balanced the wailing baby on one hip while attempting to focus her camera. Before Krista could offer to hold the baby, Tracy thrust the child at Alex. "Would you hold her, Santa? That way I can get both kids in the shot."

Alex didn't have a choice. He took the baby and settled her on his knee, his hand supporting her back, his white teeth showing through his beard. The baby stared up at him out of watery eyes and quieted.

"Would you look at that?" Krista remarked to no one in particular. "It's a Christmas miracle."

Laughter sounded from behind Krista. The blonde. Tall and slender with the bone structure of a fashion model, the other woman was even prettier when she was amused.

"It's no miracle," the woman said. "It's Alex."

"You know Santa?" Krista asked.

"I'm here because of Alex," the woman said. "See the blond boy in line? That's my five-year-old son, Derrick. He chickens out every time I take him to see Santa. I'm hoping this time will be different."

"Alex is really that good with kids?" Krista asked.

"Look how that baby loves him." The blonde gestured to the little girl, who was laughing and tugging on Alex's white beard. "When Alex and I were together, my nieces and nephews couldn't get enough of him. Neither could I."

That didn't sound like something a married woman would say. Krista checked the blonde's left hand for rings. It was bare except for the faint outline of pale skin on her fourth finger.

"Alex is an ex-boyfriend, not my ex-husband." The

woman had misinterpreted Krista's look. "It never went far between us, probably because he was on the rebound."

Krista couldn't stifle her curiosity. "I didn't realize Alex had been serious about anyone."

The woman's expertly made-up eyes widened. "Do you know him well?"

Krista squashed a sudden impulse to lie. "Hardly at all."

The blonde seemed to relax. "Alex and I knew each other in high school but we didn't date until a couple of years after graduation. I was crazy about him, but some woman did a number on him. I think she moved to Paris or someplace like that."

Krista inhaled sharply. It would be easy to confuse Prague with Paris after so many years had passed.

"Funny how these things work. I married the very next guy I dated. Our divorce was final last month," the woman continued. "Oh, look! Derrick's next!"

The woman dug her camera from her stylish black leather purse and hurried past Krista. Derrick hung back, his feet frozen in place. Alex patted his knee.

"You're a pretty big boy," Alex called to him. "Just promise not to squash me. Okay?"

"Okay," Derrick parroted, a giggle in his voice. He ventured forward and climbed on Alex's lap.

A flash went off and then another as the blonde snapped photos. Tracy spotted Krista and they exchanged pleasantries before her baby started crying again. It wasn't much quieter after Tracy left the store. Conversation hummed and carols played, making it difficult for Krista to puzzle through what the chatty blonde had told her.

Krista didn't think she'd "done a number" on Alex. But who else could the blonde have meant?

The timing was right, but everything else about the blonde's theory seemed wrong. Krista and Alex had only dated for two weeks. If he'd had strong feelings for her, wouldn't he have asked her to reconsider moving to Europe?

"Excuse me, but could you tell me where to find Leona Novak?" The man asking the question was roughly her grandmother's age. He'd lost most of his hair, but not his appeal. His chin was strong, his cheekbones high, his forehead wide.

This had to be Burton. His smile and the hint of mischief in his eyes made him immediately likeable. Grandma, it seemed, had made a good decision.

Krista shoved aside her questions about Alex and gave Burton her full attention. "She's behind the cash register."

"Oh, yes. I see her now," he said. "She's even lovely dressed as Mrs. Claus, isn't she?"

Krista had been under the impression her grandmother and Burton had never met. "You already know my grandmother?"

"Your grandmother? Then you must be Krista." He affected a bow. "I'm Charlie Crosby, your grandmother's suitor. I stopped by to surprise her."

Charlie? Not Burton?

"Nice to meet you, Charlie," Krista said, the wheels in her brain turning. Burton could show at any time. "I've heard about you, too."

"That's a good sign." Charlie winked at her. "Hopefully your grandmother is as smitten with me as I am with her."

He tipped his nonexistent hat and sauntered away.

The blonde was finally through snapping photos. She lifted her son from Alex's lap, planting a lingering kiss on Alex's cheek before she straightened.

It very much seemed like the blonde wanted Alex back. Krista couldn't worry about that now, not even to puzzle through why she was concerned about it.

She needed to figure out how to keep her grandmother's men from bumping into each other.

"IT'S LOVELY TO SEE YOU again, Alex." Julia Merrifield lingered beside the Santa display when it was time to break for lunch. "I'm so glad I ran into your dad and he told me you'd be here. You were awesome with Derrick."

Alex returned his attention to Julia from where Krista was talking to an elderly man in a trench coat. His white hair stuck up like the mad scientist in the *Back to the Future* movies.

"Derrick must have been ready to sit on Santa's lap this year," Alex said. "Look how eager he was to get to the ball crawl with that friend of his."

"That could be true." Julia leaned toward him. "But you *are* pretty great."

"Thanks." Alex wasn't sure what else to say. Julia was warm, caring and indisputably gorgeous. He had no desire to get involved with her again, though. Eleanor Novak had been on the mark about his desire to settle down and raise a family. On some level, he'd always wanted that. As the years went by and he got older, the realization had grown stronger.

Considering Julia's numerous positive qualities, she should have been the perfect woman for him. Alex still couldn't explain why she wasn't.

Neither was Krista, who'd be thousands of miles

away in just a few days. That fact didn't stop Alex from thinking about her proposition every time he looked at her. The elf dress didn't help. Even wearing green stockings, she looked damned sexy.

"Will I see you at Timeout after Christmas?" Julia named a local sports bar popular for its happy hours and the variety of beers it served. "You've probably heard Malt Green is getting the old crowd together."

"I didn't know Malt was in town," Alex said slowly. He and Malt had once been as close as brothers, sharing a love for mountain bike riding and landscape photography. "How is he?"

"You two didn't keep in touch?" Julia sounded surprised. "He's doing fantastic. His company's really taken off so he says he can afford better than malt liquor."

"Good for him." Alex had to force out the words, although he wished Malt nothing but the best.

Julia wrinkled her nose. "Am I remembering wrong or didn't you used to talk about going into business with him?"

Together Alex and Malt had dreamed up a company that sold calendars and date books depicting professional-quality landscape photographs. Malt now ran Greenscapes Ltd. alone out of Toronto.

"I joined my dad's landscape business instead." Alex reminded himself it was the right decision.

"I imagine you're great at it." Julia affixed a bright smile to her face. "I better get Derrick out of the ball crawl. Hope to see you at Timeout."

Alex nodded but didn't commit. "Catch you later."

The moment Julia was gone, Alex zeroed in on Krista. She was still with the man in the trench coat, but it now seemed as though they were dancing.

When the man stepped to his left, Krista countered by moving to her right. When the man went right, she stepped left.

Whatever was going on, it was too intriguing to resist.

"I keep telling you I don't want an artificial tree!" the man exclaimed, loud enough that Alex could hear him as he approached.

"How can you be sure until you look at them? If you don't care to buy now, pick one out for our after-Christmas sale." Krista noticed Alex and grabbed him by the arm. "We have a fabulous selection. Don't we, Santa?"

Alex felt like a conspirator who didn't know what the end game was. "We sure do."

"I'm not here to look at trees," the man protested. "I'm here to see Leona Novak."

"I've already told you," Krista said, "I'm not sure where she is."

As far as Alex knew, Grandma Novak hadn't budged from the cashier's station. "I think she's—"

An elf shoe kicked Alex in the shins.

"Ow," Alex said.

"Why don't I try to find her for you? In the meantime, Santa, will you show *Burton* the trees?" Krista put emphasis on the man's name.

"But he doesn't want—" Alex began. Krista squeezed his arm hard, causing him to lose his train of thought.

"Excuse us a moment," she told the man and pulled Alex aside. Her hair smelled great, as clean as a winter breeze. Alex was tempted to take her in his arms and breathe in the scent. He doubted she'd be amenable to that at the moment.

"You're not taking the hint," she hissed. "I want you to distract that man, not take him to Grandma."

"Why?"

"It's *Burton*." Krista obviously expected him to know who that was. He shrugged to convey that he didn't. "Come on! Burton! The man she met online and told he could stop by the shop."

Oh, yeah. Now Alex remembered. "So what's the problem?"

"Charlie Crosby's here," Krista said. "I need to get Charlie out of the store before he sees Burton."

Her logic still didn't compute. "What's the big deal if the two men run into each other?"

Krista settled her hands on her hips, in the place where the hem of the elf dress started to flare. She shook her head, and her long brown hair swung. "Burton could mess things up for Grandma with Charlie."

"Or he could start a healthy competition," Alex countered. "Maybe Grandma Novak even arranged to have both men here at the same time."

"Charlie told me he came by to surprise her. Besides, Grandma hasn't dated in twenty years! Believe me, the woman doesn't know what she's doing." Krista narrowed her eyes. "Now are you going to help me or not?"

The fire in her expression warned Alex what she'd think of him if he refused. "Okay. I'll distract Burton."

"Thank you." She smiled at him and bustled off, taking a circuitous path, probably so Burton wouldn't gaze in the direction of the cashier's station.

Alex adopted a helpful expression. He rejoined Burton, whose face was pinched underneath his wild mop of white hair.

"Don't you dare try to show me any trees," Burton said.

"Hey, I'm Santa Claus," Alex tried reminding him. "I aim to please."

Burton seemed to relax. "Between you and me, I met this Leona Novak on the internet. Didn't realize how old she was 'til after I put on my reading glasses. By then, I'd already emailed her."

"Excuse me?" Alex injected his tone with heavy disapproval.

Burton kept on talking. "Would've canceled but I figured why disappoint the old gal."

"That *old gal* is younger than you," Alex said. "What makes you think she won't be disappointed in you?"

"It's different for men," Burton said. "Everybody knows we get better looking with age."

Grandma Novak would see right through this guy, Alex thought. Krista was across the store, ushering Charlie Crosby toward the exit. Showing Burton the door would have been the better move.

"Go ahead and share that theory with Leona," Alex suggested. "She'll enjoy it."

Burton perked up. "You think so?"

"Sure do," Alex said. "She's behind the cash register. You can't miss her."

"Got it." Burton strutted off, a lamb to the slaughter.

Alex spotted Krista the instant she reentered the store. She looked well pleased with herself, her smile lighting up her eyes as she walked toward him. He was proud of himself for noticing her eyes, considering how much willpower it took not to let his gaze dip to the rest of her.

"Mission accomplished," she said. "I think Charlie's a keeper."

"Burton's not." Alex gestured to the cashier's desk in the distance where the elderly man was talking to Grandma Novak. "Your grandmother's sure to send him packing any moment now."

No sooner had Alex uttered the words than Grandma Novak shook a finger in Burton's face. He reeled back, pivoted and walked quickly toward the exit with his head down.

"How did you know she was going to do that?" Krista asked.

"Lucky guess," Alex said. "I'm gonna grab a quick lunch. There are sandwiches, chips and drinks in the back room. Want to join me?"

"I can't," she said. "I'm going to relieve my mom at the ball crawl. She needs the break more than I do."

"Good luck convincing her of that," Alex said.

"Oh, I'll do it," Krista vowed. "I can be very persuasive. It's a Novak family trait."

She sashayed away from him, her elf dress swishing as she walked. He watched her until she rounded an aisle and was out of sight, helpless to look away.

If she carried through on her threat to proposition him, he wasn't entirely certain he'd be able to resist.

Especially if she added persuasion into the mix.

RAYNA NOVAK HURRIED through the parking lot to the flat gray building, her scarf shielding her face from the wind. She pushed through one of the double glass doors, expecting to be enveloped in warmth. Then she remembered.

An ice hockey rink was not the place to go in the winter if you wanted to be cozy. She unwrapped her scarf, slipped off her gloves and followed the sounds of men's voices and blades sliding on ice.

Peering through the glass that partitioned off the rink to the scoreboard, she determined the ice hockey game was tied at two goals a piece in the third period.

A team of men in mismatched dark hockey sweaters, some with numbers affixed with masking tape, skated against players wearing white.

The swiftest of them wore the number seven because he claimed it was lucky. He stole the puck at the center line and streaked toward the goal with two much slower defenders in pursuit. He faked left, shot right and missed the goal entirely.

He swore, loud enough that Rayna heard from off the ice.

"Showing off for your girl doesn't count unless you finish, Trey," one of his teammates yelled.

Trey ignored him and narrowly lost out to an opposing player as they both chased down the puck.

Trey Farina's girl.

Rayna supposed that was who she was. They'd been dating for about a year even though neither she nor Trey had ever discussed where their relationship was headed. They hadn't agreed to be exclusive, either. They just were.

Rayna shivered. She hugged herself, not sure whether her tremble was from the cold or from what she had to tell Trey. Rayna had only found out herself that morning, a few minutes before her absentee sister woke up. The revelation had consumed Rayna so that she'd barely been able to perform her duties at the dentist's office today.

In an alternate universe, she would have confided in Krista. An alternate universe where her sister was a friend rather than a stranger she hadn't seen in eight years.

"Rayna, over here." A petite woman in her twenties with a mass of curly red hair motioned to Rayna from mostly empty silver bleachers. Her name was Mimi. She moved over, patting the metal surface beside her.

"Trey's having a good game," Mimi told Rayna as she sat down. "He scored one of the goals and assisted on the other."

"How about Bob?" Rayna asked, referring to the woman's husband.

Mimi laughed. "Scoreless, the same as always. What are you doing here anyway? I thought you were too busy at the dentist's office to come to the games."

Rayna wouldn't be here today, either, if she didn't need to get Trey alone, a nearly impossible feat. He lived in a house with three other guys, one of whom was always around.

"The office closed early today," Rayna said. "I stopped by to remind Trey he's supposed to come Christmas caroling tonight with my family."

"Smart girl," Mimi said. "There's already talk of going drinking after the game. You've got to keep your guy in check. That's why I'm here."

A tremendous shout erupted from the ice. Arms upraised, Trey stood in front of the net and a sprawling goalie. The referee signaled a good goal with a tomahawk chop of his arm. Trey's teammates on the ice mobbed him with hugs.

"Applaud," Mimi told her. "That way Trey will think you saw him score the winning goal."

Less than a minute remained in the game. The trailing team pulled its goalie to get an extra skater on the ice, but this was low-level ice hockey. The offensive players weren't skilled enough to keep control of the puck. The buzzer sounded, signaling the end of the game.

Trey let out a victory whoop. He skated past Rayna, stick raised in the air. She smiled and gave him a thumbs-up. While Trey went through the postgame handshake line, Rayna walked to the spot where the players came off the ice.

Trey finished shaking hands with the opposing team members first and skated full tilt toward her, executing a hockey stop before he reached the exit. Ice shards sprayed in the air.

"Woooo-hoooo!" he cried.

He stepped onto the threadbare carpet. Trey wasn't the best-looking man Rayna had ever dated, but his looks were compelling. Thick brown hair, blue eyes that danced with excitement, well-shaped lips that were almost always smiling.

Rayna thought she'd fallen in love the first time she'd seen him, when he'd sauntered into the dentist's office for a checkup.

"Did you see that goal?" Trey yelled.

Before she could answer, Trey bent down, swept her into his arms and kissed her. She had to stand on tiptoe because in his skates, he was about three inches taller than normal. His cool lips sent hot sensation sweeping through her—nothing new. She always reacted to him that way. She never wanted his kisses to stop, either, though they inevitably did.

"Mimi said you had two goals today," Rayna said.

"It was a good day at the office!" Trey didn't actually work at an office. He was twenty-two, a year older than Rayna but not as sure what to do with his life. He was currently working as a manager at a trendy clothing store and talking about going to bartending school. Sometimes when Alex and his father were particularly busy, Trey helped out at Costas Landscaping.

"I'll shower and change clothes," Trey said. "Wait for me, okay?"

"Sure." Rayna moved toward the now-empty bleachers and took a seat. She wasn't sure where Mimi was but Trey had stopped outside the locker room to drink at the water fountain.

Trey's teammates skated off the ice, laughing and talking. None of them looked toward the bleachers, probably because they typically had so few fans in attendance.

"You're really not coming with us, Bob?" the stockiest player asked Mimi's husband.

"Can't," Bob said. "Mimi has plans."

"Cancel 'em," the stocky guy said. "A guy should do what a guy wants to do."

"Unless he's married. Then he's screwed," another of the players joked as they duck-walked on their ice skates to the locker room. Trey held the door open for them. "You're coming with us, right, Trey?"

"Damn straight," Trey answered.

"Your girlfriend won't mind?"

"She's cool," Trey said as he disappeared inside the locker room. Rayna could just make out his next words. "We're not serious or anything."

"But—" Rayna started to protest but nobody could hear her. She probably wouldn't have finished the sentence anyway. If Trey didn't want to go caroling tonight, she wouldn't force him.

Not after finding out he wasn't serious about her.

Rayna got up and headed for the exit, vaguely crossing paths with Mimi. She called to her friend to let

Trey know she'd had to leave, then rushed out of the arena, tears already streaming down her face.

She wouldn't tell Trey she was pregnant, either.

CHAPTER FOUR

IN ALL HER YEARS OF caroling, Krista had never heard a more off-key rendition of "Silent Night."

Not everybody in their group of eight was hitting sour notes. Krista, her mother and her grandmother could sing a little. Charlie Crosby had a pleasing baritone, Milo Costas was more or less on key and the neighbors who'd joined them were mainstays in the church choir.

That left Alex.

He was singing about sleeping in heavenly peace, confidently belting out the word *peace* so it sounded as though it had two syllables.

The elderly man and woman just inside the threshold had been smiling since they opened the door to a care basket and a choir. The man's smile grew. He laughed. The woman poked him in the side with her elbow.

Mirth rose from Krista's diaphragm, begging for release. She stopped singing and clamped her hand over her mouth. Her chest rose and fell in silent guffaws.

The song ended, and the couple applauded. The elderly man caught Krista's eye and winked.

Alex was standing next to Krista at the rear of the group. He edged closer and whispered, "Are you and that man laughing at me?"

Krista removed her gloved hand from her mouth to

issue a denial, leaving nothing to hold back the laughter. It burst forth, like a car horn. She swallowed it back, only half-successfully.

"No," she said on a half giggle.

"Yes, you were." Alex placed a hand over his heart. "I'm wounded."

"You sounded like it when you were singing," Krista quipped in a voice only loud enough for Alex to hear and broke into more laughter.

The flat line of Alex's lips crinkled. Then he laughed, too.

"Shall we sing another carol?" Krista's mother sent Krista and Alex a withering look. "Mr. and Mrs. Dombrowski enjoy the religious ones."

Krista clamped her lips together. So did Alex. They exchanged a guilty look, and Krista felt about ten years old. She giggled again. Her mother looked more stern.

"Let's do 'Angels We Have Heard on High,'" Grandma Novak suggested.

Krista caught Alex's eye and placed a shushing finger to her lips. "Not as loud this time. It's okay to hear the angels, but not you," she whispered.

"Smart aleck," he said without heat.

With Krista's mother directing frequent warning glances in their direction, Krista got through the carol without laughing. It helped that Alex took her advice and turned down the volume.

While the couple thanked them, Krista grabbed Alex's hand. "Let's get out of here before my mom has a chance to scold us. I know the way to the next house."

Krista wasn't so much afraid of her mother as she was eager for an adventure. Caroling had never been so much fun. "Faster," she said over her shoulder, smiling at Alex.

He smiled back. He wore gloves and a brown winter jacket made of a fabric that retained heat. He was hatless, his thick black hair rustled by the wind. With his skin ruddy from the cold, he looked vital and alive.

For the hundredth time that day, Krista thought about what the blonde had said at the Christmas shop. Was it really possible that Krista had broken Alex's heart? She couldn't put much credence to it. Their relationship, however intense, had been too brief. Neither could she get the possibility out of her mind.

"Krista! Alex! Wait!"

They'd barely made it twenty yards down the sidewalk before Krista's mother hailed them. She was securely wrapped in order to fend off the cold, with only her face showing through an ice-blue scarf. "What got into you two back there? The seniors want to hear you sing, not laugh."

Krista remembered the delight in Mr. Dombrowski's eyes when his gaze met hers. "I think Mr. Dombrowski liked it."

"Only after you started to behave," Krista's mother said. "I know you haven't been home in a long time, Krista, but you know how important this program is to your grandmother."

Krista did know. Grandma had come up with the idea years ago to deliver holiday care baskets accompanied by Christmas carols to the elderly and shut-ins of the community. Grandma got lists of names and addresses of the willing from area senior centers and assigned caroling teams routes, with most of the stops within walking distance. This year, the Novaks' group had five destinations.

"We'll be good from now on." Krista caught Alex's eye and waggled her brows. "Won't we, Alex?"

He did a nice job keeping a straight face. "We will."

"You have to hold up your end of the bargain, too, Mom," Krista said. "One house and then you go home."

Her mom had only struck the deal after the Novaks threatened en masse to call off the caroling.

"I know your tricks, Krista Novak." Her mother wagged a finger. "You're trying to deflect attention from yourself. If you think that will work, you—"

"Look, there's Rayna," Krista interrupted, nodding toward her sister, who was walking toward them with the rest of the group. "Didn't you say she was bringing her boyfriend, Mom?"

"Why, yes. Trey's supposed to be with her." Her mother's forehead creased. "I'll go find out what happened."

She left Alex and Krista and headed for Rayna.

"Nice misdirection," Alex said.

"Thank you." Krista executed a little bow. "I learned that from my Grandma. Anytime Mom says something Grandma doesn't like, Grandma changes the subject. That's probably how she's been able to live under the same roof with my mom all these years."

"I think it's because Grandma Novak doesn't take herself too seriously." Alex had resumed walking toward the next house on their list, and Krista fell into step beside him. "She keeps things in the house light."

"You mean because my dad's in a wheelchair?" Krista couldn't hold back the question, both wanting to hear how her father was coping eight and a half years after the accident and not wanting to know. Except couldn't she make an educated guess? Her father had been mostly sequestered in the office by himself since she arrived. That didn't paint a picture of a well-adjusted man.

"Well, yeah," he said, "but not only because your dad's paralyzed. Rayna's twenty-one going on thirty-one, and your parents…how can I say this…? They like to agree to disagree."

Krista couldn't have summed up her family more succinctly than that, especially Rayna. She didn't know her sister well enough to make an astute observation.

"Diplomatically put," she said.

"Eleanor and Joe don't put anything diplomatically," Alex said with a grin. "Used to freak me out until I caught on that was the way they interacted."

It had taken Krista most of her childhood to reach that realization. "You know my family awfully well."

"That happens when you live next door," he said.

Even though he openly disapproved of her own dealings with her family, Krista couldn't pass up this chance to find out more about her sister's life. She already knew Rayna had five months of school left. It was the personal stuff that interested Krista more.

"Do you know what the deal is with Rayna's boyfriend?" she asked. "Any guess why he didn't show tonight?"

"Trey? It's hard to sum him up. He's a bit of a free spirit."

"So he's irresponsible?" Krista asked.

"More like irrepressible. It's impossible not to like the guy. If there's a good time to be had, Trey will find it," Alex said. "But he's not the caroling type."

"Neither are you," Krista pointed out.

"Hey, I come every year," he said.

"Do you always sing so loud?"

"Pretty much. I fake confidence." He laughed. "That's what us guys do when we're in over our heads."

"Good thing I'm here to keep you in line," Krista said.

"Oh, yeah. I just love having a woman around who's blunt enough to tell me I sound like I'm dying."

"Not dying—wounded," Krista said. "The wounded have greater lung capacity."

He threw back his head and let out another deep chuckle. Krista joined in. They'd laughed a lot in the past, too, including over the spilled poinsettias. She found it attractive that he didn't take himself too seriously.

Grandma Novak caught up to them on the sidewalk with Charlie Crosby next to her. "We're sticking with you two. You're having more fun than everyone else."

"It does the heart good to see a young couple enjoying each other," Charlie remarked.

Krista shook her head. "We're not a couple."

"Really?" Charlie wore a long black coat with a top hat that might have looked foolish on anyone else. On Charlie, it looked dignified. "You've never been a couple?"

Krista exchanged a look with Alex, silently requesting help in how to handle the situation. He shrugged.

"Aha! I saw that look!" Grandma cried. "I knew something went on between you after the poinsettias dropped!"

"It was a long time ago, Grandma." To Charlie, she clarified, "Eight years."

Charlie tipped his top hat. "Bully for you for managing to keep the spark alive."

Charlie could tell there was still fire between them?

That could only lead to problems. "Alex and I didn't keep in touch."

"So the spark reignited?" Charlie asked.

"There is no spark," Krista lied. She tugged on Alex's arm. "Tell them, Alex."

"No spark," he agreed.

"Can both the lady and gentleman protest too much?" Grandma asked.

Krista was about to object more vigorously when her grandmother laughed. "You should see your face, Krista. We're teasing!"

"I wasn't," Charlie stated. "I really think they look like a couple."

The rest of the carolers were gaining on them. Krista expected her mother to be leading the way, demanding to know what they'd been discussing. Her mom, though, must have kept her word and returned home.

"Appearances can be deceiving," Krista told Charlie with more levity than she felt.

At the next house, Milo was deputized to ring the doorbell because he carried the care basket corresponding to the address.

Alex stepped aside so his father could move to the front of the group. "It's come to my attention that it's better if I keep to the rear," Alex remarked.

Milo patted his son on the shoulder. "Somebody finally told you that you can't sing, huh?" He nodded at Krista. "Good girl."

"I took it like a man," Alex said. "Didn't even cry."

Krista grinned at him. Alex smiled back.

"You two are the cutest couple!" the neighbor lady who sang in the church choir remarked as she passed by with her husband to their rightful place at the front and center of the carolers.

"Did I hear right?" Rayna was the last to arrive. She addressed her question to Alex, not even glancing at Krista. "Do you and my sister have something going on?"

"Nope," Alex said. "Not a thing."

Krista listened to Alex's casual denial with dismay. He seemed to think this troubling development was no big deal. If she were a member of just about any other family, she'd be inclined to agree. Priority number one was getting Alex alone so she could explain the precariousness of their situation.

It was either that or suffer through a couple days of hell.

ALEX HAD NEVER BEEN more glad for a song to be over.

The temperature seemed to have dropped at least ten degrees since they'd started caroling, although there was no sign of the snow that was in the forecast.

Grandma Novak had invited everybody to her house for hot chocolate and eggnog. The group made excellent time traveling the few blocks back to White Point Road, possibly because the wind was at their back.

"Mulled wine would be good, too," Grandma remarked before she went into the house. "I know we have mulling spices but I'm not sure how much wine we've got."

"We have some wine," Alex offered. "I'll stop by next door and get a bottle."

"I'll come with you," Krista offered.

Alex wondered at her change of heart. Since they'd been mistaken for a couple, Krista had maneuvered to keep one caroler between them at all times.

"I'm anxious to see what Alex and his dad have done with the house. I used to play over there all the time when I was a kid." Krista broadcast her reason as though she were a politician addressing an assembly. It gained her curious looks.

"We haven't done much." Milo stomped his feet and rubbed his hands to keep warm. "Why do you think we always hang out at your parents' house?"

"Go on, you two." Grandma Novak swept her right arm toward the house next door. "And take your time. There's no rush on the mulled wine."

The inside of the one-story ranch-style home where Alex lived with his father was nearly identical in layout to the Novaks'. A living room, kitchen and dining room accounted for one side of the house. A hall leading to the bedrooms and bathroom took up the other. The warmth from the radiator heating system made it feel cozy after the chill of the outdoors. Alex cocked an eyebrow at Krista's scarf, hat and red winter coat.

"If you take all that off for the tour, you'll just have to put it back on again," he said.

"I'm not here for a tour!" Krista sounded as though she were stating the obvious when the situation was anything but.

"If I didn't know better," Alex said, slowly drawing out the words, "I'd think you were trying to get me alone."

"That's exactly what I'm doing."

Alex's muscles tensed, and the temperature in the room seemed higher than it had mere moments ago. Was Krista finally following through on the hypothetical she'd posed in the car? Was she propositioning him?

"We need to put a stop to this couple nonsense straight away," Krista said.

Alex felt like a fool. The entire caroling group knew he and Krista were alone in his house. Of course she hadn't been about to propose they make wild, passionate love. "And here I thought you were open to the idea."

"To having another fling! Not to being a couple! Can you imagine what my mother would make of that?"

Alex wasn't looking to build a lasting relationship with Krista, either, but hearing her reject the idea so forcefully stung. "Hate to break this to you," he said, "but you added fuel to the fire by insisting on coming over here."

Alex headed for the rear of the house and the wine rack he'd had built into the cabinetry a few years back when they'd had the kitchen remodeled. He examined the selection, aware without turning that she was close behind him.

"How else could I get a private moment with you?" Krista asked. "We need to discourage people from thinking we're an item."

The twelve-bottle wine rack was half-full, with a number of different types of red wines represented. "Any idea what kind of wine is best for mulling?"

"What? No," Krista said. "I don't have the faintest idea."

"Maybe a merlot." Alex had a choice of two brands, pulled out the less expensive bottle and held it up to her. "I got this one at the grocery store. I'm no connoisseur but I wouldn't put mulling spices in fine wine."

"Neither would—" Krista stopped talking midsentence. "Why are we talking about wine? We're wasting time. We need a strategy."

She'd taken off her hat, the only concession to being indoors, and the static electricity in her hair caused it to frizz. Her nose, the one he disagreed was too long, was red from the prolonged exposure to the cold. So were her lips. She'd looked so put together since arriving that he enjoyed seeing her frazzled.

"Why?" he asked. "What does it matter what your mother thinks?"

"You know what she's like, Alex," Krista said. "She'll use any means possible to get me to move back to Pennsylvania. If she believes we have something going, that's leverage."

"I still don't get it," he said. "If you know you're staying in Prague, what's the big deal?"

"The big deal is that she'll make my life miserable!"

"So tell her there's nothing going on," Alex suggested.

"It'll have to be the truth." Krista touched him on the sleeve of his jacket. "This flirting we've been doing, it can't go any further."

"We've been flirting?" he asked.

"I have." She squeezed his arm. "I can't forget how great we were in bed together. You were there. You must remember, too."

Oh, yeah. He remembered.

"The past is the past," Alex said. "The present is a whole new ball game."

"So you're not attracted to me anymore?" she demanded.

Alex debated how to answer. No matter how different their outlooks on home and family, he liked Krista. He always had.

"You're very attractive," he said, "but I've moved on."

"Does that mean you're getting back together with that blonde who was at the Christmas Shoppe today?"

"Julia Merrifiled? How do you know I dated Julia?"

"She told me," Krista said. "Well, are you?"

"And this is your business why?" Alex asked.

"If you were dating Julia, people would be less likely to believe you were interested in me."

Her rationale held a twisted sort of logic. "So you want me to date her?"

Krista removed her hand from his arm, and threw it up in the air. "Pay attention. I don't *want* you to date Julia. It would just be easier if you did."

The exhilaration that rushed through Alex was at odds with the circumstances. "I'm not going to date Julia."

"Because of me?"

He shook his head. "This is the most bizarre conversation I've ever had."

"Then your life's been boring," Krista shot back.

Although he wouldn't describe it that way, Alex silently admitted having Krista around livened up his days. "Things didn't work out before between Julia and me. Why would they now?"

"Timing. Julia said years ago when you dated her, you were hung up on a woman who broke your heart." Krista stared straight into his eyes, regarding him with careful intensity. "Was that woman me?"

"Julia said that?" Alex was stunned by his ex's take on the situation. He remembered the past another way. He'd ended his association with Krista before he had a chance to fall for her. "We didn't know each other long enough for my heart to be involved."

He stepped to the side, effectively breaking eye contact. "Let's get out of here before your family really starts gossiping about us."

Without pausing to hear whether she agreed, Alex left the kitchen and strode through the living room. He held the front door open, waiting for Krista to precede him into the cold night.

"So you think you can do it?" Krista paused to ask the question, cutting her big brown eyes at him while she brushed by him, her lips almost close enough to kiss. "The no-flirting part, I mean."

She was past him before he could reply. Sure enough she'd discombobulated him again, with ease no less. He didn't answer until they were both outside and walking between the two houses.

"I can manage to control myself." He was pleased that his voice sounded strong and steady. "I haven't been pining for you for the past eight years, you know."

That would be insanity. Alex wouldn't lie to himself. His initial reaction to Krista had been so strong that he wanted more than a few weeks of fun. Her departure had smarted, propelling Alex to dive back into the dating game to forget about her. As the days, months and years had passed, the sting had faded.

The sidewalk wasn't wide enough to walk two abreast, not with the illuminated toy soldiers standing guard on either side. Krista preceded Alex and climbed up the first step of the porch before gazing at him over her shoulder.

"Let me get this straight." Faint horizontal lines appeared on her forehead. "You haven't thought about me at all?"

It would have been impossible to banish Krista entirely from mind while living next door to her parents. For years, whenever Eleanor Novak had brought up the subject of her daughter, Alex had focused on how badly he'd misjudged Krista.

"I got over you a long time ago," he said.

Krista pivoted sharply in his direction and lost her footing. He caught her under the arms, dimly noting she smelled better than the cold air, and helped her to stand upright. One porch step up, she was at eye level with him.

"Did you really?" she asked in a soft voice.

By the time what she was asking registered, she'd threaded her gloved fingers through his hair and kissed him.

Her lips were cool against his but a familiar heat flared inside him. His reaction to her had been this immediate years ago, too. Sometimes it hadn't even taken a kiss. A mere touch would have him ready to haul her into the bedroom.

The tip of her tongue teased his. He gathered her closer against him, deepening the kiss, realizing that despite everything he'd wanted her back in his arms the instant he saw her in the Novak kitchen. His reaction to her hadn't lost any of its intensity. If possible, it was even stronger now.

Somebody was making low-throated sounds of pleasure. Alex wasn't sure whether it was one or both of them. He couldn't identify where the thudding, scraping noise was coming from, either, although it seemed out of context.

"There you two are!" a familiar female voice cried.

Alex and Krista sprung apart. Krista turned her head one hundred and eighty degrees. Alex angled his to the side to see around her.

The sound had been the door opening. Eleanor

Novak stood inside it wearing a smile that couldn't have been brighter had she strung Christmas lights on her teeth.

EVEN IF MULLED WINE were an acquired taste, Krista would never develop a fondness for it.

She wouldn't have minded soothing herself with alcohol after her plan to get Alex alone had backfired so completely, but not with wine this hot, sweet and awful.

Krista gravitated to the back of the group in the Novak living room, then made a break for the kitchen when it seemed like nobody was watching her. Of course, that might not be the case. It seemed Krista's mother had monitored Krista's every move since The Kiss. Mom had even beckoned a few times with a crooked finger Krista pretended not to notice.

The kitchen had an unexpected inhabitant. Milo Costas stood at the stainless-steel sink, an empty wineglass in one hand, a guilty grimace on his face.

"Please don't tell your grandma I think her mulled wine tastes like boiled beets," he said.

Krista joined Milo at the sink and dumped her nearly full glass down the drain. "It tastes like cold medicine to me, the icky liquid kind kids refuse to drink."

"I think I like you." Milo leaned back against the kitchen counter. He had the same charming smile as his son and a similar easygoing manner. "So tell me, what did you think of our house?"

Had Milo bought her excuse? If so, he was the only one who believed she'd gone next door to tour his house.

"It's a very nice house," she said.

"It's okay for a place where a color-blind guy lives." Milo jerked a thumb at his chest. "Alex got rid of the green walls and pink kitchen when he moved in."

"Sounds colorful," Krista said.

"In a ghastly sort of way, I'm told." Milo could laugh at himself, another attractive trait he shared with his son.

"Where did you live before?"

"A condo on Grover Street. Before that, a four-bedroom place in Shenandoah Acres. I bought the condo after my wife died but it wasn't for me. I like having a yard and more space."

"How did Alex come to live with you?" Krista should probably have swallowed the question in light of the speculation about her and Alex, but found she couldn't contain her curiosity.

"He offered," Milo said. "Surprised the heck out of me because he had a nice place in town. Took me a couple of years to figure out why he did it."

"Why?" Krista asked, totally absorbed.

"He was worried about me," Milo said. "His mother had been gone for almost five years and I was still sad all the time."

"I imagine you never truly get over a loved one's death," Krista said.

"You're right about that," Milo said, his smile turning sad. "But I'm no longer depressed."

"Because Alex lives with you?"

"Because Alex fussed at me 'til I saw a doctor," Milo said. "Turns out I'm prone to clinical depression and losing my wife made it worse. The meds I'm on help."

"Sounds like Alex is a good son," Krista remarked.

"The best," Milo said. "He's a great business partner, too. Got to say, though, it surprised the hell out of me that he went into landscaping."

"My parents are the opposite," Krista said. "I never pretended to like working at the nursery, but they still thought I'd go into business with them. My mom, especially."

"It might have been wishful thinking on Eleanor's part," Milo said. "I know how much she likes having you home."

"Yeah," Krista said. "You also know what she did to get me here."

"Didn't you want to come?" Milo asked. An innocent question with a complicated answer. Hadn't Milo noticed that even with company in the house, her father was shut away in his office?

Her mother swept into the kitchen before Krista could reply. "There you are, Krista. I wondered where you were hiding. Alex is probably looking for you, too."

Just as Krista feared, the matchmaking had begun. "I wasn't hiding, Mom. I was talking to Milo."

"Your daughter and I have been getting acquainted," Milo said. "I like talking to her. Krista reminds me of Joe."

"Seriously?" Krista was surprised the synapses between her brain and tongue didn't short-circuit. "In what way?"

Milo smiled. "You both come out and say what's on your minds."

"If you ask me, Joe should keep quiet more often," her mother said, as though she agreed with the comparison. Hadn't either of them noticed that Krista and her father barely spoke to each other? "Speaking of the devil, he should have joined us by now. Krista, could you tell your father people are asking about him?"

Krista's impulse was to refuse, but she couldn't very well do that without raising questions. "All right."

She squared her shoulders, silently assuring herself she could handle a brief moment alone with her father. His office was down a hall plastered with family photographs, mostly of Krista and Rayna. Despite the gap in their ages, the photos commemorating their milestones were arranged side-by-side, highlighting the family resemblance. There they were as babies, gaptoothed second-graders, teenagers dressed for the prom and high-school seniors in caps and gowns.

The photo that leaped out at Krista, however, was of the Novak family of four at the beach when Rayna was about two years old. The ocean was at their backs, and Rayna was perched on their father's shoulders, thin bare legs dangling. Next to him, wearing a sarong-type bathing suit, Krista's mother posed with one leg in front of the other. Krista was front and center, her father's large hand resting on her narrow shoulder. All four of them were smiling.

Since her arrival, Krista hadn't seen her father smile.

She drew in a lungful of air, continued past the photograph and rapped on the closed door to the office. In response, she thought she heard a muffled groan.

"Dad?" she called in a loud voice. "It's Krista."

No answer, but Krista was almost positive about the groan. Even though the door was constructed from a sturdy hardwood that would block sound, there was a sliver of air where the bottom of the door met the floor.

"I'm coming in," she warned.

Krista pushed open the door and gasped. Her father

lay on his stomach, his upper body raised a few inches off the floor and his elbows supporting his weight. The muscles in his arms strained as he tried to pull himself toward his empty wheelchair.

"Dad!" Krista rushed forward, her heart beating heavily. Another image of her fallen father flashed in her mind, this one at the nursery beside the forklift. "What happened?"

Her father didn't look at her. "What do you think happened? I fell out of the wheelchair," he said gruffly.

His flip answer stung her, but only for a moment. She shoved aside the hurt and focused on the crisis. "What can I do to help?"

"Get Alex."

Krista assessed the situation. Her father, never a large man, didn't weigh as much as he had before the accident. He already had himself in position to get back on the wheelchair.

She ventured forward a step. "Maybe I can—"

"Just get Alex," her father barked.

Krista reeled backward, a hand at her throat, unshed tears burning the backs of her eyes.

"Please," her father added, the plea much softer than his order had been. He still wouldn't look at her.

Krista rushed out of the office and ran down the hall, stopping at the entrance to the living room. Alex was facing her direction, in conversation with the neighbor couple who sang in the choir. He excused himself before Krista could say a word and came to her. "What's wrong?"

"It's my dad. He fell out of his wheelchair." She tried to be circumspect, because that was what her father would want. Tears brimmed over her lower eyelids. She wiped them away.

"Hey, look at me." Alex laid a hand on her shoulder and tipped up her chin. "I know it's scary but this has happened before. He'll be okay."

She blinked back more tears and nodded. Alex let her go and walked swiftly down the hall, with Krista following. She paused outside the door. Her father had made it abundantly clear she was an interloper in his office.

"Are you okay, Joe?" she heard Alex ask. "Is anything hurt?"

"Just my pride," her father bit out. "I dropped a pen, of all things. I reached over to pick it up and fell flat on my face."

"The brake on the wheelchair isn't set," Alex said. "It must have accidentally dislodged when you bent over."

"Figured that was what happened," her father grumbled. "The chair rolled backward and down I went."

"I'll lift you under the arms on the count of three. Ready? One. Two. Three."

For long moments, the only sound was her father's labored breathing. Krista leaned against the wall, her own breaths ragged.

"There you go," Alex said. "You sure you're not hurt?"

"The advantage of being a paraplegic," her father said wryly. "Usually you feel no pain."

Alex chuckled, although Krista didn't find the remark funny. How could she when she was the reason her father would never walk again?

"You've got a houseful of guests out there," Alex told her father. "Care to join us?"

"No, thanks," came the quick rejoinder. "I've had enough excitement for one night."

"Okay, but Krista's pretty worried about you. She'll want to see for herself that you're okay."

"No!" Her father's caustic refusal cut through Krista, ripping into her heart. "Don't let her come in here."

Alex might have said something in reply. Krista didn't know. She could no longer hear past the roaring in her ears. Neither could she bring herself to move.

Alex walked through the open door, missing a step when he spotted her in the hall. He pulled the door shut, his expression filled with empathy. "You heard that, didn't you?"

She nodded, not trusting herself to speak. She blinked but felt another tear escape. She didn't know what was wrong with her. She couldn't even remember the last time she'd cried. Alex lifted a hand and gently brushed her cheek.

"Joe didn't mean it like it sounded," Alex said. "He's just a bit embarrassed, that's all."

Why was Alex being so sweet to her? He'd lived next door to her parents for years. He must know her father wouldn't be in the wheelchair if not for Krista.

"You said my dad has fallen out of his chair before," Krista said when she trusted herself to speak. "Does it happen often?"

"Not often," Alex said. "But I was here once when he dropped a vitamin and the same thing happened."

Krista swallowed. How humbling it must be to have simple tasks elude you like picking up pens and vitamins from the floor.

"I'm glad you were here when he dropped the vitamin." Krista laid a hand on Alex's cheek, feeling the bristly beginnings of his five o'clock shadow under the warm skin. "I'm glad you're here now."

Their eyes locked, and she felt the same powerful connection that had compelled her to kiss him on the porch. "Thanks for looking out for my dad."

"Think nothing of it," he said.

But she did.

CHAPTER FIVE

THE TOWHEADED LITTLE BOY in the ball crawl tossed red and green plastic balls into the air, laughing uproariously when they bounced off his head.

"Time's up, buddy," Krista called to him. "The store's closing."

The boy giggled, picked up a green ball with his left hand and flung it at her. It would have hit Krista square in the forehead if not for the netting around the apparatus.

"Hey, careful!" Krista called. "It's Christmas Eve. Haven't you heard about the naughty and nice list?"

The boy selected another ball, red this time, and threw that one at Krista, too. He couldn't have been more than three years old, which put Krista at a distinct disadvantage. Most of her friends in Europe were single and none of them had young children. The last time she'd spent any significant time around a child had been years ago, when Rayna was young.

Her sister, who Krista gathered helped out at the store when school and her job allowed, was approaching now. Rayna's blond hair was tied back from her pretty face with a festive ribbon that should have made her look young and carefree. Instead the ribbon emphasized the touch of melancholy in Rayna's expression.

Something in her sister's world wasn't right. Krista

wished she could get Rayna to confide in her. Too bad she was as unsure how to deal with her now-adult sister as she was the child.

"The boy's mom sent me to get him," Rayna said. "Grandma's almost done ringing up her purchases. She's our last customer."

The store was closing at 2:00 p.m., several hours earlier than usual because heavy snow was in the forecast. The Novaks had learned from experience that once the snow started, customers were reluctant to navigate the hill to get to the shop.

"Good luck getting our friend here to budge," Krista told her sister. "He doesn't want to stop playing."

Rayna parted the netting, a gutsy move considering the kid was destined to put on a baseball uniform and pitch fireballs to opposing batters one day. "Hey, sport. Ready to go home and wait for Santa Claus to come?"

"Santa!" the boy cried. He crawled through the balls on his hands and knees, breaking speed records to reach Rayna's outstretched hand.

"Impressive," Krista said.

Rayna lifted the boy from the ball crawl and set him on the floor, her hand rustling his floppy blond hair. "I know a couple tricks, is all."

"Mommy!" The boy let go of Rayna's hand and dashed to a tall, thin woman who was approaching them with a large bag in one hand. "Go get chimney ready!"

"Sounds good to me." The boy's mother beamed at the child and enfolded his hand in hers. To Rayna and Krista, she called, "Merry Christmas!"

"Same to you," Krista responded.

"Have a good one," Rayna said with less enthusiasm. She started to head away from the ball crawl.

"Rayna, wait!"

Her sister stopped and regarded Krista with a stoic look. A memory surfaced of Rayna as a child no older than the boy, following Krista around the house, eager to spend time with her. It seemed like a very long time ago.

"Is everything okay?" Krista ventured.

"Why wouldn't it be?" Rayna asked.

"You don't seem to be yourself," Krista said.

"You don't know me well enough to say that."

A terrible sense of déjà vu overtook Krista. Last night her father had rejected her help and now Rayna was doing the same. "What I meant is I'm here for you if something's wrong."

Rayna stared at her long and hard. "When you say you're here for me, you mean until the day after Christmas, right?"

"Well, yes." Krista had booked her flight to Switzerland the very night she'd arrived in Pennsylvania, just as she said she would. "But I hope we'll keep in better touch once I'm back in Europe."

"You never know what'll happen." The corners of Rayna's mouth turned up, as though she were mimicking the motions of smiling. "I appreciate your concern, but I'm good."

"Really?" Krista asked.

"Really," Rayna said. "I've gotta go help close up."

"Right behind you," Krista said to her sister's retreating back. A wave of frustration threatened to overtake Krista. She fought through it, focusing on the minor straightening up that needed to be done in the shop before they locked up and ventured into the cold.

A short time later, feathery snowflakes fluttered from the sky, sticking on the grass in the nursery yard and the pavement of the parking lot.

"Oh, goody. It looks like we'll have a white Christmas," Grandma said.

Rayna held up a piece of paper with what appeared to be an itemized list. "You still want me to stop at the grocery store for you, right, Grandma?"

"Yes, dear." Grandma planned to prepare a traditional Czech Christmas Eve dinner of fish soup, fried carp, potato salad and other favorites. Krista's mom should already have started on the desserts, probably the only reason she hadn't insisted on working today. "Don't forget that crusty, dark bread Alex and Milo love."

Delicious anticipation ran through Krista. She wished she could attribute it to the dinner, but was honest enough to admit to herself that she looked forward to seeing Alex tonight.

"Remember I'm having dinner with Trey's family at five-thirty," Rayna said.

"That's why we're not eating until seven-thirty," Grandma said. "Just remember to leave room."

"Won't be a problem," Rayna said. "I usually only eat half of what I'd like."

The dusting of snow in the parking lot made for slippery going. Krista took gentle hold of her grandmother's arm as a precaution. "Be careful driving, Rayna," she said.

"You, too," Rayna mumbled before treading carefully through the lot to her car.

Krista didn't release her grandmother's arm until the older woman was seated safely in the passenger seat of her sturdy Volvo. With only a few days left in her visit, Krista had given up on the notion of a rental car. Now she was glad. Not only did her grandmother's Volvo have snow tires, but Leona also preferred that Krista drive it.

When she was behind the steering wheel, Krista switched on the ignition and started the wiper blades. The snow was coming down just hard enough that the roads could be slick driving home, but the conditions weren't what weighed on Krista's mind.

"Rayna will come around," Grandma said. "You just need to be patient."

"How did you know I was thinking about Rayna?" Krista asked.

"I've been with the two of you all day," Grandma said. "I can see what's going on."

Krista turned on the heater before she replied, getting a face full of cool air. "Rayna's been pretty standoffish."

"She's like her father," Grandma said. "She takes a while to warm up to people. Give her a couple of days."

"I only have a couple of days."

"Such a shame you can't stay longer," Grandma said. "And not just because I like having you at the store. I miss you terribly."

"I miss you, too, Grandma." Krista squeezed the words past the lump in her throat. She hadn't realized how much she longed for her grandmother's company until she came home.

Krista backed out of the parking space, glad she was in a car with an excellent safety rating. She hoped the crews had pretreated the roads. In case they hadn't, she drove under the speed limit and increased her following distance.

"Would you mind if we stopped by the coffee shop?" Grandma asked. "It's on the way."

"You sure you want to do that?" Krista asked. "The roads won't get any better, and I thought you were eager to start cooking."

"I don't have much of a choice." Grandma shifted in her seat, appearing uncomfortable with what she had to say. "I told Martin I'd meet him for a cuppa."

"Martin?" Krista slanted her grandmother a sideways look. "Oh, no. Please tell me he's not another internet date."

"I can't tell you that, dear," Grandma said. "Martin's really a very nice man. He says I have a lovely nose."

"Nose?"

"He's a nose man, of all things. The smaller, the better. He couldn't say enough nice things about mine the last time we had coffee."

"The last time? So you've already met this man?"

"Martin was my first internet date," Grandma said. "I think he wants me to be his girlfriend."

"What do you want?" Krista asked.

"To be Charlie's girl," Grandma said. "I want to be Martin's friend, only I don't know how to tell him that."

Obviously, Krista thought. Her grandmother hadn't even managed to convey that she was too busy to meet the man at a coffee shop on a snowy Christmas Eve.

"How about saying, 'I'm busy. Oh, and by the way, I'd like us to be friends,'" Krista recommended.

"You make it sound so easy!" Grandma said.

"It is easy."

"For you, maybe. But I can't bear the thought of hurting Martin's feelings," Grandma said. "There's the coffee shop on the right."

Krista pulled into a parallel parking spot in front of the store, unsurprised to find one available. With the combination of the holiday and the snow, downtown Jarrell was nearly a ghost town. She shut off the engine. "How would Charlie feel if he found out you were still meeting other men?"

"Charlie can't know!" Grandma cried.

"Then you have to be straight with Martin," Krista said.

Grandma put her hands together, as though in prayer. "Can you tell Martin for me?"

"No, but I can be on hand for moral support," Krista offered. "I'll sit at another table. Look over at me if you need courage."

"Shouldn't I introduce you to Martin?" Grandma asked.

"And give him the impression you're serious enough about him to meet the family?"

Grandma wrinkled her nose and puckered her lips. "I hadn't thought of that."

Krista's sister and father might not need her, Krista thought, but Grandma certainly did.

ALEX PUSHED THROUGH the door of the coffee shop, causing the Christmas bells that announced the arrival of a customer to jingle. He spotted Grandma Novak immediately. She sat at a table across from an elderly gentleman with a ruddy complexion, a full head of white hair and a nose that appeared to have been broken a few times.

The only other occupied table was in the farthest corner of the shop. Alex glanced toward the woman with the long brown hair who was nursing a tall cup of coffee, then did a double take.

What was Krista doing here?

Their gazes locked and he felt transported to the first time he'd seen her eight years ago. Except what passed through him didn't feel like electricity as much as a current that swept him toward her. Something had changed last night when he'd looked into her tearful eyes after her father's fall. Alex realized it was his determination to keep Krista at arm's length.

What was the point of resisting the sexual pull? As long as he understood that was all that could be between them, Alex could handle it. Not only would Krista be gone in a few days, but he was also older and wiser now. He'd never allow himself to fall for a woman with such vastly different priorities from his own.

When Alex reached Krista's table, he cocked his head in the direction of Grandma Novak, who was laughing at one of the white-haired man's remarks.

"What are you doing over here when Grandma Novak is over there?" Alex asked.

"Providing moral support from afar," Krista said. "She's trying to get up the courage to tell her latest internet conquest she only wants to be friends."

The cell phone call Alex had received ten minutes ago suddenly made sense. "Did she try to get you to tell him for her?"

Krista's brow furrowed. "How did you know that?"

"Educated guess. She lured me here, too. On the cell phone, she said it was an emergency."

"That little stinker must have called you when she went to the ladies' room!" Krista grabbed his hand. Hers felt warm from her cup of coffee. "You can't go over there."

Alex gazed down at their hands, then at her. "If I stay, will you keep holding my hand?"

She immediately let go of him. "I wasn't holding your hand. I was…" Her voice trailed off and her eyes narrowed. "You're teasing me."

"Yep."

"Would you sit down?" She looked cute when she was irritated. The color in her cheeks heightened and her nose wrinkled.

"Gladly." He pulled back a chair and settled in across from her at the café-style table for two.

"I was about to explain that Grandma needs to learn to handle these situations by herself," Krista said. "I already told her that."

"That must not have sat well with her," Alex said. "Otherwise, she wouldn't have called me."

"She's a sneaky one, all right," Krista said. "But if she's going to continue with this internet dating thing, she needs to be more savvy."

A loud, boisterous laugh reverberated through the shop. Alex watched as the man with Grandma Novak reached over and touched her nose.

"See! That's exactly what I mean," Krista hissed under her breath. "Grandma shouldn't let him do that. Martin—that's the guy's name—apparently has a nose fetish."

Alex couldn't stop his smile. "As far as fetishes go, that's pretty mild. It's nothing compared to mine."

"What's your fetish?"

Alex put both elbows on the table and leaned forward as though he were about to reveal a deep secret. Krista's body tilted toward him, her eyes growing huge. "Cranky women in coffee shops," he said.

She pursed her lips. "You're teasing me again."

"Why would you say that?" He tapped her nose and straightened in his chair before she could bat his hand away.

She folded her arms over her chest. "And for your information, I'm not cranky—I'm concerned. There's a difference."

Behind Krista, the teenage girl at the counter motioned to Alex and silently held up a white mug.

"Excuse me," Alex told Krista, rising to his feet. "My hot chocolate's ready."

"I didn't notice you place an order," Krista said.

"I didn't," he said. "I always get the same thing. She probably remembers because I'm a regular who doesn't like coffee."

After Alex paid for the hot chocolate and returned to the table, he raised the steaming cup to his mouth and closed his eyes in bliss as the warm liquid slid down his throat. "I needed that after being out in the cold all day."

"Were you working?" she asked.

He'd been traipsing through the woods searching for a vantage point where he could take the perfect photo. Some people might call that work, but not Alex. "Dad and I aren't busy over the holidays so I headed up a mountain and went for a hike. It's been snowing for a few hours at higher elevations."

"The scenery must have been amazing."

"No argument there." Alex thought fresh snow provided the most pleasing vistas, with the branches of the trees outlined in slivers of white. "Pennsylvania's beautiful in any season, but I'm partial to winter."

"Me, too," Krista said.

Yet another thing the homebody and the wanderer had in common, Alex thought.

"I'm glad I ran into you." He'd been thinking about her all day, unsurprising after what had happened last night. "How did things go with your dad this morning?"

The warmth leeched out of her expression. "He was asleep when we left for the Christmas Shoppe."

"How about your mom, then?" Alex asked. "Did she say anything about the kiss?"

"Not yet," Krista said. "She was asleep, too."

"Maybe you're wrong," Alex said. "Maybe Eleanor won't give you a hard time about us."

"Yeah, right," Krista said. "And maybe Santa really will come down the chimney tonight."

He laughed. "You brought it on yourself when you kissed me."

"It was your fault for saying you could control yourself around me," she shot back.

"I can control myself," he said. "You're the one who has trouble with your impulses. *You* kissed me."

"You reacted."

"I'm a red-blooded American male. A beautiful woman kissed me. Of course I reacted." It wasn't quite that cut-and-dried. The intensity of the sexual attraction he felt for Krista was off the charts. "As long as you keep your hands off me, we'll be fine."

"I can do that," Krista said.

He cocked an eyebrow.

"I *can*." She narrowed her eyes. "You're not planning to hang around our house for the rest of the afternoon tempting me, are you?"

"Nope," he said, smiling. "I'm braving the snow and heading over to the mall to pick up my dad and finish my shopping. Are you done?"

"I'm giving gift cards," Krista said.

His smile faded. "Wow. It really has been a long time since you've been home for Christmas."

"What does that mean?"

He held up a hand. "Never mind. I'm supposed to stay out of your business."

"You think gift cards are too impersonal, don't you?" she persisted.

"Okay. Yes," he said. "Your family makes a big deal out of picking out the perfect gifts. I'm surprised you didn't know that."

"I do!" Krista responded as though he'd criticized her, and he supposed he had. "But I live in Europe. The cost to mail presents is too high."

"You're here now." Alex tapped the face of his watch. "And there are still more than two shopping hours left until Christmas."

"I don't—"

"Some help you two were." Grandma Novak was suddenly beside the table, heedless of the fact that she was interrupting their conversation. "Did you see what Martin tried to do?"

Martin was no longer present in the coffee shop, although Alex couldn't recall hearing the bells ring when the man left.

"He tried to kiss me!" Grandma Novak cried. "Right on the smacker."

"Did he succeed?" Alex asked.

"I dodged him," she said. "Then he had the nerve to say he wasn't in the market for a relationship with a prude."

"So you got rid of him," Krista concluded. "That's good."

"Good? I'm not a prude," Grandma Novak said with

asperity. "I can kiss with the best of them when I find a man I want to kiss!"

Alex's gaze fell on Krista's lips. It must run in the family, he mused. He immediately squelched the thought. How much more proof did he need that he and Krista were only compatible when it came to sex? She couldn't even understand that giving gifts to her family was about more than fulfilling an obligation.

"Let's get out of here," Grandma Novak said.

"Good idea, Grandma." Krista got to her feet, slanting Alex a meaningful look. "Alex is taking me shopping after we drop you home. We don't have much time before the mall closes."

FORGET A TEAM OF REINDEER leading a sleigh. For peace of mind, Krista preferred a snow blade attached to the front of a pickup truck, even if Alex kept it in the upright position as he drove north on the snowy highway to the mall.

"Will I see the plow in action on the way home?" Krista had learned that like many Pennsylvania landscapers, Alex and his father supplemented their income during the winter months by offering their clients snow-removal services.

"Nah. The forecast is calling for the heaviest snow to hit tonight," Alex said. "Besides, Dad and I aren't contracted to clear the main roads. We mostly do parking lots for our commercial clients."

The lot at the mall was in decent shape. It was also nearly full, causing Alex to drive up and down the long aisles a few times before he found a spot.

"What are all these people still doing at the mall?" Krista asked before they got out of the pickup. "Don't they know it's snowing?"

Alex raised his index finger and waggled it back and forth. "Don't underestimate the desperation of the last-minute Christmas shopper. What made you change your mind about coming, anyway?"

She groaned. "This isn't easy to admit, but you were right. I can't hand over gift cards when everybody else is exchanging presents. Who knows when I'll be home for Christmas again?"

"You could make the trip home an annual tradition." He posed the statement like a challenge.

"I'm not planning on it. This trip alone is costing me a fortune." She changed the subject before he could say something like "spending time with your family is priceless." Krista already knew that. "The minutes are ticking away. We better get going."

Inside the mall the walkways were filled with customers laden with colorful shopping bags. Garland wrapped around banisters, wreaths hung from walls and lights strung from store windows created a festive feel. Underneath the decorations, store fronts sparkled and floors gleamed. Even out of season, the mall would be an inviting place.

"I hardly recognize it in here!" Krista said. "We used to drive to Harrisburg to shop because this place was such a dump."

"An investment group bought the mall a few years back and did an extensive renovation," Alex said. "It paid off. Sales have really picked up."

"I'll bet."

Most of the shoppers were female. A few of them remembered Krista from high school and said brief hellos. Most turned to admire Alex as he passed. Krista didn't blame them. Today Alex wore a black jacket. Underneath was a beige mock turtleneck that brought out his dramatic coloring and emphasized the planes and angles of his face.

A woman swinging an oversize bag passed too close to Krista. Krista stepped sideways toward Alex, and he put a hand at the small of her back. After the woman was gone, he kept it there.

"So we don't get separated," he told her.

Krista didn't particularly care if that was the real reason. She liked being this close to Alex. The spot on her back where his hand rested felt warmer than the rest of her but could that even be possible? Beneath her red coat, she wore a thick sweater.

"We'll do my shopping last. I'm picking up gourmet food gift baskets I'd rather not lug around," he said. "So where to?"

The array of choices was dizzying. Reluctant to admit she wasn't sure where to start, Krista picked the nearest women's clothing store. She wandered around aimlessly for a few minutes before stumbling across a gold V-necked sweater shot through with glitter. She snatched it off the rack.

"This would be great for Grandma when she's being wined and dined," Krista said, relieved that she'd gotten one present out of the way.

Shopping for the rest of her family didn't get any easier. After the clothing store, Krista's mind went blank. They passed a half-dozen shops that sold everything from hats to body lotion, but Krista didn't suggest stopping at a single one. It wasn't enough to pick out any gifts. She needed to choose the right ones.

"You can ask me for advice, you know," Alex said.

"I'm afraid if I do, you'll rub it in my face that you know my family better than I do," Krista said.

"Ouch," he said. "Do you really think I'd do that?"

"Probably not," Krista said.

"Probably?"

"Okay. No," Krista admitted. "I guess I said that because I wish I had a better handle on them. I can't even figure out what to buy Rayna."

"Anything dealing with cats," Alex said. "Since she got Casper, she's crazy about them."

"So I wasn't hallucinating!" Krista said. "There was a white cat in the basement one morning when I woke up, but I haven't seen it since."

"Why do you think her name is Casper?"

"Oh, I get it," Krista said. "Casper the ghostly cat."

"That's right. I'm surprised you saw her at all. Other than Rayna, Casper's slow to warm up to people."

"She was wearing silver bells on her collar," Krista said.

"That was supposed to make her easier to find," Alex said. "But I hear she shook them off."

Almost immediately they stumbled across a mall kiosk filled with tote bags. Krista bought one featuring a Cheshire cat, then gladly took Alex's suggestion that they hit the bookstore. It was one of those huge chain stores that appeared to stock every title on every imaginable subject.

"Your dad likes action adventure," Alex said. "Authors like Tom Clancy, Jeffrey Archer, Ken Follett. Pick up a new release from any one of those and you can't go wrong."

Krista hadn't even been aware that her father liked to read. Growing up she couldn't remember seeing him with anything other than the newspaper. She sobered. Of course his circumstances had changed since then. It wasn't like he could still play racquetball or get out on the golf course.

After she'd chosen a few books for her father and picked up one on impulse for her grandmother, Alex suggested checking out the DVD section for her mother. Krista stopped at a display of travel DVDs and picked up one featuring some of the top destinations in Europe.

"I'm getting this," Krista decided. "It could inspire Mom to visit me."

"Not gonna happen," Alex predicted. "She won't leave your dad. She's devoted to him."

"She could get away for a week." Krista added the DVD to the stack of books she was carrying. "It would do her good."

"Not if something happened to him while she was thousands of miles away," Alex said.

"That's why we have airplanes," Krista said.

"Airplanes can't always get you where you're going quickly enough," he retorted.

Krista examined Alex's serious expression. "I never pegged you for a fatalist."

"I'm not. I'm a realist," he said. "So you better get in line for the cashier before the mall closes."

She had a strong sense that he was changing the subject but he also had a point. The stores wouldn't be open much longer and he still needed to buy his gourmet food baskets.

A short time later, their arms filled with packages and their shopping complete, Alex and Krista took the escalator to the lower level of the mall and walked toward the towering Christmas tree in the atrium.

"I mentioned I'm giving Dad a ride home, right?" Alex asked. "He's on Santa duty but he should be about through."

"Why didn't he drive?" Krista asked.

"With the snow coming, I wasn't comfortable with it," Alex said. "Eventually he'll need cataract surgery in his right eye. His vision's still okay but I figured why take chances."

Krista was struck with how different Alex's life was from hers. Although she admired his devotion to his father, she refused to feel guilty about her own choices. She didn't love her family any less because she lived apart from them.

The strains of a Christmas song Krista hadn't heard in years came over the mall's sound system, transporting Krista to another time and place. She was twenty-one years old, home on winter break from college and carrying on in secret with a man who could make her straight hair curl.

The same man walking beside her.

"Remember this song?" she asked him.

A woman with a lovely voice was wishing her darling merry Christmas, telling him her one wish on Christmas Eve was to be with him.

"I think about you when I hear it," Krista confessed. "Remember that crazy call I made to you from the bathroom in my parents' house?"

"Remind me," he said.

She could call the incident to mind as though it happened yesterday. Because of family obligations on Christmas Eve, she hadn't been able to get away to see him.

"My house is so crazy on Christmas Eve, the bathroom was the only place I could get privacy," Krista said. "Oh, I wanted to be with you so bad that night."

"You could have invited me over," Alex said.

"You're forgetting I hadn't told my family about

you," Krista said. "And that's not exactly what I meant. I wanted to be in bed with you."

He stopped walking, and so did she. Shoppers swerved to the left and right of them. To Krista, however, it felt as though she and Alex were the only two people in the mall. She couldn't be sure whether the attraction she still felt for him was new or a leftover from the past. She only knew that it was real.

"You shouldn't say those things," Alex said.

She reached up with her free hand to see if his lips felt as soft as they looked. She'd been wanting to do that since the coffee shop, she realized. "Why not?"

He caught her hand, drawing it away from his mouth but keeping it enfolded in his.

"You're leaving soon," he said. "Even if I was open to a fling—"

"You are open to one," Krista interrupted.

"For argument's sake, let's say I am." Alex brought their joined hands to her cheek and ran his thumb over her lower lip. "It's Christmas Eve. You're visiting your parents and I live with my dad. For privacy, we might have to sneak off to your bathroom again."

The bathroom at her parents' house, with its sky-blue tile, white porcelain toilet and handicap modifications, was decidedly not sexy.

"Then the mall might be as private as we get." Krista edged closer to him until their mouths were inches apart.

"Are you going to kiss me again?" He sounded out of breath.

"I'd much rather you kiss me this time." Her words were so soft and breathy she barely recognized her own voice. His pupils dilated, his eyelids becoming heavy. He lowered his head, starting to close the gap.

"Hey, Alex! Am I glad to run into you!" The volume of the man's greeting nearly split Krista's eardrum. Alex pulled back from her, frustration and regret in his expression. She felt the same.

"Malt. It's good to see you." Alex extended his hand. The man ignored it and enfolded Alex in a back-slapping embrace that lasted several seconds.

"Krista, this is Malt Green," Alex said when they broke apart. "Malt, Krista Novak."

The man pumped Krista's hand with enthusiasm. He had sandy blond hair, a square build and pleasant features. Krista was relatively sure his overcoat was cashmere and his teeth appeared to have been professionally whitened.

"The name's actually Mark Green. Malt's a high school nickname I can't shake. Go ahead and call me that, too, Krista. Just be aware I've graduated from malt liquor."

Krista smiled. "So you two go way back?"

Malt slung an arm around Alex's neck, highlighting the contrast between his blond hair and fair skin and Alex's darker good looks. "Used to be like brothers. I'm still not sure how we lost touch."

"You moved to Toronto," Alex said.

"Toronto, not Timbuktu." Malt let go of Alex. "I called the last couple times I was in town but never reached you."

"I've been busy," Alex said, which Krista thought was a strange response. Alex didn't strike her as the kind of guy who wouldn't make time to get together with an old friend.

"I hear you're still working with your dad," Malt said. "How's that going?"

"Fine," Alex said.

Malt gave Alex a penetrating look. "You don't ever think about what might have been?"

"No reason to," Alex said. "I'm a happy guy."

Malt made a point of smiling at Krista. "I've been happy, too, since I met my girlfriend. With all the hours I spend building the business, I'm just hoping I can keep *her* happy."

Krista had been about to correct Malt's misconception about her and Alex, but he didn't give her a chance.

"I have a company that produces high-end calendars, date books, stationary and other paper products," he told her. "It's called Greenscapes. Check us out on the web."

"I might do that," Krista said.

"Great!" Malt clapped Alex on the shoulder. "Hey, I'm getting the old crowd together the day after Christmas at Timeout."

"I heard," Alex said.

"Make sure you come. And bring Krista with you." Malt was backpedaling, talking so quickly Krista had no possibility to interrupt and say she was leaving for Switzerland December twenty-sixth. "I've got a business proposition to discuss with you."

"I'm happy where I am," Alex called after him.

"Never hurts to talk. Nice meeting you, Krista. Merry Christmas to all and to all a good night!" Malt gave a jaunty wave and melted into the crowd.

"It's hard to get a word in when he's around, isn't it?" Krista asked. "We didn't even tell him we weren't dating."

"He'll figure it out when I show up at the bar without you," Alex said.

"You're going?" Krista tried to put her thoughts

into words. "I got the impression Malt was somebody you've been avoiding."

"Nope," Alex said. "He lives in Canada, is all."

That could be the gist of it, but Krista didn't believe it. "What did he mean by a business proposition?"

"Nothing important." Alex avoided looking at her when he answered. "We should get a move on. Dad's probably waiting."

Krista complied, deep in thought while she walked beside him. If she went to the get-together at Timeout, she'd almost certainly discover what Alex didn't want to discuss.

For the first time since she arrived in Jarrell, she wished she'd booked a later return flight.

CHAPTER SIX

TREY'S MOTHER DIPPED a tablespoon into the pot simmering on her kitchen stove later on Christmas Eve. Withdrawing some hot liquid, she blew on it.

"I'm experimenting with a new clam chowder recipe." Jackie Farina extended the spoon to Rayna. "Try this and tell me if it's any good."

The fishy smell of the soup penetrated Rayna's nostrils, and her stomach churned. She reeled back, battling sudden nausea.

"Rayna, are you okay?" Jackie put the spoon back in the pot and regarded her with anxious eyes.

"I will be in a minute." Rayna backed away from the stove and sank into a kitchen chair. She felt beads of sweat form on her forehead.

"You don't look so good. Let me get you a glass of cold water." Jackie hurried to a cupboard, pulled out a glass and filled it with tap water. She handed the glass to Rayna. "Drink slowly."

Rayna did as she was told. The cool water slid down her throat, and the nausea receded.

"Feel better?" Jackie asked.

"Much better," Rayna said. "I'm sorry about that."

"No need to apologize." Jackie waved a small, slim hand. She was a petite blonde in her mid-forties who had been divorced from Trey's father for ten years. "I just hope you're not coming down with something, especially over the holidays."

Rayna was pregnant, not sick. She dimly remembered hearing somewhere that women who were expecting were sensitive to smells. Jackie's kitchen was a collection of them.

"I'm fine now." Rayna tried to concoct an explanation that would make sense. "Or I will be once we have dinner. I'm on this diet and—"

"You don't need to be on a diet!" Jackie cried. "You have a beautiful figure."

"Thanks." Rayna would prefer being naturally thin like Jackie. Saying so would be dumber than claiming to be on a diet had been. Rayna was about to gain weight, not lose it. "The holidays are a bad time to cut down anyway."

"They most certainly are," Jackie said. "But we can fix that right up if a lack of food is all that's wrong with you."

Rayna made herself nod so Jackie wouldn't suspect anything. She even ate the handful of grapes Jackie offered her. Rayna couldn't let Jackie find out Rayna was carrying her grandchild before Trey knew he was going to be a father.

Rayna hadn't seen Trey since the ice hockey game, although he'd phoned her last night when he got home from drinking with his buddies. He hadn't asked how Christmas caroling went or why she hadn't waited for him to come out of the locker room.

He had half-drunkenly serenaded her with the song "My Gal."

"Trey said he was spending the day at your house," Rayna said. "Where is he?"

Jackie hadn't given Rayna a chance to ask about

Trey's whereabouts until now. When Rayna arrived, Trey's mother had barely given Rayna time to shake the snow from her boots and take off her coat before ushering her into the kitchen for the taste testing.

"Where do you think?" Jackie rolled her eyes. "Down in the man cave with Buddy."

Buddy was what everyone in Trey's family called his fifteen-year-old brother, the youngest of the three Farina boys.

"I'm going to say hi," Rayna said.

"Tell them I said to come upstairs and set the table," Jackie said. "Their brother should be here any minute with his wife and little girl."

Rayna stopped moving. "I didn't know Bruce was in town."

The eldest Farina brother had taken a government job and moved to Washington D.C. before Rayna and Trey started dating. Rayna had never met him.

"They just got in yesterday," Jackie said. "They're staying with Bruce's wife's parents about a mile from here. Otherwise, they wouldn't be able to make it tonight with the snow still falling. Wait 'til you see their Katelyn. She's precious."

A kitchen timer sounded.

"The rice is done. I'm gonna start the shrimp scampi," Jackie said. "Don't stay in the basement too long."

Rayna descended the stairs, following the sound of male voices to a finished basement with Berber carpeting and dark wood-paneled walls.

"I'm in the lead!" Buddy yelled. "You can't beat me now."

"Don't bet on that," Trey retorted.

The brothers sat side by side on an overstuffed sofa,

their bodies leaning forward, their attention riveted on the television screen. In their hands were twin controllers.

Cartoonish characters driving colorful race cars sped across a split screen. Trey and Buddy leaned left and right, depending on which direction the track curved. The finish line loomed ahead.

"I'm comin' for you, Buddy!" Trey yelled.

"Not gonna catch me!"

The brothers shouted in unison. Rayna couldn't tell who had won until Buddy pumped a fist.

"Told you I'd win!" Buddy shouted.

"You were lucky." Trey put down the controller, caught sight of Rayna and grinned. "Hey, babe. How long have you been standing there?"

"Long enough to see you lose!" Buddy called.

"Just for a few moments." Rayna moved closer to the sofa.

Without warning, Trey's hand shot out and captured hers. He tugged, and she lost her balance. For a moment, she was airborne and then she was dropping straight into his lap.

Trey laughed and kissed her on the mouth until she was even more confused about which way was up. Her senses swam.

"Mmm," he said against her mouth. "Am I glad to see you."

"I'm outta here," Buddy said.

Rayna was about to tell Trey's brother his mother needed him to set the table but then Trey was kissing her again, deeper this time.

She closed her eyes, helpless against the sensations that swamped her. Because of her hourglass figure, Rayna had always been popular with the opposite sex.

Before Trey, she'd kissed countless boys and made love with a few. None had come close to affecting her like this.

Rayna repositioned herself on Trey's lap, encircling his neck with her arms. She felt him growing hard. Almost immediately he ended the kiss. She tried to pull his head back down to hers, but he resisted.

"Whoa," he said, his eyes slightly unfocused. "The family's upstairs. If we don't stop now, I won't be able to."

Of course he was right. Rayna was usually the one with more restraint. Her hormones were seriously out of whack. She slid off his lap. "Sorry."

"Nothing to be sorry about." He gathered her close with an arm across her shoulders, planting a kiss on her hair. "I've missed you."

They'd spent precious little time together lately. Rayna avoided looking at him. Gazing into his beautiful blue eyes, she could forgive him anything.

"You're the one who skipped caroling last night," she pointed out.

"I thought that was okay," Trey said. "If you really want me somewhere, I'm there."

Rayna turned to tell Trey that she shouldn't need to ask. Of course she'd wanted him along at caroling. Sincerity fairly shone out of his face. He really didn't get it.

"Yeah," she said. "I know."

He kissed her again, tenderly this time.

Maybe she'd overreacted at the hockey rink when she'd heard him say he wasn't serious about her, Rayna thought as she fought not to deepen the kiss. Men said all sorts of things when they were with their friends that weren't necessarily true. Although Trey had never told her he loved her, he obviously cared about her. Hadn't he just demonstrated as much?

Maybe she could tell him she was pregnant after all.

Trey lifted his head. "Somebody's coming."

Rayna heard heavy footsteps on the stairs and grimaced. How could she have forgotten she was a dinner guest in Trey's mother's home?

"I was supposed to tell you to go upstairs and set the table," Rayna said.

Trey made a comical face. "What do you think? Did Mom send someone down here to scold us?"

"Where you hiding, Trey?" A deep male voice preceded its owner into the main room of the basement. The man's features were coarser than Trey's and he had a thicker build, but it was obviously Trey's brother Bruce.

He stopped in his tracks.

"I didn't know you had company," Bruce said, his brows drawing together.

"Just Rayna," Trey said. "She's my girl."

"You've got a girl?" Bruce strode forward, shaking his head. "Sorry, Rayna. I'm just surprised anybody would put up with this guy."

"Thanks a lot," Trey said.

Bruce laughed. "You two can't have been dating long."

Rayna swallowed. "A year."

"Wow," Bruce said. "How come I didn't know about this?"

Rayna's heart thudded slowly and painfully. She'd told everyone in her family about Trey, including aunts, uncles, cousins and relations distant enough she couldn't say for sure how they were connected to her.

"You don't know everything about me," Trey said.

But surely Bruce should have known Trey had a serious girlfriend.

Bruce's eyes flicked to the television screen before settling back on Rayna. "I think I see the attraction. You're a video game fan, too, aren't you, Rayna?"

"Actually, no," Rayna said.

"Daddy! Daddy!"

This time Rayna hadn't heard heavy footsteps on the staircase. The tiny feet of the girl with the curly brown hair who dashed into the room wouldn't produce much sound. She was only about three years old.

"Grandma gave me present!" she announced, holding out a pretty gold-and-red bow.

"That's not a present, baby girl." Bruce lifted his daughter into his arms. Her laugh was light and high-pitched. "That's part of the wrapping."

"Hey, Katelyn," Trey said, giving the girl a wave. "Remember me?"

The girl buried her face in Bruce's shoulder.

"Still shy around your uncle Trey, huh?" Bruce asked his daughter, who didn't lift her head.

Trey stood up, extended a hand to Rayna and pulled her to her feet. "Katelyn always does that when she sees me."

"I'm not sure why," Bruce said. "She's usually pretty friendly."

"I'm not good with kids." Trey shrugged as though that fact didn't trouble him in the slightest. "We better get upstairs before Mom sends a hunting party down here for us."

Rayna had to consciously signal her feet to move. Trey slung an arm around her yet she'd never felt more distant from him.

In a year of dating, she'd never once thought to ask him whether he wanted kids.

Judging by his reaction to his niece, she feared the answer might be no.

"SO WHAT'S GOING ON between you two?" Eleanor Novak demanded.

Alex had to give Krista's mother credit for patience. She'd waited until Christmas Eve dinner was served and enjoyed, the dishwasher was running and everybody was gathered around the fireplace to ask the question.

Krista exchanged a long-suffering look with Alex, who indicated with his raised eyebrows that she should answer the question.

"I'm glad you asked," Krista said. "We've been meaning to tell you we've fallen madly in love."

Alex swiveled toward Krista. "We have?"

"Oh, yes. We're as mad as a couple of hatters," she said, her face deadpan. She was sitting beside Alex on the short end of the L-shaped sofa set that faced the fireplace, more by coincidence than design. After they'd cleared the table, it was the only space available.

Eleanor clapped her hands. The glow from the fireplace lit up her smile, which was warm enough to melt the snow that still fell outside. "Oh, my gosh. That is so wonderful! You two are perfect for each other!"

Krista released a long, slow breath. "Mom, I'm teasing. We're not in love."

Eleanor pinned him with a look. "Is this true, Alex?"

The others in the room regarded them with various degrees of curiosity. Grandma Novak and Alex's father seemed intent on the answer. Joe sipped his red wine. Rayna seemed preoccupied. Her boyfriend, Trey, leafed through a *Sports Illustrated* magazine he'd found on the coffee table.

"True," Alex said. "Krista and I are not in love."

"Are you sure?" Eleanor asked. "I saw you kissing on the porch."

That got Rayna's attention. "Alex and Krista were kissing?"

Eleanor ignored the interruption. "And you two do make a lovely couple."

"Leave it alone, Ellie," Joe scolded. "If Alex and Krista say they're not in love, they're not in love."

"How can they know for sure?" Eleanor shot back. "Love's a tricky thing. Unless you know what it feels like, you don't know what it feels like."

Joe made a dismissive noise. "If you listened to yourself, Ellie, you wouldn't talk."

Krista leaned close to Alex. Her hair smelled fresh and clean, like the outdoors after a rain. "Uh-oh. Look what I started," she said in a quiet voice.

"See that!" Eleanor cried. "They're whispering! Sweet nothings, for all we know. Doesn't that prove there's something between them?"

"Oh, come on, Mom. All it proves is that we're whispering." Krista sent imploring looks at the other people in the living room. "Help me out here."

Rayna said nothing, but Trey glanced up from the magazine. "Sorry. What are we talking about?"

"Whispering," Grandma answered. "That's what it looked like to me."

"Me, too," added Milo.

"We were whispering," Krista conceded. "We're not in love."

Eleanor couldn't have appeared more crestfallen if

somebody had died. "Well, that's a good way to burst somebody's bubble." She got up abruptly and stalked from the room.

A few beats of silence passed before Grandma Novak said, "You better go apologize, Krista."

"For what?"

"For egging her on," Grandma Novak said. "You know better than that."

Krista blew out an audible breath before she rose and left the room.

"Well?" Grandma Novak arched an eyebrow at Alex. "Aren't you going with her?"

"What did I do?" Alex asked.

"Don't ask, dude," Trey said. "Just go along."

Alex wasn't convinced getting between two strong-minded Novak women was the right move. He stopped at the entrance to the hall when he spotted Krista and her mother facing each other about ten feet away. Neither woman seemed aware of his presence.

"I'm sorry, Mom," Krista said.

Eleanor folded her arms over her chest. "Your grandmother sent you to apologize, didn't she?"

"As a matter of fact, she did," Krista said.

"So you're not actually sorry for teasing me like that."

"Are you sorry for not telling me the whole truth about the ulcers?" Krista asked.

"That's not the same thing," Eleanor said. "I really believed you'd fallen in love with Alex. I thought you might be moving back home to Jarrell."

"Oh, come on," Krista exclaimed. "You have to know how far-fetched that would be."

"I saw you kissing him."

"I hate to break this to you, Mom, but I've kissed a lot of guys I don't love."

Alex wondered where he ranked in that group. He started to back away, remembering an old adage about the eavesdropper never hearing anything good about themselves.

"Then you don't have a special man in your life?" Eleanor asked.

Alex stopped backpedaling, interested in the answer despite himself.

"No, I don't," Krista said.

"When you were a girl," Eleanor said, "you always said you wanted to get married and have children."

"That might happen," Krista said. "One day."

"That's what Alex wants, too," Eleanor said.

"Alex is a friend, Mom," Krista said. "Besides, I've only been back two days. Nobody falls in love that quickly. And even if I did, that doesn't mean I'd move back to Jarrell."

"I can hope," Eleanor said.

Krista shook her head. "You don't quit, do you?"

"How can I quit?" Eleanor asked. "You live half-way across the world. Sometimes I wonder if you've forgotten about me."

"You can't be serious." Krista put her free hand over her heart. "You're right here, Mom. No matter where I live."

Eleanor sniffled. Alex moved away from the hall, half ashamed of himself for eavesdropping, half glad he had. He'd been guilty of the same misconception as Eleanor, believing Krista didn't care about her family the way she should.

Since that obviously wasn't the case, why had she stayed away for so long? And now that she was home,

why was she so eager to leave? She'd given the Switzerland trip as a reason. To Alex, it sounded like an
excuse.

Back to the living room, he gave Grandma Novak a
thumbs-up signal and sat back down. Dad and Joe were
discussing the latest weather report, but Alex barely
heard them. Eleanor rejoined them a few minutes later,
her eyes suspiciously damp.

"Where's Krista?" Grandma asked.

"Downstairs wrapping presents," Eleanor said.
"We're supposed to stay upstairs until she's through."

"I can do that," Joe said dryly.

Trey laughed. "Good one, Mr. Novak."

Alex stood. "I know what she bought. I'll go help
her wrap."

"You sure about that, Alex?" Joe asked. "Ellie here
might start planning a wedding if you go down there."

"You're a real smart aleck, Joe." Eleanor made a
face at her husband. "I don't know why I went through
with our wedding."

"Went through with it?" Joe snorted. "You begged
me to marry you."

"In your dreams, buster."

Alex didn't hear the rest of their exchange because
he was already halfway down the stairs. The basement
was divided into three sections: a large paneled-room
with a bar, television and sofas; Rayna's bedroom and
adjoining bath; and an unfinished space with storage,
a sewing room and a work area.

"Don't come in here!" Krista called when Alex was
halfway down the steps. "I'm wrapping."

He found her in the unfinished part of the basement
at a table littered with red- and green-striped wrapping

paper, tape and scissors. She held something behind her back.

"It's only me," Alex said.

Krista's shoulders relaxed. From behind her back, she pulled out the glittery, gold sweater she'd brought for her grandmother.

"It might not be safe for you to be down here," Krista said, chewing her bottom lip. "My mom hasn't given up on a romance between us."

"Your dad's up there right now making sure she knows we're not going to fall in love," Alex remarked.

"Could be trouble," Krista said. "Mom doesn't pay attention to anything Dad says."

"What matters is that we know it's not love," Alex said.

"Agreed." Krista placed the sweater in a box lined with tissue paper and closed it before looking up. "So what is between us, do you think? Lust?"

He let out a surprised breath. "I'll never get used to you blurting out things like that."

She arranged the box in the middle of a precut piece of wrapping paper. "I think it's cute that you're shy."

He picked up the roll of tape, ripped off a piece and handed it to her. "I'm not shy," he denied.

"More shy than me."

"Everybody's more shy than you."

Their fingers brushed when he handed her the tape. He thought it was deliberate on her part.

"If I was staying longer, I'd show you how shy I'm not," she said.

Instead of rising to the sexual bait, Alex rocked back on his heels. "Why aren't you staying longer?"

She seemed taken aback by the question. "You know why. I'm going skiing in Switzerland."

"Yeah," he said, "but there's something I don't know."

She stopped wrapping. "What's that?"

"Why haven't you been home before now?"

That had been the reason he'd come down to the basement, he realized. To discover the answer to that question.

Krista's eyes flicked away. She went back to wrapping the present. "It just hasn't worked out."

"Why?" he persisted.

"It's tough to get time off work," she said.

Alex needed to accept that Krista wasn't going to tell him the real reason. And why should she?

Like she'd said, they were in lust, not love.

CHAPTER SEVEN

KRISTA HUGGED HERSELF on Christmas morning, fighting off the shivers as she surveyed the wintry scene outside the large picture window in her parents' living room. The snow feathered down from the sky, blanketing everything in sight.

Grandma shuffled to her side, handing Krista a cup of steaming coffee. "When do you think it will stop?"

"The radio report said not until later this afternoon," Krista said. "I'm still amazed we got to church this morning."

"Thanks to Alex," Grandma said.

He'd gotten up early to clear both driveways with his snow blower. With the snow blade already attached to the front of his pickup, he'd forged a path on the half-plowed neighborhood road to a church partially filled with other hardy souls. Only Krista's father had been unable to attend.

"Thank the Lord he's our neighbor," Grandma declared.

"Shhhh." Krista bent her head down to her much shorter grandmother's level. "We can't have all that praise going to his head."

Alex was across the room, having deposited presents under a Christmas tree so thick with miniature lights it could burn eyeballs. He wore black dress slacks and a long-sleeved shirt in a rich burgundy that complemented his black hair. With a fresh shave, he looked younger, his angular features more prominent.

"It won't," Grandma said. "Alex is very level-headed."

"He's determined, too," Krista said. "When I woke up, I thought it would take a Christmas miracle to get to church."

"Too bad more people couldn't make it," Grandma said. "The service was lovely."

A warmth at odds with the frosty scenery outside spread through Krista as a memory surfaced. On the way into church that morning, Alex had told Krista she looked lovely.

"We're ready to open presents!" Krista's mother announced from the velour armchair closest to the tree. Krista and Rayna used to refer to it as her throne, the seat from where she could survey all her subjects.

"Oh, goodie!" Grandma exclaimed. "I'm dying to see what Alex got you, Krista."

"Alex didn't get me anything."

"He most certainly did," Grandma said. "It's one of the biggest presents under the tree. I saw the name tag."

"But I didn't buy Alex anything!" At the mall on Christmas Eve, Krista had been focused on shopping for her family.

"I'll tell you what," Grandma said in a conspiratorial voice. "I got Charlie two presents. You can give Alex one of them."

Relief cascaded through Krista. "You sure you don't mind?"

"Not at all. Charlie can't make it today anyway because he's snowed in. Just follow my lead."

"Did you hear me over there?" Ellie projected her

voice so it drowned out the ubiquitous Christmas music. "What are you two murmuring about anyway?"

"If we told you, Ellie, it wouldn't be a secret," Grandma said with good cheer. She hooked her elbow through Krista's and walked with her to where everybody was gathered.

Two seats were vacant. One was next to Milo on the long end of the L-shaped sofa and the other beside Alex on the short end.

"Sit next to Milo, Grandma," Krista's mother ordered. "That way Alex and Krista can be next to each other."

Grandma complied even as Krista groaned. Her mother had maneuvered it so Krista and Alex were side by side at church, too. Krista sat down next to Alex, forcing herself to count to five before she replied.

"Would you give it a rest, Mom? It won't work."

Ellie made her eyes go wide and innocent. "I don't know what you're talking about."

Krista blew out a disbelieving breath. Her mother had kept such close watch on them at church that Krista had a hard time concentrating on the service. She might have anyway, with Alex so close, but her mother definitely hadn't made things easier.

"You do, too," Krista spluttered.

"Down, girl," Alex said near her ear, his warm breath chasing away her lingering chill. He smelled wonderful, like soap, shampoo and the outdoors. "It's Christmas morning."

Krista clamped her lips shut. Alex was right. No matter how infuriating her mother could be, Krista was thankful to share this time with her family. She remembered Christmases when she ached from missing them.

The holiday had always been special. Because of the age gap between Krista and Rayna, someone had believed in Santa at the Novak house for a very long time. To keep the legend alive, her father used to climb up on the roof a few nights before Christmas, hollering down the chimney in the guise of Santa Claus to ask his daughters what they wanted for Christmas.

Krista avoided looking at her father's useless legs, instead meeting her mother's fake expression of innocence.

"Never mind," Krista mumbled.

"Good, then we can start." Her mother gestured to Rayna. Krista's sister sat cross-legged at her traditional place on the floor next to the presents. "Rayna's going to distribute."

"Just call me Rayna Claus." Rayna smiled faintly, which was animated for her that morning. She'd been quiet on Christmas Eve, too, letting Trey do the talking. Her boyfriend was absent this morning, although he was supposed to stop by later.

"Let's start with my gift for Milo," Grandma suggested. "It's the big one with red snowmen on it."

The present was at least three feet square and one foot deep, but Rayna managed to hand it to Milo with little effort. Milo raised his brows at Grandma before ripping off the paper and opening the lid of the box. He rummaged through volumes of tissue paper, finally pulling out a miniature orange life jacket.

Milo held it up, a quizzical look on his face. "Is this for a doll?"

"No, silly," Grandma said. "Read the label. Out loud."

Milo glanced down at the label, then shook his head before reading, "Golf ball life jacket."

Everybody erupted into laughter, Krista excluded.

"Dad just started golfing last summer." Alex leaned his head close so Krista could hear over the laughter. "He and Grandma Novak try to outdo each other every year by giving the funniest gift."

"Time to open yours," Milo told her grandmother. "Rayna, it's the present wrapped entirely in red."

"Oooo," Grandma said. "I can't wait to see what's in it."

The box contained an oversize T-shirt imprinted with the shapely body of a bikini-clad young woman. Grandma shouted with laughter. She stood up, pulled the T-shirt over her clothes and posed with one hand on her hip. "Va va va voom!"

"I thought you could wear that on your internet dates," Milo said.

Krista shared an amused look with Alex. Her father covered his eyes. "I can't look at my mother this way."

"I think we can all agree that Milo wins for best gag gift this year," Krista's mother said.

Grandma gave a few exaggerated shakes of her hip. "Can't argue with that."

The lighthearted mood continued as more presents were opened. As the gifts to Krista piled up—a silk scarf, cashmere-lined black leather gloves, fluffy slippers—she was increasingly glad she'd saved the gift cards for another occasion.

Grandma's sweater, Rayna's tote bag and the books for her father were all hits. Krista's mother was harder to read when she opened the DVD of Europe's favorite destinations. Her brow creased as she examined the description on the back of the package.

"You're always watching those travel shows so I thought you'd like it," Krista said.

Mom set the DVD aside. "I might."

Krista knew she should let her mother's comment go. Alex even gave her arm a brief squeeze, undoubtedly a signal to do exactly that.

"You *might* decide to visit me so you can see some of those places in person," Krista said.

"No, I won't." Her mother's denial was lightning quick. "I'd rather see the sights in New York City. If you move back to the United States, you can take me."

"Do you have to say things like that, Ellie?" Her father spoke before Krista could snap off a reply.

"I'm only speaking the truth," her mother said. "What? You want me to lie?"

"On Christmas morning, yeah," he said. "I want you to lie."

Krista's mother glared at her father. Her body visibly tensed as though she were ready to go to battle. She opened her mouth.

"Let's see what Alex got Krista," Grandma suggested.

Krista's mother shut her mouth and turned away from her husband. "Oh, yes! Let's!"

"Let me help Rayna with it." Alex rose to take a large, flat gift from Rayna, carefully setting it on the coffee table in front of Krista.

"I bet it's a painting," Krista guessed. She carefully peeled away the wrapping paper to reveal a framed photograph of a landscape, but not just any landscape.

Snow blanketed a panoramic view of farmland and a tiny town nestled on the banks of the frosty Susquehanna River. The white stuff clung to the branches of evergreens and oaks, contrasting vividly with the bark of the trees and the crystalline sky. An eagle soared above the beauty.

"I recognize this view. It was taken from that scenic overlook at the park," Krista said, awe in her voice.

The first day she and Alex had spent together, they'd driven into the mountains and stopped at the overlook. The breathtaking scenery had stirred her soul, especially after Alex had given her something to remember it by.

A first kiss so amazing she could recall it in detail eight years later.

"Isn't Alex talented? He took that photo, too." Grandma gestured to the gorgeous landscape of the wildflowers Krista had noticed when she'd first arrived. Krista's focus, however, was on her gift.

Too much snow was on the ground for Alex to have snapped the shot during yesterday's hike. Krista's mind reeled with questions she couldn't ask until they were alone. When exactly had he taken the photo? Had he always intended to give it to her? Did he remember the significance of the spot?

"It's a very pretty picture." Mom was never good at masking her emotions so her disappointment shone through. She'd probably hoped Alex would buy Krista jewelry, not realizing that the landscape was far more personal.

"Thank you," Krista said, touching Alex's arm. "I love it."

Alex shrugged, not quite meeting her eyes. "I thought you might."

He *thought* she might?

"We only have a few presents left," Rayna said.

"I think that red one is for Alex from Krista." Grandma caught Krista's eye and winked, snapping

Krista back to the present. Krista could puzzle through why Alex had given her the photo later.

"That's right," Krista said.

Krista was fairly certain Alex hadn't seen Grandma's wink. He regarded her quizzically, probably wondering where she'd found the time to shop for him and what could be inside the box. Come to think of it, Krista hadn't thought to ask Grandma.

The first tinge of unease hit Krista while Alex was unwrapping the present. When he reached inside, she held her breath.

Alex pulled out something sleek and black and unfolded it.

"It's a bathrobe!" Ellie sent Krista a pointed, triumphant look. "What a wonderful gift to get your *friend,* Krista."

Grandma Novak beamed at Krista, unmindful of the damage she'd wrought.

"I love it," Alex said.

Krista swung her gaze to Alex's laughing eyes in time to see his wink.

NEVER MIND THAT IT was after 5:00 p.m. on Christmas day. If the neighborhood held a popularity contest, Alex believed he and his dad would trounce Santa Claus.

The jolly fat man didn't have snow-clearing capabilities and an industrial-strength snowblower like they did.

"Looks like about eighteen inches on the ground," his father said after Alex climbed into the cab of the pickup and shut out the cold. The senior center was one of their clients. Alex had used the snowblower to clear the pathways while his father plowed the lot.

"At least that much," Alex agreed. It had snowed throughout the morning and the sumptuous Christmas lunch the Novaks had served after the gifts had been opened. Now, at nearly five in the afternoon, it seemed to have finally stopped.

His father whistled long and low.

"Good thing most people have tomorrow off," his father said. "It'll take most of the day to get the parking lots cleared."

Costas Landscaping dealt solely with commercial clients, which meant larger-scale jobs.

"I already lined up some subcontractors," Alex said. "That way, we can get everything done."

Today Alex and his dad had stayed close to home, plowing the neighborhood streets and a fair number of driveways as favors to their neighbors. From experience Alex knew it was best to stay off the main roads after a big snow to give the crews a chance to do their jobs. Besides, it was Christmas day.

"We should be getting back," his father said. "It'll be dark soon, and Ellie and Joe invited us over to help them get rid of the leftovers."

After serving bountiful spreads for Christmas Eve dinner and Christmas lunch, the Novaks traditionally took the night off from cooking. Family and friends were expected to raid the refrigerator and eat when they were hungry.

"Let's go," Alex said.

His father turned the truck from the senior center parking lot onto a neighborhood street and lowered the plow. Another inch or so of snow had accumulated since they'd made their initial pass on the way to the center. Deep mounds bracketed the pavement.

"When is Krista going back to Europe?" his father asked over the scrape of the plow.

"Tomorrow," Alex said and felt his spirits dip.

"You sure about that?" his father asked. "After all this snow, won't her flight be canceled?"

"We didn't get as much as some other places in the northeast," Alex said. "I heard on the radio that the crews at the Harrisburg airport are managing to keep the runways clear."

"Where does she catch her connecting flight?"

"Washington D.C.," Alex said. "They didn't get any snow."

"That's too bad," his father said. "Not about the airports, about Krista leaving."

Alex suppressed a sigh. "You're not going to ask if I'm into her, too, are you, Dad?"

"I don't need to," his father said. "I know my son."

Was his attraction to Krista that obvious? Alex wondered a little while later as he approached the Novaks' house.

It was out of character for him to act on impulse without regard for the consequences tomorrow would bring. And yet only yesterday Alex had dug the framed photo of the view from the mountain out of storage and wrapped it up. He'd meant to give the photo to Krista years ago to assure she remembered their first kiss.

She'd moved to Europe while the gift was at the frame shop so Alex tucked it away. He couldn't say for sure why he'd dug it back up. Certainly not because he'd harbored feelings for her all these years.

From the awe on her face when she'd opened the gift, however, Alex might have a hard time convincing her that sometimes a photograph was just a photograph.

Alex was barely inside the Novak house when Eleanor sprang up from the armchair and blocked his way into the living room. "Would you do me a favor?"

"Do I have a choice?" Alex asked.

Eleanor laughed and batted his arm. "It won't be hard. I need you to check if Krista needs help getting our snowblower home. She was helping some of the neighbors clear their driveways."

Alex tugged the zipper of his jacket back up, wondering why Krista wasn't home yet with darkness encroaching. "Will do."

"One more thing." Eleanor detained him with a hand on his arm. "Mention how much we enjoy having her home and how hopeful we are that she'll stay."

Alex narrowed his eyes. "How many times did you tell Krista that today?"

"Not many," Eleanor said. "Three or four, tops."

Now Alex understood why Krista wasn't back yet. He hadn't noticed Krista or the snowblower on the way back from the senior center so he walked up the street in the opposite direction, listening for the sound of a blower.

The quiet was almost absolute. Darkness had fallen, although light reflected off the white snow and the Christmas lights on the neighborhood houses, illuminating the way.

Alex spotted the Novaks' snowblower in a cleared driveway five houses down from his own. The two-story Colonial belonged to the Snyders, a friendly retired couple in their late sixties.

"Come in! Come in!" Mrs. Snyder told Alex after he explained why he'd rung the doorbell. "Krista and I were just sitting down to some hot chocolate. Such a dear she was for clearing our driveway."

Mrs. Snyder wore her gray hair in a short stylish cut that worked well with the thin frames of her black glasses. Alex often saw her walking in the neighborhood.

"Pete's next door trying to fix a broken hot-water heater," Mrs. Snyder said, referring to her husband. "He used to be in the heating and air-conditioning business, you know."

Alex had known that. Pete had used his connections to get Alex's father a good price on a new hot-water heater when their old one gave out.

"Look who the snow blew in, Krista!" Mrs. Snyder announced on the way into her spacious kitchen.

"Alex!" Krista sat on a stool at the breakfast bar with a cup of hot chocolate. Her nose and cheeks were still red from the cold, and her hat, gloves and jacket lay on one of the kitchen chairs. "Mom sent you to find me, didn't she?"

"How'd you guess?" he asked with a smile.

Mrs. Snyder filled a mug with hot water and put it in the microwave. "I'll give Ellie a call and let her know you'll both be here awhile. Krista was just about to tell me about her life in Europe!"

"I took French from Mrs. Snyder in high school." Krista had gone to Jarrell High, one of the two public schools that served the students in the area. Alex had attended the other. "She's the teacher who got me excited about languages."

"Krista was one of my favorites," Mrs. Snyder said, then held up a finger while she spoke into the phone. "Ellie? Merry Christmas. It's Susie Snyder calling to tell you Krista and Alex are over here with me."

While Mrs. Snyder finished the phone conversation, Alex took off his jacket and sat down on the stool next to Krista at the breakfast bar. There was a lot about Krista he didn't know, he realized.

"How many languages can you speak?" Alex asked.

"Fluently? Four," she said. "It's not as impressive as it sounds, though. Mrs. Snyder will tell you each subsequent language gets easier to learn."

"But not Czech!" Mrs. Snyder replaced the phone back on its cradle. "It's notoriously difficult."

"Mluvíš česky?" Krista asked Mrs. Snyder.

"Jen trochu," Mrs. Snyder answered. To Alex, she said, "Krista asked if I spoke Czech and I told her just a little. I'd love to hear how you picked it up, Krista."

"My Grandpa Novak used to speak to me in Czech when I was younger," Krista said. "I went to Penn, which happens to have a Slavic language department. I jumped at the chance to take Czech and some of the words and phrases came back to me."

"That doesn't explain how you became fluent." Mrs. Snyder removed the mug from the microwave, stirred in some instant mix and slid the cup across to Alex. He nodded his thanks. "Did you do a study abroad program?"

"No, but I roomed with a Czech student for two years," Krista said. "My professor suggested it. She said it would be good for my Czech and Ana's English. And it was."

"Fascinating," Mrs. Snyder said. "So how did you end up in Prague?"

"On a lark." Krista glanced at Alex. This part of the story, he knew. "A friend of Ana's runs a translation and interpreter business. He was looking to add an American to his team. Ana told him about me, he offered me a job and off I went."

"I heard from your mother that it happened just like

The Reader Service—Here's how it works:

If offer card is missing write to: The Reader Service, P.O. Box 1867, Buffalo, NY 14240-1867 or visit us at www.ReaderService.com.

NO POSTAGE
NECESSARY
IF MAILED
IN THE
UNITED STATES

BUSINESS REPLY MAIL

FIRST-CLASS MAIL   PERMIT NO. 717   BUFFALO, NY

POSTAGE WILL BE PAID BY ADDRESSEE

THE READER SERVICE

PO BOX 1867

BUFFALO NY 14240-9952

Play the Lucky Hearts Game

and get...
2 FREE BOOKS and
2 FREE MYSTERY GIFTS...
YOURS TO KEEP!

Yes! I have scratched off the gold card.
Please send me my *2 FREE BOOKS* and
2 FREE MYSTERY GIFTS (gifts are worth about $10).
I understand that I am under no obligation to purchase
any books as explained on the back of this card.

Scratch Here!
Then look below to see what your
cards get you...*2 Free Books*
& 2 Free Mystery Gifts!

❏ I prefer the regular-print edition
135/336 HDL FJA2

❏ I prefer the larger-print edition
139/339 HDL FJA2

FIRST NAME

LAST NAME

ADDRESS

APT.#   CITY

Visit us online at
www.ReaderService.com

STATE/PROV.   ZIP/POSTAL CODE

Twenty-one gets you
2 FREE BOOKS and
2 FREE MYSTERY GIFTS!

Twenty gets you
2 FREE BOOKS!

Nineteen gets you
1 FREE BOOK!

TRY AGAIN!

▼ **DETACH AND MAIL CARD TODAY!** ▼

H-SR-11/11

that." Mrs. Snyder snapped her fingers. "One minute you were here, the next you were gone."

"My mother thought I should have stayed and finished my last semester of college," Krista said.

"I don't agree!" Mrs. Snyder exclaimed. "You have your college degree now, don't you? And you've gotten to see some of the world."

"A lot of the world," Krista said. "Prague is pretty central. Airfare between European cities is reasonable so I've been to most of the major cities in Europe."

Mrs. Snyder placed her hand over her heart. "I would love to have the opportunity to travel like that. You don't happen to have photos with you, do you?"

"On my computer," Krista said. "I have a folder for each city. It's kind of corny but I arranged them into slide shows and set them to music."

"You simply must come to the senior center and share those photos," Mrs. Snyder said. "Your grandmother and I volunteer on the programs committee. You could be a special guest."

"I can't," Krista said. "I'm leaving tomorrow."

Mrs. Snyder's face fell. "That's disappointing. Is there any chance your flight will be delayed because of the weather?"

"It takes more than a little snow to shut down Harrisburg International," Krista said. "Some flights were delayed today, but things are expected to be back to normal tomorrow, especially because there's no snow in the forecast."

Evidently Krista and Alex had heard similar weather reports. Alex took a gulp of hot chocolate, realizing when it scalded the roof of his mouth that he should have let it cool.

"What is normal for you in Prague?" Mrs. Snyder

asked. "I'd love to hear about your day-to-day life and your job."

"The job's okay," Krista said, "but it's a job, like any other."

With her response, Alex felt as though Krista had cracked open a window into herself he'd never seen before. "What do you mean?" he asked.

"After eight years doing the same thing, the challenge isn't so great anymore. Lately the bulk of my work has been translating documents," Krista said. "I work to live, not the other way around."

"Where do you live?" Mrs. Snyder asked. "The central city?"

"Close to it," Krista said. "The district is called Vinohrady. It's quiet and safe, like most of Prague. There are cafés, shops, tree-lined streets, parks. You name it. The area's popular with ex-pats."

"Are your friends ex-pats or natives?" Alex asked.

"Half and half," Krista said. "I met the majority of the Czechs I know through Ana. Funny thing, though. She's lived in Manhattan for the past five years."

"The grass is always greener," Mrs. Snyder said, laughing.

"Aby oprávněný," Krista said, then translated her own words. "That's true."

"Do you ever get lonely?" Alex didn't know where that question came from.

Krista considered the question before replying. "I can't say that I do. I have a group of friends I see often so I guess I don't have time to be lonely."

For the first time Alex was able to picture Krista in Prague, immersed in the life she'd built for herself.

No matter how much Eleanor wished it, Jarrell was no longer Krista's home.

THE SIDEWALK LEADING BACK to the Novaks' house was clear of snow, thanks to Krista's efforts. Alex walked abreast of Krista, keeping his hand at the small of her back, ready to steady her if she should slip.

Because of the heavy treads on her snow boots, Krista was not going to trip.

She was content to let him keep his hand where it was anyway.

"Did you really come looking for me because of the snowblower?" Krista asked. Since they'd opened presents that morning, she'd been waiting all day to get him alone. She wouldn't waste this opportunity. She intended to fire questions at him fast and furious.

"It's a heavy piece of equipment," Alex said. "I would have pushed it home for you if you hadn't left it with the Snyders."

Mr. Snyder had returned home as they were leaving and asked to borrow the machine until tomorrow morning. Not everybody farther down the street had completely cleared their sidewalks and he meant to do it for them.

"But I'm strong." Krista flexed her left arm in a Charles Atlas pose that was ruined by her parka. "You must have known I could get the snowblower home myself."

Alex slanted her a perplexed look. "What's your point?"

"My point is that the blower couldn't have been your only reason for coming to the Snyders'," she said. "Seems to me you wanted to spend time with me."

"Guilty as charged," he said without missing a beat. "But come on. What did you expect after you got me that sexy black bathrobe?"

Krista stopped walking and pivoted sharply so she

was facing him. She poked him in the chest with a gloved finger.

"I've been meaning to talk to you about that," she said. "You saw Grandma wink at me, didn't you?"

"Maybe," he said.

"So you knew the bathrobe was from Grandma for Charlie," she accused.

A grin teased the corners of his mouth. "A logical assumption."

She balanced both hands on her hips. "Then why did you say you loved it? You must have known how my mom would take that."

"I wasn't thinking about your mom," Alex said. "I was thinking I really would love it if you got me a bathrobe."

"Since when?" she asked.

"Since I realized I'd be all for it if we could squeeze in some sex before you left."

Krista resumed walking, trying to camouflage the rush of blood to her face. Had Alex really just said that? Why had he said that?

"Too bad nothing's changed," she said with forced lightness. "We still have no privacy."

"It's more than too bad," Alex drawled. "It's damn near a tragedy."

Now that was a remark Krista couldn't let pass unquestioned.

"Does this have something to do with the gift you gave me?" she asked.

"I don't understand," he said.

"Surely you remember what happened at that overlook," Krista said.

"What happened?" he asked.

"That was the place we first kissed," she exclaimed.

His brow furrowed. "I guess it was."

He'd had to be reminded? For once Krista didn't blurt out what she was thinking. How could such a momentous moment have made such a faint impression on him?

"You didn't take that photo eight years ago and keep it for me all this time?" she asked.

"Why would I do that?" he asked.

Krista fought back disappointment. She'd started to believe Alex had once harbored strong feelings for her. For the past few hours, Krista wondered if any remnant of those feelings extended into the present. A part of her had even wanted them to.

"Around the house I have a bunch of photos I've taken over the years," Alex continued. "Now I understand why I thought you'd like that one."

They were approaching the driveway of the house he shared with his father. A sane amount of white lights lit up the bushes in the Costas' front yard and flanked the door, from which hung a tasteful wreath. The inside of the house, however, looked dark.

"Dad must already be at your house." Alex swept a hand in front of him with a flourish, indicating the sidewalk leading to the Novaks' front door. "Shall we?"

Krista groaned, momentarily forgetting her damaged ego. What was the matter with her anyway, wishing she meant something to Alex? She lived in Prague. She couldn't afford to get involved with Alex on anything more than a superficial level. That didn't mean she couldn't complain to him about her mother.

"I know it's Christmas day but I am not looking forward to going back in the house," Krista said. "It's like my Mom thinks the more times she mentions me moving back to Jarrell, the likelier it is to happen."

"I noticed that," Alex said, "and I've got something that might help. It's called ouzo."

"What's that?"

"A Greek liquor that'll mellow you out so you don't care what your mom says," he said. "I've got a bottle inside the house."

"That's tempting," Krista said, "but it'll be dinner-time soon."

"Not so. Lunch is the big meal for your family on Christmas. The rest of the day, everybody snacks on leftovers," Alex said. "Nobody's expecting us because they think we're still at the Snyders'."

"You're right," Krista said. "When Mrs. Snyder called my mom, she didn't say how long we'd be over there."

Alex cut his eyes toward his house. "Well?"

Krista captured his bare hand in her gloved one and tugged.

"Quick. Let's get inside before anyone sees us."

CHAPTER EIGHT

THE DINING ROOM WAS DARK enough that Alex had to feel his way along the edge of the table to the cabinet where they kept the ouzo.

"Are you sure we can't turn on a light?" he asked.

"Positive." Krista was giggling, the same way she had when they'd entered the darkened house and shed their outerwear in the kitchen beside the dim light over the stove. She'd claimed turning on any other light would be too conspicuous. "This room faces my parents' house. We can't let them know we're over here."

His shin connected with something hard. "Ow."

"What was that?" Krista asked from the archway between the kitchen and dining room. They'd decided he should retrieve the booze because he knew where it was.

"A chair, I think." Alex didn't move for a moment while his eyes adjusted to the darkness. "I'm starting to make out shapes, I think because of the Christmas lights from your house."

More laughter erupted from Krista. "The yard art has its uses, after all."

Alex reached the china cabinet without another mishap. He leaned down, pulled open one of the doors to the buffet and felt around for the ouzo bottle.

"Got it," he said. "Now for the shot glasses."

He straightened, opened the hutch and felt around

for small glasses with thin sides and thick, protruding bases. After a few unsuccessful moments of searching, he grabbed the two nearest glasses.

On the way back to the kitchen, he bumped into the same solid object. "Damn chair. Remind me again why I didn't get a flashlight?"

"How could you find one without turning on a light?" Krista asked.

Alex supposed her reasoning had a warped sort of logic.

"I'll take the ouzo." She reached for the bottle, then for his hand. "You might not know this about me but I have excellent night vision. I can get us to where we're going."

"Where's that?"

"The kitchen," she answered. "We're going to imbibe by the light of the stove."

The bulb emitted barely enough brightness to illuminate the way to the kitchen table. They sat down at an angle to each other, with their knees touching.

Alex set the long-stemmed glasses with the cone-shaped bowls on the table, unscrewed the cap on the ouzo and tipped the bottle.

"Are you trying to get me drunk, Alex Costas?" Krista asked. "Because I swear those are martini glasses."

"I couldn't find the shot glasses so I super-sized," Alex said as he poured. "It's the American way to drink Greek booze."

"They why is the ouzo bottle almost full?"

Alex slid one half-filled glass across the wooden tabletop to Krista and went to work pouring ouzo into the second one. "We only bring out the ouzo on special occasions."

Krista lifted her glass. "What special occasion is this?"

"Are you kidding me?" He smiled at her. The light softened her features, making her look almost ethereal. "It's Christmas night and I'm alone in the dark with a beautiful woman."

He waited for her to pick up her glass before raising his own and clinking it against hers. "*Stini Yamos!* That's a Greek toast to your health and happiness."

"*Stini Yamos!*" she repeated.

He watched her over the rim of his glass as he downed half the drink. She took a healthy swallow, too, blinking rapidly as the liquor slid down her esophagus.

"It tastes sort of like licorice," she said, "but I don't get a strong sense of alcohol."

"The alcohol content is pretty low but it'll get you drunk fast because it's high in sugar," Alex said. "Sugar delays the absorption of alcohol in the stomach. In Greece, it's considered poor form to drink ouzo without food."

"Have you been to Greece?" Krista asked.

"Nope."

"Why not?" she asked. "You have family over there, right?"

"Not that I'm aware of," Alex said. "My dad's parents were born in the United States. So there's nobody to visit."

"Aren't you curious to see the land of your ancestors?"

Alex's father had proposed a trip maybe five years ago. They'd both gotten passports but plans had fallen through when they'd gotten busy at work. His dad hadn't mentioned going to Greece since.

"I'd never really thought about it." Alex raised his glass again, unwilling to enter a discussion about distant places. Krista would be jetting off to one of them tomorrow. For now, though, she was right here. "Bottoms up."

"Your plan *is* to get me drunk!" she exclaimed. "Then you'll try to have your way with me, won't you?"

His hand froze with the glass suspended in midair. He'd never been good at living in the moment, but the past few days with Krista had taught him that moments were sometimes all two people had.

"What if I were?" he asked softly.

The silence between them turned so absolute that Alex could hear the wind whistling past the kitchen windows. If he listened more closely, he could hear Krista breathing.

She reached across the table and took his glass, her fingers brushing his. She set his glass down on the table. "Then I'd rather not let ouzo dull the experience."

All the blood in his body rushed straight to his groin. Despite the years and the distance, one thing hadn't changed. Krista didn't even need to touch him for his body to respond.

Their eyes connected in the semidarkness and held. He stood up and she did the same.

"I'd race you to your bedroom," she said in a husky voice, "except I don't know where it is."

"Are you suggesting we turn on a light?" he asked.

She shook her head, advanced a few steps toward him and walked her fingers up his chest. "I was looking forward to feeling my way."

He made a sound between a laugh and a groan and

took her hand, leading her down a hall that was almost pitch-black. He stumbled on what he realized was the place where the carpet wasn't stretched tight enough and steadied himself with a hand on the wall.

"Alex Costas, if you fall and break something," Krista said in a warning tone, "I'll be seriously annoyed."

He laughed. He was still laughing when they reached his room and he pulled the door shut behind them. It seemed incredible that he could be amused and aroused at the same time. What was it about Krista that he found so irresistible?

He concluded it didn't matter. All that was important was kissing her.

Their lips connected in the darkness, molding together as though they were two halves of a whole, their tongues tangling, the heat building between them.

He'd missed this immediate bond, this dizzying speed of his body's response to her, this excitement.

His hands roamed over her body, encountering layers of material. She was wearing a shirt under her sweater and blue jeans. Too many clothes.

"Where's your bed?" she rasped against his mouth.

He didn't know. With Krista in his arms and the room pitched in darkness, he couldn't tell east from west or up from down.

His back hit a wall. No, that must be a door. He could feel the edge of the knob against the top of his thigh.

Suddenly he knew what had to be done.

He switched on the light.

She blinked up at him, her pupils constricting, her mouth agape. With her well-kissed lips, the heightened color in her cheeks and the slight haze in her eyes, she'd never looked more beautiful.

"What did...you do that...for?" Her voice was breathy, her words disjointed.

Alex's bedroom was on the side of the house opposite from where her parents lived. It was unlikely that his father or one of Krista's relatives would notice the light and figure out what was going on.

But even if his bedroom were directly in their line of sight, Alex might have taken the risk.

He held her face in his hands and gazed deeply into her eyes. She'd once blindsided him with the news that she was moving to Europe. It wouldn't happen again.

He understood that she was getting on a plane tomorrow. He didn't harbor any illusions that she would leave the life she'd made for herself in Prague and move back to Jarrell.

"I need to see exactly what I'm doing," he said.

He picked her up and carried her to his bed, depositing her on the mattress and joining her so their bodies were aligned.

Then he kissed her with his eyes wide open.

LANGUOR SPREAD THROUGH Krista, so complete she couldn't imagine a more perfect spot than Alex's king-size bed. With his arm encircling her and their naked bodies flush against each other, she was so delightfully warm it could have been summer in the tropics rather than winter in Pennsylvania.

"That was incredible," she said.

"Thank you."

She elbowed him gently in the side. "I meant we were incredible together."

"You say tomato," he said. "I say tom-*ah*to."

She laughed. "Seriously, I haven't felt anything so intense since…well, since the last time we were together."

She waited to hear that he'd experienced the same sort of intensity. Instead she heard the ticking of his bedside alarm clock. Was this another case of the experience being better for her than it was for him, as his vague recollection of their first kiss had implied? She simply refused to believe that.

"Well?" she said. "Was it the same for you? Or do you always have that much passion?"

He let out a breath that was half-snort, half-chuckle. "I'm a passionate man."

"This passionate?" she persisted.

"Do we have to analyze it?"

"Well, yes," Krista said. "I want to understand why it's better with you than with anyone else. Don't get me wrong, I haven't slept with very many men but there have been enough for me to know this is unusual."

"So is a woman who says exactly what's on her mind." Alex sounded amused.

"It saves time and misunderstandings," Krista said. "Back to this lust we have for each other, is it powerful for you, too?"

"Very powerful," he said. "It has been since the moment I laid eyes on you, but that's no secret."

Krista had felt the same instant connection. "How about the first time we kissed?"

"I wanted to rip your clothes off," he said.

"Aha," Krista cried. "So you do remember kissing me at the overlook!"

"I remember how kissing you affected me," he said.

She still didn't quite believe that he couldn't recall every detail of that kiss. Now, however, was not the time to get immersed in another discussion about the meaning of his Christmas gift. Not when she wanted to run something else by him.

"Care to hear my theory about what's going on between us?" she asked. "It's not love at first sight, by the way. I don't believe in that."

"Me, neither. I believe you have to get to know a person before you can love them," he said. "So what's your theory?"

"Pheromones," she said. "We like the way each other smells."

"How do I smell?"

She buried her nose in his neck and breathed in his clean, warm scent. "Intoxicating, but pheromones are odorless. The brain detects them through a nerve in the nostrils."

"Are you saying humans are at the mercy of their noses?"

"Not just humans," she said. "Animal sexuality is based on olfactory senses. Did you know female rats give off pheromones when they're ready to mate?"

"I'm not sure I wanted to," Alex said. "How do you know so much about this stuff anyway?"

"It's actually a funny story," she said. "I have a friend in Prague who wears pheromone perfume."

"I thought pheromones were odorless," Alex said.

"They are. The manufacturer mixes them with the perfume to create a light, fresh scent. It's sort of citrusy."

"Does it work?"

"Becca claims it does." The pheromone hypothesis had probably occurred to Krista because Becca had called earlier that day to wish her a merry Christmas and find out when she was arriving in Switzerland.

"Of all my friends, she dates the most. It gives weight to my theory about what's up with us."

"Except you're not wearing the perfume, right?"

"I must not need to around you," she said.

She pivoted her head on the pillow to look at him at the same time he turned. Their mouths met in a slow, sweet exploration. He smoothed his hand over her hip, edging her closer to him and the unmistakable feel of his erection.

Krista anchored one hand on his shoulder and shoved, abruptly breaking off the kiss. Sitting up, she scooted backward on the bed, using the bottom sheet to partially cover her nudity.

"Oh, no," she said. "We can't do that again."

He planted his right elbow on the bed and propped his head on one hand. With his five o'clock shadow, uncombed hair and eyes at half-mast, he exuded sex appeal. "Who are we to fight our pheromones?"

"We have to! Sooner or later, my mother will figure out we're not at the Snyders' anymore. We can't let her find out about this."

Krista scooted to the edge of the bed and rummaged on the floor for her clothes. She found her bra first and looped her arms through the straps. Alex watched her so intently her fingers shook when she fastened the front clasp. She could feel her nipples hardening. Again.

Krista felt compelled to continue with her thought. "My mother wouldn't understand what this is."

In truth, Krista didn't, either. Her theory sounded good. The fact she'd left out, however, was that no hard evidence existed to support the existence of phero-mones in humans.

"I'll go over to my house first." Once Krista's bra

was fastened, she located her panties. Suddenly feeling shy, she wiggled into them under the covers. "Wait five or ten minutes and follow."

"Won't that be suspicious?" Alex asked. "They know we were at the Snyders' together."

"You're right! You need to get dressed so we can arrive at the same time."

He sat up in bed and the sheet dropped away, revealing a sculpted chest lightly sprinkled with hair. He hadn't developed his muscles in a gym but through hard work. Krista clenched her right hand into a fist so she wouldn't repeat the sensation of tracing the musculature of his bare skin.

"How many feet should we keep between us at all times?" he asked. "One or two?"

"One would probably be…" She trailed off when she noticed his smirk. "You do love to tease me, don't you?"

"Only because it's so easy," he said.

The first few notes of a Linkin Park song that happened to be one of her favorites rang out. "That's my text tone," Alex said.

He reached for his jeans, fished his cell phone from one of the pockets and checked the display screen. "It's from Rayna." He pressed a few keys, checked the message and handed the phone over to Krista.

Stay at Snyders as long as you can, the text read. *My parents in rare form.*

"That means nobody's expecting us for a while longer." Alex's eyes met hers and held. "What do you want to do about that?"

Krista should tell him it made no sense to further indulge themselves. The longer they spent together, the greater the chance somebody would find them out. It shouldn't be worth the risk. This unfathomable something between them, however pleasurable, had no future.

As Alex had pointed out, however, she was leaving tomorrow. If she passed up this opportunity to make love to him again, she might never get another.

Krista unfastened her bra, letting her breasts spill free.

"I want you," she said.

LATER THAT EVENING Rayna waited approximately thirty seconds after her parents said good-night to put on her coat and head for the door.

She passed through the living room where Grandma sat in the armchair beside the Christmas tree, leafing through the book of dating tips Krista had bought her for Christmas.

"What do you think of this, Rayna?" Grandma was so intent on the page, she didn't lift her head. "If you think you're in love with two men, go with the second. You wouldn't have fallen for him if you really loved the first."

Rayna paused beside the chair and considered the quote. Since meeting Trey, she'd barely glanced at another man. "Makes sense to me."

"I thought so, too." Grandma finally looked up, peering at Rayna over her reading glasses. "Are you going somewhere, dear? I was going to suggest you, me and Krista have a nightcap when she gets out of the shower."

Rayna could no longer hear water running, giving her more cause to hurry. Between clearing snow for the neighbors and visiting with the Snyders, Krista hadn't been around much today. That was fine with Rayna.

"Sorry, Grandma. I can't." Rayna was careful to speak in a voice too soft to carry through the closed door of her parents' bedroom. "I'm going to Trey's."

Grandma appeared about to say something, possibly about this being Rayna's last chance to spend time with Krista, but then she smiled. "Have fun, dear."

"Thanks, Grandma," Rayna said and left the house.

She was grateful Grandma didn't give her a hard time about spending nights with Trey like Mom did. Never mind that Rayna was twenty-one. Just last week, her mother had suggested withholding sex was a good way to get a guy to ask you to marry him.

Thankfully Mom's outdated notion was wrong.

Because Trey was going to propose tonight.

Excitement raced through Rayna at the thought, so powerful the baby must feel it, too. Trey had stopped by earlier in the afternoon to give her a pretty silver watch, a gift she'd opened while her parents looked on. He'd whispered in her ear that she should come to his place tonight. He had another, much more special present for when they were alone.

What else could it be besides an engagement ring?

After hearing Trey minimize their relationship at the hockey rink and discovering his brother didn't know about her, Rayna feared committing to her was not even on his radar.

It felt like a dream come true that Trey could actually be ready to settle down.

Rayna was flying so high she barely remembered getting in her car, starting the engine and driving the five miles to the house Trey shared with his buddies. Thankfully the road had been plowed, and she arrived safely.

With the piles of snow in the yards and on the sides

of the street, Trey's house was nearly indistinguishable from the others in the neighborhood.

She operated on auto pilot, parking the car, walking up the shoveled sidewalk, climbing the short set of steps to the porch, ringing the doorbell.

She wouldn't tell Trey about the baby tonight. It was important to Rayna there be no question Trey was marrying her because he loved her and not because she was pregnant.

If he were ready to take this huge step and pledge himself to her, he'd commit to the baby, too.

The door swung open. Trey grinned at her, looking darkly handsome with stubble on his face and hair that needed combed.

She smiled back, her heart swelling with love.

"Come into my empty house," he said, his eyebrows dancing.

She stepped inside what was a typical bachelor pad. Trey and his housemates had purchased the few items of furniture they owned secondhand. Posters hung on the wall instead of paintings. The only nod to Christmas was a sparsely decorated tree about three feet high.

"Nobody else is here?" Rayna could hardly believe it. Trey lived with three guys, each one more omnipresent than the next.

"It's just you and me, babe," he said.

She came into the house and he backed up. He was barefoot, his jeans unsnapped, his shirt unbuttoned so that she could see his six-pack.

Rayna took off her coat and draped it over the back of the sofa. "I've been thinking about what you said this afternoon all day."

"You mean, about the present?" He looked absolutely delighted with himself.

"Yes," she said, "about the present."

"Then I won't make you wait any longer," he said. "Let's get this party started."

"Let's." She bit her lower lip to keep it from trembling with happiness.

He peeled off his shirt and started to pull down the zipper of his jeans, all the while with a devilish smile playing about his lips.

"What are you doing?" Rayna asked.

"Isn't it obvious? I'm unwrapping your present."

A terrible weight settled over Rayna's heart. "You? Naked? That's my special gift?"

"Yeah," Trey said. "You've never been here before when the house was empty. We can make as much noise as we want."

Rayna opened her mouth but nothing came out. She stared at him, shaking her head.

"Babe?" Trey took a step toward her. "What's wrong?"

Snatching her coat from the sofa, Rayna backed away from him. "I'll tell you what's wrong! You and me. It's over, Trey."

The look of shock on Trey's face might have been comical had the circumstances been different.

She stormed out of the house without putting on her coat, not bothering to see if he was following as she ran down the porch steps and ate up the ground to her car.

"Rayna! Come back and talk to me," Trey cried from the porch. "I don't understand."

"I know," she murmured under her breath.

That, in a nutshell, was the problem.

CHAPTER NINE

ON THE MORNING AFTER Christmas, piles of rolled-up clothing covered the downstairs sofa bed where Krista had lain awake until nearly dawn. Impressions and images from her brief trip to Jarrell had raced through her mind, but now one worry superseded everything.

She'd reached the moment of reckoning.

Krista eyed her empty suitcase, unable to tell anything by sight alone. Picking up the framed photograph Alex had given her for Christmas, she took a deep breath and tried to lay it at the bottom of the bag.

It didn't fit.

"Oh, damn." Something that felt suspiciously like tears burned the backs of Krista's eyes.

"Is something wrong, dear?" Grandma asked.

Krista whirled. Her grandmother was walking toward her wearing a look of concern along with her red-and-green plaid sweater. Krista must have been so preoccupied she hadn't heard her footsteps on the stairs when she descended into the basement.

"Everything's fine." Krista blinked a few times to counteract the burning feeling. At her grandmother's frown, Krista held up the landscape. "Well, almost fine. I brought my smaller suitcase so I didn't have to check any baggage. This doesn't fit inside."

Grandma came over to get a closer look, rubbing

her chin. "If you had a wooden frame box, you could check it separately."

"Except I don't," Krista said, her voice unsteady, "and there's no time to buy one."

Grandma patted her on the back. "Don't sound so glum. I'll go to a shipping store. They'll pack it up and send it to you."

Krista nodded and leaned the photo against the wall, once more taking in the majestic beauty of the scene Alex had captured with his camera. Leaving it behind felt wrong. What other option did she have, though?

"Thanks, Grandma," Krista said. "I'd appreciate that."

"Do you need any help repacking?" Grandma asked.

"No thanks. I travel so much I have a system." Krista picked up a pair of pants in the shape of a fat sausage. "You can fit more clothes in your bag if you roll them."

"Even ski clothes?"

"I didn't bring any," Krista said. "I wasn't sure if I'd get to Switzerland so figured I could always rent them."

Grandma sat down on the far edge of the day bed. "Where exactly in Switzerland are you going?"

"A place called Zermatt. It's this beautiful mountain town that doesn't allow cars. Once I get to Geneva, I'll need to take a train there."

"How many friends are you meeting?"

"Five," Krista said. "We've been planning this trip forever. It's a ski-and-stay package. The chalet has three bedrooms, two fireplaces and amazing views."

"Sounds expensive," Grandma said.

"It is, even split six ways. We prepaid so I can't get my money back."

"Now I understand why you're eager to leave," Grandma said.

Krista swallowed. She wouldn't have used the word *eager*. Not when she'd awakened this morning thinking about making love to Alex and regretting that she couldn't repeat the experience.

"Is Alex coming over to say goodbye?" Grandma asked, almost as though she'd read Krista's thoughts.

Krista shook her head. "We said our goodbyes last night."

She was referring to their final lingering kiss after they'd made love for the second time.

As if by mutual consent, Krista and Alex had kept their distance once they'd joined their families in the waning hours of Christmas.

Alex had wished Krista good luck at the end of the night. The rueful curl of his lips was the only hint that he was sad to see her go. But maybe that regret hadn't been there. Maybe Krista had only wanted it to be.

"I think you like Alex," Grandma said.

Krista didn't look up from her repacking. "I think you have romance on the mind since you started online dating."

"Only since I met Charlie," Grandma said. "That man is fine!"

Krista had to laugh. "I could tell you thought so from that bathrobe you bought him."

"I decided to only give him the tie even before I pawned the bathrobe off on you," Grandma said.

Krista winced. "Isn't a tie kind of impersonal?"

"It was a very nice tie," Grandma said.

"What did Charlie get you?"

"I can't believe I didn't show you!" Grandma extended her arm. From her wrist dangled a dainty gold bracelet. "Isn't it beautiful?"

"Very." Krista arranged the last of her clothes in the suitcase, not able to make sense of her grandmother. "Why did you decide to only give Charlie a tie?"

"Because I don't want him to know how much I like him," Grandma said. "Men prefer it when you play hard to get."

Krista frowned. "I'm not sure that's true, Grandma. I think men value honesty."

"Too much of that can ruin a relationship, dear," Grandma said, shaking her head.

"Krista!" Her father's booming voice carried into the basement. "If you don't hurry it up, you'll miss your plane."

Krista felt as if he'd slapped her across the face. Her father had barely spoken to her since she'd gotten home. Now that he finally initiated an exchange, it was to urge her to leave.

She walked over to the foot of the stairs. Her father had the door to the basement open. His mouth was set in a straight slash. "My flight doesn't leave for a few hours yet, Dad," she called up the stairs.

"It's best to be early," he said. "Planes don't wait."

He closed the door and she heard the whir of the chair's wheels on the hardwood. Krista stared at the closed door, then rejoined her grandmother.

"Was it my imagination," she said with more levity than she felt, "or did it sound like he's trying to get rid of me?"

"You know your father, dear." Grandma was behind her. "He hates to be late."

"But he's not going to the airport," Krista said.

"Well, yes." Grandma nodded. "I think he is."

"Really?" Krista could hardly believe it until an explanation occurred to her. "He probably wants to make certain I get on the plane."

"I'm sure he wants to see you safely off." Grandma entirely missed the irony in Krista's statement. At least her grandmother didn't add that her father had enjoyed having her home. They'd both know that wasn't true.

"That's everything." Krista shut the suitcase and held the top down while she zippered it closed. "I'm sorry I can't help you at the store today, Grandma. I hope you're not too busy."

"Rayna's going to help," Grandma said. "And your mother will be by after she drops you at the airport."

Krista would have liked more time with both of them, especially Rayna. Despite Krista's attempts to reconnect with her sister, Rayna spoke to her barely more than their father. Krista couldn't shake the feeling that something was troubling Rayna. Now she didn't have a prayer of discovering what it was.

"Where is Mom, anyway?" Krista said. "I haven't seen her this morning."

"Probably trying to figure out a way to keep you here," Grandma said at the same time they heard a distinct cry that sounded like, "Hallelujah!"

"What was that?" Krista said.

"I think it was Ellie."

Grandma headed for the stairs and rushed up them with vigor, with Krista trailing. Krista's mother was sitting in the living room in front of the television, which was switched to the Weather Channel. She was beaming.

"What is it, Mom?" Krista asked.

"Your connecting flight is out of Washington D.C., right?" Mom asked.

"Dulles International," Krista confirmed. "Why?"

"D.C. was just hit by an ice storm. Its airports are closed." Mom's smile got wider. "It doesn't look like you're leaving today, after all."

ALEX PULLED INTO the parking lot of Novaks' Nursery and Christmas Shoppe and shut off the engine of his company pickup.

He'd had two cravings during a long day while he cleared snow from the parking lots of his commercial clients. Krista had flown back to Europe today so he could only satisfy one of them.

Although peppermint bark candy was a poor substitute for having Krista in his bed, maybe it would lift his spirits. If the candy didn't do it, Alex would down a few cold ones when he met Malt Green and the old crowd tonight at Timeout.

As much as he'd enjoyed having Krista around these past few days, he needed to get on with a life without her in it.

Above all, he couldn't let himself miss her.

Alex was about to get out of the truck when a young woman in a black coat and a knit cap exited the shop. Alex could hardly believe his eyes.

Krista was still in Jarrell!

The drudgery of the day faded and he felt his mood lift along with the corners of his mouth.

Except, wait. The woman moved like Krista, but as she neared the parking lot it became obvious she was a few inches taller and a few pounds heavier. The hair stuffed under her hat was blond, not brown.

Because the woman was Rayna.

Krista's sister stopped beside her car to rummage

through her purse for her keys, providing Alex with a clear view of her face. She was crying.

Shoving aside his disappointment, Alex got out of the pickup. "Rayna? Are you okay?"

Her head jerked up. She lifted a hand to brush away her tears. She shook her head, her expression miserable.

The wind whipped through the parking lot, chilling an already cold day. Rayna appeared to be unsteady on her feet, as though another gust might knock her over.

Alex crossed to where she stood and put an arm around her shoulders, shielding her from the cold.

"It's warm in my pickup," he said. "We can talk there."

She let him usher her to the cab, offering not a word of protest when he opened the passenger door and helped her inside. Alex hurried to the driver's side, hopped in and shut the door on the whipping wind.

Rayna found a tissue in her purse and mopped up her face. She pulled out another and blew her nose.

Had something happened to Krista? Her plane should be en route to Switzerland. Surely somebody would have called him if there'd been an accident.

"I'm probably scaring you," Rayna said, her voice punctuated by sobs that weren't quite under control.

"A little bit," Alex said.

"I'm sorry. Everyone's fine. I mean, everyone except me." She drew in a deep, shuddering breath. "Trey and I broke up last night."

"Sorry to hear that." Alex gave Rayna's shoulder a brief squeeze. "He's a fool."

Rayna sniffled and turned watery eyes to him. "I broke up with Trey."

"Oh."

"You're surprised, right? You thought that if anybody was going to cut and run, it would be Trey." Rayna shut her eyes tight. When she opened them, she said, "That's why I had to do it."

Alex scratched his head. "I'm not following."

"You know the theory that one person in a relationship always loves more?" Rayna didn't seem to realize this wasn't a popular belief. "With Trey and me, that's me."

"So you broke up with him before he could break up with you?" Alex guessed.

"No," Rayna said. "I broke up with him because he didn't ask me to marry him."

The conversation was making even less sense by the minute. Rayna and Trey were both barely the legal drinking age. Trey flitted from job to job, not sure exactly what he wanted to do for a living. Rayna had yet to finish school.

"Why do you want to get married?" Alex asked the obvious question.

"Because I'm pregnant," Rayna blurted out.

Alex wasn't sure what to say. The possibility hadn't occurred to him.

Rayna covered her mouth with her hand, then let it drop. "I've only known for a couple of days. You're the first person I've told."

"So Trey doesn't know?"

Rayna shook her head, looking even more miserable.

"Are you having the baby?" Alex asked.

She nodded, the affirmative both immediate and decisive.

"Then your timing on the breakup seems off," Alex

said. Rayna shot him a look of misery. He held up a hand. "I'm just sayin'."

"You don't understand."

"You're right," Alex admitted. "You're like a little sister to me, Rayna. I'll do anything I can to help. But I might not be the best person to talk to about this."

She held up a hand. "Don't say I should confide in my mom. She'd probably threaten to tell Trey herself if I didn't."

Within three or four months, Rayna wouldn't have to tell Trey anything. He'd figure it out for himself.

"How about Grandma Novak?" Alex asked.

"Grandma doesn't like secrets. How can I ask her to keep such a big one from my parents?"

"Then tell Krista," Alex recommended. "She has a good head on her shoulders."

"Krista and I aren't close," Rayna said. "How can we be when she lives in Prague?"

"This could bring you closer," he pointed out.

"I don't think so," Rayna said.

"It could," Alex refuted. "Look, I know Krista's gone back to Europe. But phone plans are cheap. You could call—"

"Krista's not back in Europe," Rayna interrupted.

His train of thought broken, Alex switched gears. "Maybe not yet. But her plane should be landing in Switzerland soon."

"She didn't get on a plane today," Rayna said. "Harrisburg International is open, but Washington D.C. got hit by an ice storm and closed its airports."

Alex's brain was slow to process the information. "Then where is Krista?"

"Inside," Rayna said, pointing to the store.

An emotion Alex couldn't identify rushed through

him. It could have been relief. Then again, it felt a whole lot like happiness.

"So you really think I should tell Krista I'm pregnant?" Rayna asked.

Alex brought his attention back to Rayna and her problem. "I do."

"I'll think about it," Rayna said. "Krista won't be here long. Just until December twenty-eighth. She said she couldn't get on an earlier flight."

That seemed odd. Alex wasn't well versed on the geography of Switzerland but he was under the vague impression that the ski resorts were roughly located between the airports at Geneva and Zurich. It seemed as if Krista would have lots of flight options, but with snowy weather throughout the northeast that must not have been the case.

"Then you should look at those days like a gift and take advantage of them," Alex said.

That was what he intended to do.

Until a few minutes ago, he'd been ambivalent about going to Timeout tonight. That had changed, because Alex was making damn sure Krista went with him.

CHAPTER TEN

TIMEOUT WAS A TYPICAL sports bar, with multiple television screens visible from every wooden booth in the house. An NBA game between Los Angeles and Detroit played on half the TVs. A countdown show of the year's best moments in sports was airing on the others.

"I'm glad to be here," Krista told Alex from the bar entrance, "but I'm still wondering why you were so sure I'd come with you."

"My pheromones smell good," he said, his eyebrows dancing. "Remember?"

She grinned at him. "That's the reason I gave my mom when she started in on how I must be falling for you if I'm meeting your friends."

His attention was absolute, as though she were the most important person in the bar. "How did she take that?"

"It threw her," Krista said. "She must have looked up pheromones on the internet because when I was leaving she told me I should listen to my nose."

He returned her smile, his eyes crinkling charmingly at the corners.

If Krista's flight hadn't been canceled, right about now she'd be arriving at the stunning three-bedroom chalet in the Swiss Alps. She realized with a start that she'd rather be exactly where she was.

At her side, Alex surveyed the bar crowd. "There they are. In the back beside the pool tables."

He took her hand and led her through the bar to a group of six people congregated around one of the pool tables. All of them were strangers except for Malt Green and Julia Merrifield, the single mother from the Christmas shop who used to date Alex.

"Look who showed!" Malt embraced Alex in a half hug. The two other men in the group—one sporting a sandy crew cut and square build and the other tall and thin with prematurely gray hair—gave Alex the same back-slapping treatment.

"I'm still trying to figure out how we lost touch with this guy," the man with the crew cut told Krista. "We were all real tight in high school."

Sadly Krista was no longer in contact with any of her high school classmates, but she didn't live here. She supposed Jarrell wasn't quite as small as it first appeared. Although it wasn't unusual for students from the two public high schools to know each other, Krista had never seen these men before. Until that day eight years ago at the nursery, she hadn't laid eyes on Alex, either.

It seemed incredible but there it was.

During the swirl of introductions that followed, Krista tried and failed to keep everybody's name straight. Malt Green had come stag but the two other men had brought their wives, petite brunettes who looked enough alike to be sisters.

The only name she was sure she had right was Julia's. The blonde distinguished herself from her friends in another way, too. Her smile didn't reach her eyes.

The two men went back to their game of pool. Krista wasn't exactly sure how she got separated from

Alex. One minute she was standing beside him, the next the two wives and Julia had her cornered by the dart board.

"We didn't know Alex was dating anyone," one of the brunettes said.

"Yes, it's quite a surprise," Julia remarked, and Krista imagined she was replaying their conversation at the Christmas Shoppe.

"Alex and I aren't together," Krista said, then frowned. "Well, we are. But not in the way you mean. I wouldn't be here tonight if my flight hadn't been canceled."

"I heard the snow is causing major travel headaches," the other brunette said. "Where were you flying?"

"Switzerland for a ski trip," Krista said, "but I live in Prague."

Julia sucked in a breath, and Krista remembered Julia's claim about a woman from Alex's past breaking his heart when she moved away. If the brunettes weren't present, Krista would tell Julia that wasn't true.

"That sounds so cool," the first brunette cried.

"You must have been super-bummed when the flight was canceled!" said the second.

"Not really." Krista had welcomed the chance to spend the day at the shop dealing with the after-Christmas bargain hunters. Even Rayna said she'd been a big help. "My family lives in Jarrell. It's nice to be able to spend more time with them."

"And with Alex?" Julia prompted.

"Sure," Krista said. "It's always good to catch up with old friends."

She stole a glance at Alex, who sat in a booth across from Malt Green. Alex had dressed for comfort in blue jeans and a black crew-neck pullover, clothes not much different than what most of the guys at the bar were wearing. So why did he stand out like the star at the top of a Christmas tree?

"Wait a minute! I know who you are!" The first brunette pointed her index finger at Krista. "You used to be a cheerleader at Jarrell High."

"That's right," Krista said. "I was the one with the biggest mouth. That's probably why you remember."

"Not so! I remember because you were good," she said. "I was a freshman at Jarrell when you were a senior. I wanted to be just like you."

"Thank you." Krista wasn't sure what else to say.

"Don't your parents run a nursery?" the woman asked. At Krista's nod, she continued, "I've been there a few times. Your dad's always so helpful. Once he wouldn't let me carry a bag of mulch to my car. He told me to put it on his lap and he wheeled it out."

"My dad's in a wheelchair, too," the second brunette said. "He has complications from diabetes. What about your dad, Krista?"

Krista felt herself tense. "A forklift accident."

"Oh, how awful! How did it happen?"

Guilt hit Krista hard. She thought everybody who had more than a passing acquaintance with her father knew Krista had been at fault. All three of the women stared at her, waiting for her answer. Krista cleared her throat and tried to phrase it in such a way that there wouldn't be follow-up questions.

"He got pinned between a shed and the forklift at the nursery about ten years ago," Krista said. "He's been paralyzed from the waist down ever since."

Both brunettes covered their mouths. Julia's hand flew to her throat. "But how—"

"Hey, Krista!" Malt Green's voice carried from the booth where he sat with Alex, interrupting what Julia had been about to ask. "Will you come over here?"

Krista would leap tables in a single bound to escape the curiosity of the women.

"Excuse me," Krista told the trio. She made a bee-line for the booth, barely managing not to run.

"Thanks for joining us," Malt said. "I need help convincing Alex what's good for him."

Alex sighed loudly enough that Krista heard him over the music, the TVs and the ambient noise. He slid over on the leather bench seat so Krista could sit down next to him. Krista could almost feel the tension radiating off him.

"There's no need to bring Krista into this," Alex said.

"I don't agree, buddy," Malt said. "Krista can get you to listen to reason."

"I doubt I can get Alex to do anything," Krista said slowly.

Malt threw his head back and laughed. "Then you're not trying hard enough. You've sure got a better shot at it than me."

"The matter's not open for discussion." Alex's lips were set in a tight line. "I already said no, Malt."

Krista felt as though the two men were speaking a language she didn't understand. "No to what?"

"My company is planning to expand into the United States," Malt said. "At first we'll offer products showcasing the diversity of the country's landscapes. Eventually, I'd like to put out a line of products featuring each state separately."

"Where does Alex come into that?" Krista asked.

"I offered him a job on my photography staff. The

factor that distinguishes us in the market is the artistic quality of our photographs. Like the stuff Alex shoots."

Alex rubbed the back of his neck. "You don't even know if I'm still taking photos."

"Sure I do," Malt said. "I saw some of your handi-work hanging in the window of that frame shop in the next block."

Alex stared down into a beer mug that was mostly full before raising only his eyes. "How did you figure out the photos were mine?"

"You've got a distinctive style that looks really high end," Malt said. "That's why I want you. I'm prepared to pay handsomely."

Krista had been listening to the interplay between the two men, but now she touched Alex's arm, draw-ing his attention to her. "That sounds like an amazing opportunity!"

"For someone else," Alex said. "I already said no."

"You can't tell me you prefer landscaping to pho-tography," Malt said. "It's me, Alex. I was there when you bought your first camera. You were so excited you probably slept with it. Photography's your passion."

"I'm still not taking the job," Alex said.

Krista held her tongue. Malt's stance was so strong that questioning Alex's reasons would feel too much like ganging up on him.

"You are one stubborn son of a bitch." Malt picked up his mug and drained the rest of his beer. "You think you'd take pity on an old friend who's been wallowing in guilt for the past ten years."

"You have nothing to feel guilty about," Alex said.

"How about the fact that *my* company should have been *our* company? Remember that trip to Canada and all the plans we made? Remember waking up before dawn to catch the perfect light and saying life didn't get any better than that?"

"Things change," Alex said. "So can we talk about something else?"

The conversation veered to other subjects, but Krista couldn't stop thinking about the incredible job opportunity Alex had turned down. Whatever he ultimately decided, she was on his side.

Krista was far from convinced, though, that Alex didn't want the job.

ON MOST NIGHTS, ALEX would be content to enjoy the company of his old friends until the bar closed. This, however, wasn't most nights.

Their group of eight had commandeered a table large enough to accommodate all of them, which had led to laughs and lively conversation. Krista sat next to Alex, but still too far away. He caught her attention, raised his eyebrows and delivered a silent message he hoped she could decipher.

Krista gave him an almost imperceptible nod, then yawned, covering her mouth with a hand.

"Sorry," Krista said. "I'm afraid I'm a little tired."

Alex smothered a grin and addressed his friends. "I should get Krista home."

"What? The night's still young!" Malt protested.

"Not for me," Krista said. "I must still be getting over jet lag."

Alex stood up and removed his coat from the back of his chair. Krista did the same, putting on her coat as her eyes touched on each one of his friends in turn.

"It was nice meeting all of you," Krista said with a charming smile. "Thanks for letting me crash your party."

"Anytime," Malt said. "And Alex, you know how to get in contact with me if you change your mind about the job."

"I won't." Alex shook some hands and agreed with his two friends who were locals that they should get together soon.

After they left the bar behind and were outside in the cool night air, Krista held up her hand. Alex lightly slapped her palm for a high five.

"Good job picking up on my signal," he said.

"The jet lag was a nice touch, don't you think?" She grinned, appearing not the slightest bit tired.

"Did you want to get out of there as much as I did?" he asked.

"More," Krista said. "As much as I like your friends, I'd rather have you to myself."

Alex swept a hand at the stretch of downtown Jarrell around them. Other than a middle-aged man leaving the bar alone and a couple getting into their Prius, the street was deserted.

"This is as alone as we can get with me living with my dad and you staying with your parents," he said.

"Does your pickup have a good heater?" Krista asked, her expression alighting with mischief.

"Good enough," he said. "Why?"

She released his hand and backpedaled down the sidewalk. "On the way home, we can look for a turn-off where we can park."

He laughed.

"If we fog up the windows," she continued, still walking backward, "nobody will be able to see what we're doing to each other."

An image of Krista shedding her clothes in the front

seat of his pickup crystallized. The front of his jeans felt tighter. "You're serious."

"Of course I am," she said. "I'd suggest a hotel room but if I don't come home tonight Mom might think we ran off to Atlantic City to elope."

"You're exaggerating," he said.

"What I'm doing is missing that old apartment of yours," she said.

"It was at its best with you in it." Alex hadn't regretted giving up the place until this moment.

"Flattery! I like it." The air was cold enough that he could see her puffs of breath. "I can liven up a pickup, too."

"When you put it that way…" He took a few steps toward her.

She kept retreating.

Puzzled, he jerked a thumb over his shoulder. "I parked the pickup over there."

"Before we go, I have an irresistible urge—" she paused, eyes dancing "—to see those photos Malt mentioned."

Alex groaned. "You're kidding."

"I'm not," Krista said. "I'd like to see if they're as excellent as he says they are."

"It's too cold to stay outside," he said. "It can't be more than twenty degrees."

She put up her coat collar and shoved her hands in her pockets. "It's not that cold."

He tried to think up another excuse. "It's too dark."

"Not with all the Christmas lights," she said, indicating the holiday decorations on the utility polls.

He tried one more. "You're too tired?"

"Ha ha," she said. "If you don't stop making excuses, I'll think you don't want me to see those photos."

"I don't." Despite his denial, he was walking with her toward the frame shop. "We've already talked about my photography enough tonight."

"That's why I'm interested," Krista said. "If they're anything like the landscape you gave me, they're worth seeing."

A part of Alex wanted her to see the photographs. Hell, he'd like to get a fresh look at them himself. One of the reasons he enjoyed landscape photography was that the perfect image could be enjoyed repeatedly instead of fleetingly.

They reached the frame shop. The street lamps shone on the store's large front window at an angle where the photos were clearly visible.

In the first one, trees in the full burst of fall color flanked a lake of such a clear, glimmering blue it was only surpassed by the hue of the sky. The second photo depicted a rustic house on the banks of the lake, the mist of the morning hugging it like a cloud.

"Wow," Krista said. "These are incredible."

"Thank you." Alex couldn't stop his swell of pride. Landscape photography awarded the early riser when the light was soft and the air was still. He'd taken both these photos moments after dawn broke.

"How'd they end up at the frame shop?" she asked.

"The owner's a friend," Alex said. "He has a lake house in the Poconos. He asked if I could take some shots he could frame and use in the window as an advertisement."

"Sounds like a good way to make some extra money."

"Nah, I didn't charge him," Alex said. "Unless you count the use of his lake house as payment."

"Your friend got a good deal." Krista tilted her head, examining the photos from several angles. "You must know you could make money at this."

"It's not that easy," Alex said.

"It would be if you said yes to Malt Green."

He crossed his arms over his chest, but not because the temperature felt like it was dropping by the minute. "You're not going to start in on me, too, are you?"

"Of course not," she said. "I'm on your side, whatever it is. It's kind of tough to tell with the limited information I have."

He said nothing.

"If you don't explain what Malt meant about how you should have gone into business with him, I'll probably keep working it into the conversation until you do," she said.

"Why?" he asked.

She didn't even pause before she responded. "Because I want to know you better."

If she'd said anything else, he might have clammed up. Suddenly it seemed important not only that she understand why he'd given up his dream, but that he revisited the reasons, too.

Seeing Malt again had made him nostalgic for what never could have been.

"Malt and I were in a photography class together in high school," Alex said. "We used to talk about how cool it would be to take photos for a living. Not wedding photos or studios shots. Landscapes."

"So you came up with the idea for Greenscapes?" Krista shuffled her feet back and forth, no doubt in an attempt to keep warm. She was probably as cold as he was.

"Pretty much, except we didn't call it that. We didn't have any start-up money, either. So the idea kind of fell by the wayside for a couple of years."

"Until your trip to Canada?" Krista guessed.

"Yeah," he said. "I was working for my dad and taking classes at the community college, not real sure what field I wanted to go into. Malt was going to Penn State and caddying at the country club in the summer."

A gust of wind blew over them, a reminder that most sane people were home snug in their beds. Or at least somewhere with access to a heater. "This isn't a good place to have this conversation."

"Then come over here." Krista grabbed his hand and pulled him with her into the short alcove that led to the door of the frame shop. The area was protected from the wind.

"Go on," she urged.

He'd revealed this much of the story. He might as well tell the rest of it.

"Malt overheard one of the golfers say he was looking for an investment," Alex continued. "The guy was intrigued by our idea and told Malt we should come up with a presentation."

"Whose idea was it to go to Canada?" Krista asked.

"Mine. The guy was Canadian. I thought our chances of impressing him would be better if we showed him familiar scenes in new lights. We got some fantastic shots."

"The investor liked the photos, right?" Krista asked. "That's how Malt was able to start the business?"

"He loved them," Alex said. "He offered to pay for

start-up costs in exchange for a cut in profits. Malt quit school on the spot to focus on the business."

"Sounds like a sweet deal," Krista said. "Why didn't you get in on it, too?"

"There were strings attached," Alex said. "The investor stipulated that we focus on Canadian landscapes and base the business in Toronto."

"I don't understand why that was a problem," Krista said.

She wouldn't, Alex thought. She'd moved three thousand miles from her family. But he wasn't being fair to her. She didn't know his whole story.

"When Malt and I took the Canada trip, we didn't tell anyone exactly where we were going. We didn't know ourselves." Alex swallowed a lump of emotion. To this day, he blamed himself for not checking in with his parents every few days. "It turned out cell phone reception is poor when you're camping out in the mountains."

Krista must have an inkling of what he was going to say, because she reached for his hand and hung on. She didn't interrupt his story, though. He'd come this far. He had no choice but to go on.

"My Dad couldn't reach me. It was about my mom." His chest felt thick and heavy. "She had a brain aneurysm that ruptured. She didn't make it."

Krista gasped softly, compassion in her eyes.

Something seemed to be blocking Alex's windpipe. He cleared his throat. "It happened the day after Malt and I left for Canada. By the time we got home two weeks later, she'd already been buried."

"Oh, my gosh," Krista said. "That's terrible."

"The worst time of my life. But what made it even harder was that I wasn't there for my dad." He took a deep, ragged breath. When he exhaled, the condensation from his breath seemed to form a cloud. "So now you understand why I couldn't go into business with Malt."

They both fell silent. In the entire time they'd been talking, no cars had passed. A blue minivan that needed a new muffler rattled by. Long moments passed before the street was quiet again.

"Actually," Krista finally said, drawing out the word, "I don't understand."

It was the last thing Alex expected her to say. He slipped his hand from hers and shoved it in one of his pockets. His reason should have been as clear as the glass on the frame-shop window.

"It's pretty simple," he said, disappointed that he had to offer a clarification. "I couldn't move to Canada and leave my dad here alone."

"Was that the only choice?" Krista asked. "Malt's the one with the business background, right? If he was handling the daily nuts-and-bolts stuff, couldn't you have taken trips to Canada to get the photos you needed?"

Malt had proposed exactly that years ago, insisting he'd rather not audition landscape photographers for what should be Alex's job.

"It involved too much traveling," Alex said. "That's why I turned down Malt today, too."

"What's so bad about traveling?"

He stared at her, amazed she'd asked the question. "What if something happened to my dad when I was on the road?"

"What if something happens to him when you're grocery shopping?" Krista asked. "Or at the bank? Or the movies?"

"If I were at any of those places," Alex said tightly, "I could be reached immediately."

"It'd be the same if you were taking landscape photos anywhere in the United States," Krista said. "You could hop on a plane and be home in no time."

"If I wasn't somewhere with poor cell-phone reception," Alex said.

"Cell-phone reception's more reliable than it was ten years ago," Krista pointed out.

He shook his head. "Do you really think I'd risk that?"

"What happened to your mother was tragic. I can't even imagine how terrible it must have been for you," Krista said, her voice filled with empathy. "But the likelihood of something like that happening again is remote. You can't let it stop you from doing the things that would make you happy."

"I am happy," Alex said.

"Really? You wouldn't rather make a living at photography than landscaping?"

"I'm in business with my father," Alex said. "I have a duty to him."

"So you think of landscaping as a duty," Krista stated. It angered him that he couldn't argue with that. "Does your father know you sacrificed your passion for him? I can't imagine Milo would be okay with that."

Alex had been extremely careful over the years to assure his father he was satisfied with his career. Hell, Alex had been the one who proposed they go into business together. Their partnership was one of the few things that had made his father happy after Alex's mother died.

"Let me get this straight," Alex said. "You're proposing I do what you did? Go off and chase my dream and to hell with my responsibilities to my family."

She reeled back, stunned by his comment. "Is that what you think I did?"

The first night Krista was back in Jarrell, he'd criticized her for staying away from her family for too long. Over the days that followed, he'd let himself forget how much that bothered him.

"I think you neglected your family's needs to do whatever the hell you wanted," he said.

She bristled. "My family can get along fine without me!"

"Oh, really? Then ask Rayna how she is? Or ask your parents how their business is doing?"

Krista's eyes narrowed. "Do you know something about Rayna? Or my family's business?"

Alex looked away from her, disgusted with himself. He wasn't at liberty to discuss either of those subjects. "Forget I said that."

"I can't forget anything you just said, Alex." She hugged herself, but he didn't think it was to ward off the cold. "I'm ready to go back now."

He nodded.

"Straight back," she added.

He hadn't needed the clarification. After the angry words they'd exchanged, they weren't going to make love in his pickup.

They'd probably never make love again.

CHAPTER ELEVEN

THE LONGER KRISTA WORE her fake smile the next day at the Christmas Shoppe, the more genuine it became.

She'd discovered fairly quickly it was difficult to maintain anger, even when it was justified, while working in a store that looked like it could be Santa's playground.

A store that, judging by the number of customers making purchases, was doing just fine. Krista didn't need to ask her parents how their business was faring when she could see the evidence with her own eyes.

"I hope you enjoy the yard art, Pam," Krista told a former high-school classmate after she rang up a purchase of two illuminating reindeer. One of the perks to working at the shop, Krista had found, was that she kept running into people she used to know.

"Oh, I will." Pam Ford hadn't changed much from when she and Krista had been on the cheerleading squad together. She was still bubbly, sweet and friendly. "Do you think I can keep them in the yard after Christmas?"

Krista hadn't given the matter any thought until that moment. "I don't see why not. If it makes you happy, go for it."

"That's what I think," Pam said. "When the holiday season is over, I can tell people they're deer instead of reindeer."

"I like that plan."

"It's too bad you're going back to Europe tomorrow. I would have loved to get together."

"Me, too," Krista said, meaning it. She'd forgotten how many good friends she'd had in Jarrell.

"Please tell your family I love their shop," Pam said. "How long are they staying open?"

"Until the end of February. That's when the nursery will reopen."

"So they *are* reopening the nursery." Pam seemed surprised. "I wondered if they were going to give it another go. Good for them for taking on CGC."

Even though Krista hadn't lived in Pennsylvania in years, she recognized the abbreviation. Cenzano Garden Centers was a chain of stores situated in and around the Philadelphia area known for its volume business and low prices.

"Lucky for us most people in Jarrell aren't willing to drive to Philly for plants," Krista said.

"Philly?" Pam blinked a few times. "I'm talking about the CGC that opened out by the mall the summer before last. People rave about it."

"Of course," Krista mumbled while she processed the information. Novaks' Nursery had done steady if unspectacular business over the years without competition from an industry giant. The arrival of CGC must have cut into profits. Was that why Alex had advised her to ask her parents how their business was faring?

"It was wonderful seeing you again. Hope you have a happy new year!" Pam called, wheeling away her buggy filled with yard art. Krista was too lost in thought to manage a reply.

Grandma approached the cash register where she'd stationed Krista hours ago. "I remembered we're supposed to do a cookie exchange at the senior center to-night at seven. Can we change the time for your slide show to seven-thirty?"

It took Krista a moment to process the question, a little longer to remember that after her flight had been postponed she'd been lined up to show her travel photos. "Fine with me."

Grandma balanced her hands on her hips and frowned. "Alex hasn't called and apologized yet, has he?"

Krista started. "Why do you think Alex needs to apologize?"

"I can tell when you're in a bad mood, dear, even when you try to hide it," Grandma said. "Besides, I heard you damning him under your breath when you got home last night. So what did he do?"

"It's more what he said than what he did." Krista couldn't bring herself to repeat his claim that she was unaware of what was going on in her own family. "Let me ask you something, Grandma. Why did you open the shop?"

"Because I love Christmas," Grandma said. "I already told you that."

"So it had nothing to do with the nursery falling on hard times?" Krista asked.

No customers were within twenty yards of the cash register. Grandma still edged closer and lowered her voice. "Where did you hear that?"

"Our last customer seemed surprised we were re-opening the nursery. She told me about the competition from the CGC store by the mall," Krista said. "So is it true? Is the nursery in trouble?"

Grandma sighed. "Business hasn't been good the past few years, especially with the economy the way it is. It used to be that we made enough money to get through the off months but not anymore."

"So you opened the Christmas Shoppe to bring in more revenue." Krista didn't need to hear again that it was Alex's idea. Alex, who knew more about her family than she did. "Why didn't anybody mention this to me?"

"I told your parents they should say something, but Joe was against it," Grandma said. "He said what was the point when you couldn't do anything about it."

"I could have listened."

"You never made your feelings about the nursery a secret. I guess Joe thought you wouldn't be interested."

"Of course I'm concerned about things that affect my parents. And Rayna. And you," Krista insisted. "You're my family."

"Don't shoot the messenger, dear," Grandma said.

Krista nodded, realizing she was complaining to the wrong person. She wondered what else in her family she didn't know about.

"Do you know what time Rayna finishes at the dentist's office?" Krista asked.

"Five o'clock, I think. The same time we're closing the shop this week," Grandma answered. "Why?"

"I've hardly spent any time with her," Krista said. "I'd like to meet her for dinner before I have to be at the senior center."

"What a nice idea, dear. There's a Rolodex that lists the number for the dentist. It's under R for Rayna."

As soon as her grandmother was gone, Krista leafed through the Rolodex and located the index card. A computer database of contacts made more sense but Krista wasn't surprised that her grandmother filed numbers the old-fashioned way. Until this morning when Krista put out a piece of holiday stationary beside the cash register, her grandmother hadn't been asking customers for their contact information, either.

Under Rayna's name was the number for the dental practice as well as cell-phone numbers for both Rayna and Trey. Krista dialed the dentist and got a recording about the office closing early. Her next call, to Rayna's cell, went to voice mail. On impulse Krista dialed Trey. She'd only met him the one time, on Christmas Eve, but he'd made a good impression on her. As Alex said, he was immensely likeable.

"Rayna's not with me, that's for sure," Trey said. "She's not even talking to me."

Scant days ago, her sister had been wearing a bracelet with Trey's name dangling from it. "Why not?"

"She didn't tell you?" Trey sounded surprised.

"Tell me what?"

"She broke up with me," Trey said. "On Christmas night. Wouldn't even say why. I guess you don't know the reason, either?"

"No, I don't," Krista said, although she suspected Alex did. Why else would he have mentioned Rayna when they were arguing last night?

"It's crazy," Trey said. "Do me a favor and put in a good word for me, will you? I'm giving her some space."

"Sure," Krista said and hung up the phone.

The big question was whether Krista would get the chance to talk to her sister before her flight left tomorrow morning. At the rate things were going, it didn't seem likely.

ALEX TOOK THE overhead projector from a shelf in the storage closet of the senior center and carried it past the senior citizens gathered around a table filled with cookies in the spacious lobby. The air smelled so sweet, he almost went into sugar shock. Grandma broke off from the group, walking with him to the community room.

"You're a darling to come over here and set that up for us, Alex." Grandma Novak let him precede her into the room. Rows of chairs in banks of eight, an aisle separating them, faced a wall with a drop-down projection screen. "Do you need any help?"

Alex set down the machine on the small table in the front of the room and straightened. "I'm good for now. I can't hook up the cables until Krista gets here with her computer. If you like, I'll show you how to do it."

"I remember from the last time you showed me."

"Then why did you—"

Grandma Novak didn't let him finish. "Would you like a cookie? There are some delicious ones out there. I made the lady locks that you love."

She bustled off, probably thinking she'd distracted him by bringing up the tube-shaped cookies filled with cream that made his mouth water. He'd figured out the answer to his question, anyway.

Alex left the room for the lobby and the reason Grandma Novak had called him to set up the projector walked through the front door of the center.

Krista paused at the entrance, unwrapping the colorful scarf from around her neck and unbuttoning her red coat. She wore skinny jeans, fashionable boots, a yellow sweater that hugged her perfect breasts and a half smile.

Her gaze met his from across the room, and her smile faded. She broke eye contact, headed straight for her grandmother and bent her head to whisper something. Whatever it was, Grandma Novak waved it off with a fluttering hand. She kissed Krista on the cheek before rejoining the cookie crowd.

Alex stood where he was, watching Krista approach. It would be easier if the harsh words they'd exchanged the night before had doused his attraction to her. They hadn't.

"I'm sorry Grandma tricked you into coming over here." Krista spoke before he could. "I didn't know she was going to do that."

"You told her we argued?"

"She figured it out," Krista said. "She said we'd regret it if we didn't make up before I got on that plane tomorrow."

Alex couldn't apologize for speaking the truth. "When do you leave?"

"Ten in the morning," Krista said. "There's no more ice in D.C. and no more backlog of flights."

He started to tell her that was good but couldn't get the sentiment past his throat. Instead, he nodded.

"We should get your computer hooked up," he said.

For the next ten minutes, they worked in unison, with Alex giving instructions and Krista following them. An uneasy peace existed between them, although Alex still believed every word he'd said last night.

"It's pretty simple," he told her when everything was in place up. "The overhead's acting as the computer monitor so you can flip through the slide show like you normally do."

"Could you do it for me?" Krista must have expected him to refuse, because she added, "Please."

She moved closer to him and he could smell her, an intoxicating mixture of what was probably shampoo and scented body lotion. His body reacted. She'd smelled like that when he made love to her.

"Sure thing," he said. "I'm your slide-show man."

She smiled and touched his cheek, her fingers almost instantly falling away. She stepped back. "I'll go tell Grandma we're ready. Mrs. Snyder is probably here by now, too."

Ten minutes later, after Grandma Novak introduced Krista as her travel-mad granddaughter, the slide show was underway.

The seniors—the majority of them female, some of them still munching Christmas cookies—filled three quarters of the seats. Charlie was among them, flanked by two of the more attractive women present. Both leaned toward him, their body language speaking volumes. Grandma Novak took a seat across the aisle from Charlie, occasionally stealing glances at him.

Alex polished off the second of two lady locks Grandma Novak had brought him, perhaps as a peace offering. He'd given up trying to make sense of the Novak women. Who knew why Grandma wasn't sitting next to Charlie or why Krista had asked Alex to stay? Krista certainly didn't need him here. He'd already turned over control of the slide show to her so she could pause it when necessary.

She'd started off by showing photos of Prague, her home of eight years. The capital of the Czech Republic was undeniably beautiful, and Krista had a nice eye for composition. The shots she'd taken from the watchtower of a pedestrian bridge were especially good.

Interspersed with panoramic views of the river that ran through the city and Gothic-style architecture were photos of tourists enjoying street musicians and young couples pushing prams.

"The building in this next slide looks like a Gothic castle, but it's actually a brewery in a funky old town called Žatec," Krista said. "See the hop fields in the background."

She flipped to another slide of a blond, fair-skinned couple. The young man hoisted a beer glass with relish. The woman covered her pregnant belly with a hand, frowning mightily.

Everyone laughed.

"Are those friends of yours?" Mrs. Snyder asked Krista.

"They're just people who were on the tour with me," Krista said. "I was actually in Žatec by myself."

She'd gone alone to the Wieliczka salt mine in southern Poland, too, a tidbit she'd shared after showing a photo of a different couple, this one from Britain with two small children in tow. Another slide featured Krista and a woman about her age standing outside a fortress wall.

"Where are you now?" The question came from the flashier of the women flanking Charlie. Her half-dozen bracelets jangled together as she gestured to the screen.

Krista paused the parade of slides. "In France outside a walled village called Pérouges. It's typical of the Middle Ages with cobblestone streets and the original village gates."

"The woman with you, is she a friend or another tourist?" Mrs. Snyder asked.

"That's my friend Becca," Krista said. "When I get back to Prague, I'm on the hook to help her throw a New Year's Eve bash."

Krista advanced to a slide of a toddler standing between a man and woman and holding up what looked vaguely like a slice of pizza. "These are some people I met. The little boy is eating galette vieux Pérouges, a sugary pastry you can buy on the street."

Krista continued the slide show. It struck Alex that she'd taken very few photographs of typical tourist destinations. Even in Paris, most of Krista's photos were of people enjoying the city's parks.

The drop-down screen went blank. Alex checked his watch, surprised forty-five minutes had gone by.

"Please say it's not over," a woman in the audience exclaimed. "I was so enjoying it."

"Leaving you wanting more is better than the alternative," Krista said.

"You're so lucky to have been to all those interesting places!" Mrs. Snyder exclaimed. "And how wonderful to be able to see how other people live!"

"I suppose that's why you took so many photos of random people you met," the outspoken woman sitting next to Charlie theorized.

"It must be," Krista said, but she sounded unsure of the reason. Alex's guess was that she hadn't realized she tended to photograph strangers until it was pointed out.

He leaned back in his chair, thinking about what he'd learned about Krista since she'd been back in the United States. He had a different take on the situation, one he intended to run by Krista even if it led to another disagreement.

One thing was certain. Krista wouldn't like it.

KRISTA STOOD IN FRONT of the senior citizens in the community room, fighting a silly urge to take a bow as they gave her a round of applause.

Alex clapped, too, although the quality of Krista's

photos didn't compare to his. After the disparaging remarks he'd made about her wanderlust, she supposed she should be happy he'd joined in the ovation.

"Don't leave without taking some cookies," Grandma announced. She joined the flow of people streaming from the room, no doubt to make sure they followed her order.

Stragglers from the audience approached Krista. Even as she greeted them, she noticed the woman with the bracelets waylaying Charlie, and Alex getting to work disconnecting the equipment.

"How often do you travel, Krista?" Mrs. Snyder asked. As expected, Krista's former high school French teacher was among the people eager to keep talking about distant places.

"At least a few times a month, basically every chance I get." Krista answered questions for the next few minutes until a trilling laugh sounded.

The woman who had been talking to Charlie was exiting the room with him, smiling hugely and pressing a folded piece of paper into his hand. A phone number?

"Frances has her eye on another one," Mrs. Snyder remarked. "Where did that man come from anyway? I've never seen him before."

"Neither have I, but he sure is hot for an old guy," another woman said.

Everybody laughed except Krista. Alex wouldn't have found the remark funny, either, but he'd left the room to stow away the projector. Krista wondered why Grandma hadn't made it clear to everyone that Charlie was with her.

Their questions exhausted, the few people who remained from the audience thanked Krista again and headed for the lobby. Krista walked with them, arriving in time to see the door swing open. Charlie stuck his head back inside the center.

"It's snowing and it's sticking." Charlie projected his voice so it filled every corner of the large room. "You don't want to stay much longer."

"Did you hear that, Pete?" Mrs. Snyder called to her husband, who was already gathering their coats from the rack beside the door.

"The forecast I heard didn't call for snow until late tomorrow morning." Pete Snyder approached his wife, coats in hand, concern wrinkling his brow. "You ready to go?"

"Yes, let's go home before the roads get bad." Mrs. Snyder turned to Krista and enveloped her in a quick hug. "'Bye, Krista. If I don't see you again, have a wonderful time in the Swiss Alps."

The center cleared out quickly until only Krista, Grandma and Alex remained. Krista threw away stray paper plates and napkins while Grandma wiped up the table where the cookies had been. Behind her, Alex was walking toward them from the direction of the storage room.

"What was going on with Charlie, Grandma?" Krista asked. "Why didn't you sit beside him?"

"Don't sound so worried." The deep crease between her grandmother's brows undermined her carefree smile. "I'm going to let Charlie chase me until I catch him."

"Say what?" Alex asked.

Grandma whirled, then shook her finger at him. "If I'd seen you coming, Alex, I might not have given away my secret. It's nothing new. It's called playing hard to get."

Alex stroked his chin. "Why not just let Charlie know you like him?"

"That's not how I hooked Krista's grandfather," Grandma said. "Men like the chase even if they don't know it."

"Is that why you let those two women monopolize Charlie?" Krista asked. "Aren't you worried one of them will snap him up?"

"They can try but they won't succeed," Grandma Novak said. "They're way too forward."

"But—" Krista began.

"If I give you two the keys to the center, would you stack the chairs in the community room and close up for me?" Grandma interrupted. She was obviously through talking about Charlie.

"I was planning to drive you home," Krista said. Her mother had dropped Krista off at the center, turning down an invitation to see the slide show, claiming she had things to do at home.

"I've been driving in snow all my life, young lady," Grandma said. "Alex will bring you home. He has the snow plow on his truck so no need to rush."

Grandma handed over the key and hurried to the coatrack as though that was the last word on the subject. Krista supposed it was. In no time, the door was swinging shut behind her, the wind blowing in stray snowflakes.

Krista and Alex walked together to the community room in silence and started stacking plastic chairs. The job could have waited. The cleaning crew wouldn't come in to mop floors tonight. Krista suspected this was their job, but she couldn't be angry at her grandmother for giving her and Alex time alone.

Krista finally spoke into the quiet. "Sorry about

Grandma. But I'm glad for the chance to talk to you. It's why I asked you to stick around."

She lifted another chair while she considered how to phrase her next statement. Tact wasn't her strong point, but this was important. The more she thought about their conversation outside the frame shop, the more she believed she was in the wrong.

"I feel bad about last night," she said. "I want you to know I appreciate you telling me about your mother. I'm more sorry than I can express."

"I never doubted that," Alex said quietly.

Krista's relief was tremendous, enabling her to go on. "I was also out of line about the job. It's entirely up to you whether you're comfortable accepting it."

"I agree."

"But you shouldn't have criticized me." She picked up a chair and set it down with a thump. "It's okay if we don't see eye to eye. We're very different people."

He put down his chair, too. "How so?"

"You're a homebody and I was born to travel," she said. "I can't stay in one spot."

"I don't know about that," he said.

Krista directed a sharp look at him. She hadn't expected Alex to disagree with her.

"Did you ever consider you're always traveling because you're searching for something?" he asked.

She wrinkled her brow. "What would I be looking for?"

"Your place in the world."

What was that supposed to mean? She turned it over in her mind while they finished stacking the chairs.

"Prague suits me fine," Krista finally said when they were through with the task. "Just because I like to travel doesn't mean I'm looking to relocate."

"That's not what I meant." Alex perched on the end of the small table where he'd set up the projector, his long legs stretched in front of him. "Let me ask you something. Why do you take so many photos of strangers?"

She shrugged. "You heard why. I'm curious about how people live."

"But the people you photograph are always couples or young families," Alex said. "There must be a reason for that."

Krista didn't like the direction the conversation was taking. "You obviously have a theory."

"Promise you won't bite my head off if I tell you?" Alex asked.

"No," she said, "but tell me anyway."

"Deep down you want what the people in those photographs have—love...family...stability," he said. "And once you find it, you'll be more likely to stay put."

"Wow!" Krista made the word sound like two syllables. "What was that? Pop psychology?"

"I warned you that you wouldn't like it," Alex said.

Krista was about to squash his presumption until she recalled her girlhood dream had been to marry and bear children. Her mother had pointed that out just recently.

"I *don't* like it." Krista wasn't opposed to having her own family one day, but it wasn't up to Alex to tell her what she wanted. "I haven't liked a lot of things you've said about me. Such as your claim that I don't know what's going on in my own family."

He winced. "I was hoping you'd forget about that."

The fight went out of Krista. She leaned her back against the wall where her slides had flashed across the drop-down screen, her legs suddenly too heavy to support her. "How can I when you were right? I found out today about the nursery losing money and Rayna breaking up with Trey. That's why I wanted to talk to you."

"To tell me I was right?" he asked.

"No," she said. "To thank you for keeping an eye on the people I love."

The people she was leaving behind tomorrow morning, along with Alex. An ache began near her heart that she tried to ignore. He didn't say anything for long moments, then rose.

"We should get going," he said. "The snow looked like it was coming down pretty good."

Together they went into the lobby, got their coats and put them on. Before he could move toward the door, Krista stopped him with a hand on his arm. She didn't question her motives, just went ahead with her impulse.

"Once we're in your pickup, you'll have to pay attention to the road," she said. "And you can bet my mom or Grandma will be keeping an eye out for us from the window."

She watched his body go still except for a muscle working in his jaw. "What are you saying?"

She wet her tongue with her lips, and his eyes dipped to her mouth. She could feel her pulse racing. "I'd like to kiss you one last time before I go back to Europe."

She thought she could hear his heart thudding in time with hers. He nodded toward the wintry night. "If it keeps snowing, you might not be able to leave tomorrow morning."

"If my flight's canceled, I'll count on you to figure out how to get us some privacy," she said.

"Let it snow, let it snow, let it snow," he said softly.

She chuckled. "I'd rather not take a chance on the snow stopping."

He stroked her cheek. "Then what are we waiting for?"

He lowered his head, lengthening the sweet moment of anticipation before their mouths met.

The kiss was different than the ones they'd shared before, more leisurely and not as passionate, as though both of them intended to make it last as long as possible.

With one hand Alex dug his fingers into Krista's hair, cupping her scalp and holding her head in place. With the other, he gathered her closer against him.

She'd always loved the way he made her feel, as though nothing were more important than kissing her. Even when he was in the grip of passion, she felt treasured. No matter how much she tried to convince herself otherwise, having sex with him had never felt like just sex.

As the kiss went on and on, Krista became more and more certain of one fact.

She wasn't ready to let him go.

CHAPTER TWELVE

KRISTA OPENED HER EYES to complete darkness and felt the dampness on her cheeks. Silly to cry because the snow had stopped in time for her flight to take off and she had finally made it to Zermatt. Hadn't she and her friends been eagerly anticipating this ski trip for months?

Yes, she answered herself silently. But that was before she'd made love with Alex. She ran her fingers over her lips, already missing the feel of his mouth on hers.

She groaned, turned her head on the pillow to check the glowing numbers on the bedside alarm clock and encountered only darkness. Had the power in the ski chalet blipped off?

But, no. Dim light was shining from the next room. Krista heard the soft thud of footsteps on stairs and couldn't remember how many floors the chalet had. Did she even know? Why couldn't she envision what the place looked like?

She blinked, trying to clear the cobwebs of sleep. Her eyes adjusted to the darkness and she recognized the furniture in her parents' basement.

Shoving the hair from her face, Krista sat up in the sofa bed, realizing with a start she'd only been dreaming.

She was still in Jarrell, sleeping in the basement of

the house that was only one door down from Alex's.
Gradually her situation became clear. She was downstairs because her father was using her old bedroom
as his office. Her travel alarm clock didn't have illuminating numbers. And someone was coming down
the stairs.

Rayna must finally be home.

Krista pushed aside the covers, swung her legs off
the sofa bed and got unsteadily to her feet. She could
think about Alex and what her dream meant later. Now
her priority was Rayna.

Not only hadn't her sister returned the call Krista
had left on her cell phone, but Krista also hadn't seen
Rayna at all the previous day. Fresh relief coursed
through Krista that she wasn't in the Swiss Alps. This
was her chance to talk to Rayna alone and possibly
make inroads into gaining her confidence.

Krista padded across the cool linoleum floor, her
thick winter socks making little sound. She rounded
the corner at the exact moment her sister was descend-
ing the last step.

Rayna gasped, her hand flying to her throat. Then
she blew out a long breath, shook her head and glared
at Krista.

"You scared me," Rayna said.

"I didn't mean to." Krista was about to apologize
when a childhood memory surfaced. She crossed her
arms over her chest. "Although it would serve you right
if I did it on purpose. You frightened me plenty of
times when we were growing up."

"If you stay up late watching scary movies," Rayna
said in the know-it-all tone a teacher might use, "you
should expect your little sister to jump out at you."

"Remember the time I screamed and Dad woke up

and thought somebody had broken into the house?" Krista asked.

"I'll never forget it." Rayna's smile was broader than it had been since Krista returned home. "Dad thundered out of the bedroom wearing those crazy pajamas Mom bought him for his birthday, the ones that were covered with green thumbs."

"Oh, yeah. The severed green thumbs! Tackiest pajamas in the history of sleepwear." Krista had never understood why her mother thought the pajamas were the perfect gift for a gardener. "But what I remember even better is that cast-iron frying pan he grabbed from the kitchen to use as a weapon."

"Oh, he was mad at you! Especially when you told him you'd screamed because the movie was so scary." Rayna tugged at her bottom lip with her teeth. "I never understood why you didn't give me up."

"Because you were my little sister," Krista said simply.

Rayna dropped her gaze, and the connection between them was broken. Krista desperately wanted to get it back. She cast about for something to keep her sister talking.

"Mom said you went to a party," Krista said. "Did you have fun?"

"It was okay." Rayna's response was terse. She sounded as though she regretted letting down her guard, even though it had only been for a moment.

"I would have waited up if you hadn't called and said you'd be late," Krista said. "Mom thought you might spend the night if it kept snowing."

"The party was only a mile away," Rayna said. "The roads aren't too bad when you don't have to travel far."

"Then it's still snowing?" Krista supposed she

hadn't entirely shaken off the aftermath of her dream, because she'd expected the snow to have stopped.

"A lot harder than before." Rayna took a step to the side so she could get by Krista. "It's late. I should be getting to sleep. Sorry I woke you."

Rayna was about to disappear into her room, taking with her Krista's opportunity to narrow the distance between them. Krista followed her, bracing a hand on the door to Rayna's bedroom before her sister could pull it closed.

"I'm glad you woke me," Krista said. "I tried calling you this afternoon to see if you'd have dinner with me."

"I went to the mall after work to return some presents." Rayna sat down on her bed and took off her shoes. Casper appeared as if from nowhere. It marked only the second time Krista had seen the elusive cat. Casper hopped onto the mattress beside Rayna, peering at Krista from slitted green eyes.

Rayna offered no explanation for why she hadn't returned Krista's call although she must have noticed the message on her voice mail. Maybe she hadn't listened to it when she saw the caller was Krista.

"Mom told me about the mall," Krista said. "Although at first I thought you were with Trey. I even called and asked him if he knew where you were."

Rayna sat up ruler straight. "What did Trey say?"

"He told me you broke up with him," Krista said, watching her sister carefully. "Then he asked me to put in a good word for him."

Rayna exhaled through her nose. Casper edged closer to her and rubbed her head against Rayna's thigh.

"Unbelievable," Rayna muttered. "You'd think Trey would call me and put in a good word for himself."

"What happened?" Krista ventured a step deeper into the room. If she weren't afraid of spooking Rayna, she would have sat down on the bed beside her sister like the cat had. "I got the impression you were crazy about him."

Rayna chewed on her bottom lip. It appeared to Krista that she was trying to keep it from trembling.

Krista took a few steps closer to the bed.

"If you'd gone to dinner with me, I was going to tell you that you can talk to me about anything," Krista said. "I'm here for you."

Rayna's head jerked up, her mouth twisting. "Why do you keep saying that? You're only here until tomorrow morning."

Krista was dismayed that she'd made the same mistake twice. She wasn't sure how to respond. "I care about you, Rayna."

"I believe that you do," Rayna said. "But I can't pretend we're like regular sisters when we haven't spent any time together in eight years."

The reverse wasn't true. Krista loved her sister now every bit as much as she had when they were younger even though cards and the occasional email were poor substitutes for face-to-face encounters.

"If it keeps snowing and my flight's cancelled, will you hang out with me tomorrow?" Krista asked.

Rayna's brown eyes, so like Krista's own, looked wary. Casper crawled into her lap. "Those are some pretty big ifs."

"Will you?" Krista persisted.

Rayna didn't respond for so long, Krista thought

she might not say anything at all. "Okay," she finally answered.

After bidding her sister good-night and shutting the bedroom door, Krista couldn't imagine trying to fall back asleep. Not until she saw for herself that the snow was still falling.

Careful to keep her tread light, Krista climbed the stairs to the main floor of the house. All the lights were off except for those shining inside the string of plastic Santa Claus heads that decorated the fireplace. Krista knew the layout of the house well enough that she reached the picture window in the living room without incident.

Pulling back the heavy curtain her mother kept closed at night, Krista peeked outside and lifted her gaze to the streetlight.

Fat snowflakes slashed toward the earth, the pace of their descent fast and furious. Grandma had turned off the outside Christmas lights hours ago but the blanket of white snow that covered the ground was in stark contrast to the night sky.

The windshield of the car Rayna had parked in the driveway when she'd returned home a short time ago was covered in snow. Its tire tracks were no longer visible.

Krista turned from the window and caught sight of a mantel clock that showed it was nearly 2:00 a.m. Her flight out of the Harrisburg airport was supposed to leave in eight hours.

She hesitated only briefly before going down the hall to her father's office, feeling her way along the wall. Not until she was inside the room did she switch on a light. She booted up the computer on the antique desk that had come from her grandmother's house, listened to the tone that signaled the computer was awakening and waited.

Her gaze ran over the room. Bookshelves lined the wall where her bed had once been. A beautifully rendered photo of the Susquehanna River, probably shot by Alex, hung in a spot once occupied by a poster of the Backstreet Boys.

All traces of Krista's childhood bedroom were simply gone, as though she'd never lived in the house at all.

Swallowing a lump of emotion, Krista redirected her attention to the dozens of icons that popped up on the computer monitor. She searched for an internet symbol, skipping over folders belonging to her grandmother, mother and father.

Her attention came back to her father's folder. Years ago he'd resisted computerizing their records at the nursery. She couldn't imagine him spending much time on the computer. Except maybe he did. She had no idea how he spent the long hours he was confined in this office.

With one click, Krista could satisfy her curiosity about the contents of the folder. Her finger hovered over the cursor, then relaxed. She couldn't do it. It would seem a travesty to add invasion of privacy to the sin she'd already committed against her father.

She moused over to the internet symbol and connected to the web. A widget on the toolbar at the top of the screen showed the current weather: heavy snow, nineteen degrees.

Krista typed the name of her airline into a search engine, clicked through to the site and checked the status of her flight.

Canceled.

Only when she exhaled did she realize she'd been holding her breath. Anticipation flared inside her.

It hardly mattered that she might miss the trip to the Swiss Alps entirely. There were plenty of reasons to be glad of spending another day in Jarrell.

An idea of what she and Rayna could do tomorrow afternoon crystallized. Yes, that would be perfect.

Tomorrow night, however, would be even better. Because Krista intended to remind Alex of her challenge to get her alone so they could make love.

Krista turned off the computer, flicked off the wall light switch and left the room. The sooner she got to the basement, climbed into the sofa bed and fell asleep, the sooner morning would arrive.

THE SNOW KEPT COMING DOWN early the following afternoon, the flakes soft and slightly wet, adding to the several feet of accumulation already on the ground. Krista led the way, trudging through the half-shoveled snow on the sidewalks to one of the most popular spots in the neighborhood.

"I don't know why I let you talk me into this, Krista," Rayna grumbled when they reached their destination. But she was smiling.

How could she not be?

This felt a lot like one of the snow days they'd prayed for as kids. The Christmas Shoppe and the dentist were closed. Krista's rebooked flight didn't leave for another twenty-four hours. And they were about to sled down a gently sloping hill that flattened into a field with a half-dozen laughing, shrieking children.

"What else is there to do today?" Krista asked. "It doesn't make sense to clear the driveway and sidewalks until it stops snowing."

"We could have done the adult thing and stayed indoors," Rayna said.

"What fun is that?" Krista retorted. "What happened to the girl who was up for anything?"

"That girl was a kid," Rayna said. "I've grown up."

"You're not so grown up that you refused to search the garage for these sleds." Krista lifted her lightweight piece of purple plastic. Rayna held the corded string attached to the identical model sled in orange.

"I had to," Rayna said. "You called me a chicken."

Krista threw back her head and laughed. "You haven't changed that much. That's how I used to get you to do my bidding when you were a kid."

Her sister pursed her lips, but Krista could tell she was holding back a laugh. Rayna thumped her own forehead. "How did I fall for that?"

Krista lifted her gloved hands and wriggled her fingers. "Because I am a mastermind."

Rayna's laugh burst from her. She nodded toward the sled hill. "C'mon, mastermind. Let's go make fools of ourselves."

An hour later, Krista felt more exhilarated than foolish. One of their fellow sledders clearly didn't agree with that assessment.

"How old am *I*?" Krista repeated the boy's query. She stood at the top of the hill beside her sled, shaking her head at his sheer audacity. "How old are *you*?"

"Eight." The boy was wearing so much clothing he resembled a very small Eskimo. His big blue eyes were wide and guileless, and he was missing two front teeth. "I'm a kid. I'm supposed to be outside playing in the snow."

"And I'm not?" Krista harrumphed, pretending to

take offense. "Okay, buster. That does it. You just got yourself a race."

"You're on!" the boy cried.

The kid had a much nicer sled than Krista, sleeker and shaped like a toboggan instead of a flying saucer. It looked new enough that he'd probably received it as a Christmas present. Maybe he even believed that Santa had brought it down the chimney and left it under the tree.

Getting his sled in position, the boy climbed on. Krista did the same, arranging herself in the center of her purple sled so her weight was evenly distributed.

At the bottom of the hill, Rayna had just finished a run. She rose from her sled and gazed back in the direction she'd come, her right hand shielding her eyes from the reflected glare off the snow. It wouldn't take much for Rayna to figure out a race was on.

"Ready! Set! Go!" the boy hollered. He pushed off with a small booted foot, gaining him a sizeable head start.

Krista propelled her own sled forward with her feet until it rounded the slope, then let gravity take over. The sledding conditions had steadily improved, with every run causing the hard-packed snow to become smoother and more slippery.

Adrenaline raced through Krista's veins as quickly as her sled slid down the hill. The wind and flakes of snow blew in her face, chilling her cheeks. Her stomach went into a free fall.

She zipped past the boy about three quarters of the way down the hill and dusted him at the finish line. Krista reached both arms to the sky and whooped as she and the sled glided to a stop.

Jumping to her feet, Krista dusted snow from the

weatherproof pants she'd borrowed from Rayna. "Good race," she told the boy.

The boy scrambled from the sled, the corners of his mouth turned down. "You got lucky, lady."

He checked the immediate vicinity, probably to see if his friends had witnessed him get beaten by an adult. The boy couldn't get away from Krista fast enough. He attacked the trek back up the hill with quick steps, eager to put distance between himself and his embarrassing loss.

"Can I believe my eyes?" Rayna trod through the snow to Krista's side. "Did you really just race that kid?"

"Uh-huh," Krista said. "Wasn't he adorable?"

"Adorable and gullible. You have at least sixty pounds on him. Of course you'd be faster."

"That'll teach him to ask a woman how old she is," Krista retorted with spirit.

Rayna laughed. "We are the oldest ones out here. Except for that guy at the top of the hill. Wait a minute, that's Alex!"

He stood silhouetted against the snow and the sky, looking tall and powerful. Happiness washed over Krista. She smiled and waved.

"Alex must have gotten my text," Krista told Rayna. "I knew he'd be busy plowing but I told him to stop by if he got the chance."

Rayna made a face. "Do you think that was a good idea?"

"Sure," Krista said. "Why wouldn't it be?"

Without waiting for her sister's answer, Krista towed her sled up the hill, eager to join Alex. With his appearance, the winter scenery had most definitely taken a turn for the better. Alex was bareheaded, with flakes from the still-falling snow dusting his thick black hair. His dark-colored parka was in stark contrast to the white world. He stood with his booted feet slightly apart, a smile playing across his lips.

Krista reached the top of the hill faster than she had all day. "I'm still in Jarrell."

Alex returned her smile. "I'm glad."

Krista didn't plan to hug him. She certainly didn't intend to kiss him, not with an audience of children and Rayna. Except that's exactly what she did. Or, rather, what Alex did. She wasn't sure what precipitated the kiss. She simply enjoyed it, reveling in the shot of warmth that spiraled through her on this cool day and breathing in his clean unique scent.

"Mmm," she said when the kiss ended, in no hurry to move from the circle of his arms. "Now I'm looking forward to tonight even more."

"Ah, yes. Tonight." He made a contemplative noise. "It seems to me there's something I'm supposed to do tonight."

"You're supposed to get me alone!" Krista told him, then noticed the glint in his eyes. "Which you know, because you're teasing me."

"Only because you continue to make it so easy," he said. "I could never forget an invitation like that."

Krista could suddenly breath easier. "Do you have a plan?"

"I've got some ideas," he said. "Don't worry. It's going to happen."

A delicious thrill of anticipation shot through Krista. "I can't wait."

"What can't you wait for?" Rayna asked.

Krista stepped back from Alex's arms, thinking about how their greeting might appear to have more significance than it warranted. She tried to think up a feasible answer to Rayna's question.

"We're both looking forward to tonight's football game," Alex told Rayna, coming to Krista's rescue. "Penn State is playing at the Citrus Bowl."

"Don't I know it. Our dads have been talking about it for weeks." Rayna peered at Krista. "They think of the Nittany Lions as their local team. But, Krista, why do you care? You went to Penn."

It was an excellent question, especially considering Krista had never been much of a sports fan. This one she needed to answer for herself.

"Living in Europe, I don't get to see much American football," Krista said. "It'll be fun."

Rayna didn't seem convinced, but before she could ask another question Alex gestured at the sled hill. "Speaking of fun, whose idea was sledding?"

"Krista's," Rayna said. "But you don't know the half of it. Were you here when Krista beat that seven-year-old kid in a race?"

"Hey!" Krista protested. "He was eight. And I'm not the only one acting like a kid. Rayna screams when her sled gets up to speed."

"I do not!" Rayna protested. "I whoop. There's a difference."

"If you whoop on this little mound, you'll screech when we hit the bigger hill," Krista said.

"Wait a minute," Rayna said. "I never said I'd sled another hill."

"Yeah, you two might not be up for the competition," Alex said. "I know that hill. The sledders over there tend to be at least eleven or twelve."

"If you come with us, I bet we can take 'em," Krista said.

"I can't." He raised his gaze to the still-falling snow. "There's plenty more plowing to be done."

"You'll be done by tonight, though, won't you?" Krista didn't want anything to interfere with the plan he was hatching.

"Should be," Alex said. "It's supposed to stop snowing in a few hours. We should have most of our work done by nightfall. The rest, we'll do tomorrow morning."

"Good." Krista touched him on the arm. "I'll see you later then."

"Later." His eyes lingered on Krista before his gaze shifted to Rayna. "'Bye, Rayna. Don't whoop too loud or you'll scare the children."

He left them, chuckling to himself as he walked away.

"He must have thought that remark was funny," Rayna said.

"It was funny." Krista tracked Alex with her eyes, loving the way he moved. What was it about a confident man that could get her juices flowing? What was it about Alex? He'd nearly reached his pickup when he turned and looked back at her.

"Oh, no," Rayna said, drawing out the syllables. "That is not good."

"What are you talking about?" Krista didn't take her eyes off Alex until he'd disappeared inside the truck.

"The turn," Rayna said. "A man only turns and takes another look at a woman when he's serious about her."

"Alex isn't serious about me," Krista denied. "We're just having fun."

Hot, intense, passionate fun.

"Are you sure about that?" Rayna folded her arms over her chest. "Because I'd hate to see him hurt. He doesn't do casual. I think he'd like to get married and settle down."

Krista's mother had voiced the same opinion the first night Krista had arrived in Jarrell. Alex hadn't denied it.

"Alex knows what the score is." Krista stopped short of explaining that their relationship was built on physical attraction. "I'm not going to hurt him."

"You don't know that," Rayna said. "Sometimes somebody can hurt you without even knowing they're doing it."

Rayna no longer seemed to be referring to Krista and Alex.

"Is this about Trey?" Krista asked in a soft voice. "Did he hurt you?"

Rayna cleared her throat. "I don't want to talk about it."

Krista tried not to show that her sister's refusal hurt. She tried to sound cheerful. "Okay, then. Let's leave this bunny hill and hit the black-diamond trail. The other hill's only a few blocks away."

A pained looked passed over Rayna's face. "I can't do that, either."

"Why not?" Krista asked, wondering at Rayna's answering silence. Had their relationship deteriorated so far that her sister couldn't talk to her about simple things? "C'mon, Rayna. You can at least tell me that."

Rayna stared at her, and all the levity of the afternoon vanished even though the children around them still laughed and played. "I wish I could tell you."

"You can," Krista insisted, sensing that she'd stumbled across something important but at a loss as to what it could be.

Rayna looked right, left, then back at Krista. She seemed to make a decision.

She spoke in a whisper even though nobody was within earshot. "I can't risk sledding on the steeper hill—" her eyes appeared huge in her pale face "—because I'm pregnant."

Krista's mouth must have dropped open, because she could feel the cold air rush into her lungs. A dozen questions sprang to mind. Now wasn't the time to ask any of them. She opened her arms. "Oh, honey. Come here."

Rayna let out the smallest of sobs and stepped forward. Krista wrapped her arms around her sister, holding her close. Rayna's body shook, but only slightly, as though she were holding back her emotions.

"I'm keeping the baby." Rayna spoke so softly Krista had to strain to hear her. "Trey's the father."

Rayna leaned back so she could look into her sister's unhappy face. She had one question she couldn't suppress. "Then why did you break up with him?"

Rayna sniffled. "You won't understand."

"Try me," Krista invited.

"I don't want Trey to commit to me because I'm pregnant," she said. "I want him to be with me because he loves me."

"That makes perfect sense to me." Krista kept one arm around her sister, turning her away from the hill. "So let's go home and find a quiet spot so you can tell me all about it."

Rayna nodded, unshed tears brimming in her eyes. "I didn't think anybody else would get it."

"I'm not just anybody," Krista said. "I'm your big sister."

CHAPTER THIRTEEN

THE NOVAKS WERE READY to watch some football, just as Alex had expected.

Minutes before the bowl game was about to start, the area around the television in their house was stocked with bowls of chips, a plate of brownies and crackers and cheese. Beer was just a refrigerator away. Alex could verify that because he'd added a six-pack to the stash, minus the bottle his father had kept for himself.

Alex left the kitchen and approached the crowd in the living room, his gaze focused on Krista at the end of the sofa. In worn jeans and an oversize sweatshirt, with her brown hair loose and shiny, she could have passed for a college coed. She met his gaze, but her expression wasn't filled with mischief the way it had been at the sled hill.

With a slight tilt of his head, he indicated she should meet him at the entrance to the hallway.

"Penn State's about to kick off!" Milo announced from the love seat he shared with Grandma Novak.

"Go, Nittany Lions!" Grandma Novak shook a faded navy-and-white pom-pom she took out every time Penn State played.

"It's supposed to be a good game." Eleanor sat in her favorite armchair next to her husband's wheelchair, not ten feet from the television.

"Not a *good* game," Joe contradicted. "A *great* game."

Eleanor made a face at him. "That's what I said."

"No, you didn't. You said good," he said. "Not great."

Krista got up from her spot on the sofa farthest from the TV and moved toward Alex. Nobody glanced away from the television screen. Alex couldn't look anywhere but at Krista.

She managed to appear feminine and beautiful even in a baggy sweatshirt while wearing very little makeup. She also seemed subdued.

"Here's the plan," Alex whispered. "We wait until midway through the first quarter and go out the back door to my empty house."

"I'm not so sure that's a good idea," she replied in an equally soft voice.

"Sure it is," he said. "As long as we're back by half-time, nobody will miss us."

"I meant maybe we should just ditch it."

Alex hadn't been imagining the change in her. He took Krista lightly by the arm and moved with her farther from the boisterous group in the living room. "What's going on? Where's this coming from?"

"Rayna," Krista said.

"Is she okay?" Alex asked, instantly concerned.

"She's worried about you." Krista must have noticed his confusion. "Ironic, isn't it? Seems like it should be the other way around considering what's going on with her."

"So she told you?" Alex ventured.

"She did," Krista said. "She also figured out there was something between us and warned me not to hurt you. She seems to think you're in the market for a wife and family."

Alex rubbed the back of his neck. "Why does everybody keep saying that?"

"Maybe because it's true?"

Was it? Even in his twenties, Alex hadn't been opposed to settling down with one woman. His parents had set a great example with their happy marriage and comfortable life. At thirty-two, Alex was still open to the possibility if the right woman came along.

She'd be somebody who put family first, the way Alex did.

"Relax, Krista," he said. "I'm a big boy. I know when good sex is just good sex."

She didn't respond for a pregnant moment. "Good. I'm glad."

"So is the plan back on?" he asked.

"Definitely." Her smile had returned. Was he imagining that it had lost some of its luster?

"I already stashed a pair of my boots on your porch," he said. "You'll need some, too. Just be discreet when you get them."

"Fumble!" Alex's father yelled from the love seat, half rising from the cushion.

"Penn State has the ball!" Joe cried along with the TV announcer. "What a hit!"

Grandma shook her pom-pom.

"It wasn't that good of a hit," Eleanor said. "The kick returner dropped it."

"Did not!" Joe countered. "You need glasses, Ellie."

"I'm wearing glasses," Eleanor pointed out.

Krista nodded toward the group in the living room. "We might not have to be that discreet. When did Mom, Grandma and Rayna get into football, anyway?"

"Rayna's always been a sports fan," Alex said. "Your mom and grandma probably got tired of being left out when the rest of us were watching games."

"So you're a fan, too?" Krista asked.

"Usually." He gave her a meaningful look. "Tonight, I've got better things to do."

"Go! Go!" Eleanor screeched loudly enough to puncture an eardrum. "Faster! Faster!"

Alex could just make out the TV screen from where he stood. A Penn State receiver sped downfield before a defender managed to tackle him about twenty yards from the goal line. Joe and Alex's father exchanged a high five while Grandma gave her pom-pom a workout.

"Forget about waiting," Alex told Krista. "The time to leave is now."

Heavy raps sounded before Krista could respond, followed by the door opening. Trey Farina walked into the house, a six-pack of beer in his hand, his hair rustled from the wind. He pointed a finger at them. "Hey, Krista. Hey, Alex."

The noise level in the living room was so great, it was possible nobody else had noticed him come in.

Krista advanced on him. "What are you doing here?"

"I'm here to watch the game," Trey said easily. "Your dad invited me."

"But—" Krista began.

Shouts of joy, only half of them decipherable, obliterated the rest of Krista's response. Grandma Novak's pom-poms swished left and right. Alex's father pumped a fist in the air.

"Touchdown!" Trey yelled and raised both arms to the ceiling, including the one holding the six-pack.

Everybody in the living room focused on the TV and the replay of the touchdown play with one notable exception. Rayna stared at Trey, her mouth open and her face visibly pale.

On screen, the slow-motion replay showed the Penn State fullback barreling through the opening in middle of the line and thundering into the end zone.

"What a run!" Trey exclaimed. He plopped down on the love seat beside Alex's father.

"You got here just in time, son." Joe seemed so glad to see Trey, he couldn't possibly know his daughter had dumped him.

"I brought those wheat beers I was telling you guys about." Trey took a bottle out of the sleeve. "Anybody want one?"

"I do," Joe said.

"Me, too," Eleanor said.

"Way to be adventurous, Mrs. N.!" Trey separated two more beers from the sleeve, tossed one to Joe and handed the other to Eleanor. He turned toward Rayna. "Hey, Rain. You want one, too?"

Appearing incapable of speech, Rayna shook her head. Trey shrugged, settled deeper into the sofa and went back to watching the game. Rayna's eyes flew to where Krista stood beside Alex.

A silent message seemed to pass between the sisters before Krista leaned closer to Alex, speaking near his ear. "Sorry, but I can't leave just yet. I need to stick around for Rayna."

"Nothing to be sorry for," Alex said. "Your sister needs your support."

"Thanks for understanding," Krista said.

They joined the crowd in the living room, with Krista taking the seat between Rayna and Trey. Alex noticed Krista give her sister's knee a quick squeeze and Rayna visibly relax. He'd been right when he advised Rayna to confide in Krista. Although Alex would do anything within his power to support his young neighbor, there was something special about a bond between sisters. He hoped Rayna and Krista were able to form a lasting one.

The seconds in the first half of the football game ticked down to nothing, with Penn State taking a ten-point lead into the locker room.

"Wish I could stay," Trey said, getting to his feet, "but I'm outta here."

"What!" Joe exclaimed. "You're not watching the second half?"

"My mom's a Penn State grad," Trey said. "I thought she'd like to have me home."

"What a good son you are!" Eleanor declared. "Why didn't you watch the entire game with her?"

Trey cast a look at Rayna that even Alex could tell was full of hope. "Because I got a girl, too."

Rayna opened her mouth to say something.

"Isn't that sweet?" Eleanor's question drowned out all other sound. "Rayna, you got yourself a good one."

"Did you hear that, Rain? Mother knows best!" Trey grinned at Rayna before moving quickly toward the door. "Later!"

Everybody besides Rayna called out their goodbyes. Had anyone other than Krista and Alex noticed that Rayna hadn't spoken a word to Trey? Alex hoped the dynamic between the two made more sense to Krista than it did to him. He couldn't fathom why an expectant mother wouldn't tell the man who'd impregnated her that he was going to be a father.

"How long is halftime again, Joe?" Eleanor asked.

"It's usually twenty minutes, but it'll be longer today because this is a bowl game," Joe said. "Plenty of time for a bathroom break."

"I need to turn on our outdoor lights," Alex's father said. "Would you believe Alex and I forgot about them?"

The living room cleared out, with Eleanor excusing herself to refresh the trays of food and Grandma Novak leaving to answer the ringing phone. On the television screen, a marching band was set to take the field.

"Could you believe Trey's nerve?" Rayna said when everybody else was gone and out of earshot. "Everybody knows an invitation isn't good anymore after you get dumped. And did you hear him call me 'his girl'? What gives him the right to say that?"

"You are pregnant with his baby," Alex pointed out.

Rayna glowered at him. Krista shot him a glare that was almost a carbon copy of her sister's.

"Trey was out of line," Krista told her sister. "But here's another possibility. Maybe him showing up here was his way of showing you he cares."

"You really think so?" Rayna sounded both doubtful and hopeful.

"The only way to find out for sure is to talk to him," Krista said, which Alex thought was terrific advice.

"I'll think about it," Rayna said and stood up. "If anybody asks, could you tell them I'm watching the game in my room? I need some downtime."

"You can count on me." Krista's tone was so serious, Alex thought she was talking about more than making excuses to the family.

Rayna touched her sister on the shoulder. "Thanks, Krista."

"Anytime," Krista said. Alex thought her eyes looked a little misty.

When Rayna was gone, Alex moved over to the sofa and sat down next to Krista. She leaned her head back against the cushion and turned to face him. "Sorry again."

"No apology necessary." Alex touched her cheek. "Besides, we've got an entire half to go."

"You're right." Krista brightened. "Let's sneak out when the second half starts."

"I'm up for it if you are," he said.

She cast a slow, deliberate glance from his face to his chest and points south, a teasing smile on her lips. "Not yet, you aren't. But I'll make sure you get there."

He laughed, amazed that she could amuse him and turn him on at the same time. He edged closer, breathing in her clean, sweet scent, his mouth hovering just inches above hers.

She placed three fingers against his lips and indicated with her eyes that someone was coming back into the room.

It was Grandma Novak, who walked like she was in a trance. Unsmiling, she sank into her previous spot on the love seat.

"What's wrong?" Alex asked.

"That was Susie Snyder on the phone," Grandma Novak said in a wooden voice. It took Alex a moment to remember Susie was the retired teacher's first name. "She called to tell me that Charlie made a date with Frances Brewer."

"Ah, hell," Alex said.

"I'm sorry, Grandma." Krista got up and went to sit beside her grandmother. "Is she one of the women who was flirting with Charlie at the senior center?"

"She was the one wearing too much jewelry." Grandma Novak shook her head, her expression miserable. "I don't understand why he called her. He said he was falling for me!"

Krista rubbed her grandmother's shoulder. "What did you say when Charlie told you that?"

"Thank you," Grandma Novak answered.

"That's it?" Krista asked, her tone gentle.

"I already told you, I'm playing hard to get."

"You might want to rethink that," Krista said. "Charlie might not know how much you like him."

"How could he not know?" Grandma Novak asked.

"I can give you a male's point of view," Alex interjected. "Because you haven't told him."

Grandma Novak brought a hand to her head. "Dating was easier in the twentieth century."

"I don't know, Grandma," Krista said. "Even back then men must have liked hearing they were desirable."

"Krista's right," Alex said. "Evolution works slowly. We guys haven't changed that much."

"So you both think I should let Charlie know I'm interested?" Grandma Novak asked.

"Yes," Krista said.

"Definitely," Alex chimed in.

"I'll call him right now," Grandma decided. She got up from the love seat and left the room.

Alex smiled at Krista. "You handled that well."

"She's in desperate need of dating tips," Krista said. "I'm no expert at dealing with the opposite sex but hopefully I'm better at it than my grandmother."

Alex didn't care to hear about the specifics of Krista's romantic dealings with other men. Truth was, he didn't want to think about her dating. Period.

The front door opened and his father burst through. "The second half didn't start yet, did it?"

Alex checked the TV as it cut away from a commercial to a shot of the Citrus Bowl stadium in warm, sunny Orlando. The teams had taken their respective places on the sidelines.

"It's about to," Alex said.

"Joe! Where are you?" Alex's father yelled down the hall. "Game time!"

"Coming," Joe yelled back, his voice preceding the sound of wheels rolling on hardwood.

"I'm coming, too." Eleanor reentered the room, carrying a fresh basket of chips in one hand and more brownies in the other.

"Stick to the plan," Alex told Krista in a quiet voice while their families resumed their previous positions.

It took less than a minute for their family members to get caught up in the game. Alex rose and circled around to the back of the sofa with Krista following suit. Nobody awarded them a single glance.

"That was a good catch!" Eleanor cried.

"A *great* catch!" Joe corrected.

Alex changed his mind about suggesting Krista deflect suspicion by waiting a few minutes before following him. There was no need. The back porch was through the kitchen and down a short passageway. They moved quickly, the door in sight.

"Krista! Alex!" Grandma called from beside the telephone on the wall in the kitchen, her hand still wrapped around the receiver. "Guess what! Charlie's coming over to watch the rest of the game with us!"

"Fantastic!" Krista said.

"I took your advice and told him he curled my toes!" Grandma announced.

Krista glanced back over her shoulder at Alex and grimaced comically. She composed her features before turning back to her grandmother. "I don't remember using exactly those words."

Alex grinned. "Sounds to me like a good thing to tell him. I bet he enjoyed hearing it."

"He loved it!" Grandma said. "I think I might be able to get him to cancel his date with Frances."

"I wouldn't bet against you," Krista said.

"You're always so supportive of me." Grandma Novak gave Krista an imploring look. "You'll let me know if I do anything dumb after Charlie gets here, right?"

"Of course I will, Grandma." Krista shot Alex an apologetic look, her eyes begging for understanding. She needn't have worried. Alex was aware that family came first.

Until this moment, however, he hadn't known that Krista shared that belief.

"What are we waiting for?" Alex swept a hand toward the living room. "Let's all go watch the end of the game."

Krista smiled at him, her eyes soft and shining. He banked his disappointment that they wouldn't be sneaking off to make love and consoled himself with being able to spend the rest of the night in her company.

That was when he realized he was in trouble.

Because he could no longer convince himself that what he felt for Krista was just about sex.

CHAPTER FOURTEEN

THE RAT-A-TAT SOUNDED LIKE it was coming from outside.

Krista stayed very still on the downstairs sofa bed where she'd been trying to read. Had she imagined the noise? Or had the rapping been made by a super breed of woodpecker that could withstand cold and snow?

"Yeah, right," Krista said aloud.

It was one thing to have insomnia. It was quite another to conjure up things.

The sound came again, slightly louder this time. Somebody was knocking on the basement door, she realized with a start. She swung her legs off the bed and got up, rearranging her pink flannel pajamas.

The basement was a walk out, with a heavy wooden door that opened onto canopy-covered cement steps that ascended to the ground level. A made-to-size curtain Krista's mother had sewn herself obscured the double-glass pane built into the top of the door.

Still doubting what she'd heard, Krista slowly pulled back the curtain to the dark shape of a man.

She gasped. Then she squinted.

It wasn't just any man. It was Alex. A rush of adrenaline coursed through her, quickly followed by a pang of apprehension. She dropped the curtain, hurriedly undid the lock and pulled open the door.

He came inside amidst a burst of frigid air and closed the door behind him.

"Baby, it's cold outside," he said, rubbing his bare hands together. His jeans were tucked into boots dusted with snow.

She let out a disbelieving breath. Her impulse was to jump into his arms and kiss him, but something he'd said earlier tonight held her back. *I know when good sex is just good sex.* She understood what was between them, too, but hearing it stated so baldly had smarted.

"Did you come over here just to make out with me?" Krista asked, then realized how her question sounded. For the past week or so, she'd been flirting with him relentlessly and now she was implying that she wasn't up for sex.

"I wish." There was humor in his voice, suggesting he hadn't read anything out of the ordinary into her question. "But that would be uncool with your sister in the next room and the rest of your family asleep upstairs."

Krista had a tough time identifying the mix of emotions that struck her. The disappointment was easy to spot, but something else was counteracting it, something that felt like relief. Could she want more from Alex than sex? But what?

"Then why are you here?" she asked. "It's nearly one in the morning."

"I saw the basement light on," Alex said. "I took a chance you'd be awake."

"Why?" she persisted.

"You rescheduled your flight for tomorrow afternoon, right?"

"Yes." She had a tough time getting out the word.

He shrugged. "Then I guess I'm here because I

wanted to spend time with you without your family around."

He couldn't have given a more perfect answer.

"Sounds good to me," Krista said. To keep things from getting too serious, she spread her arms wide. "As long as you're sure you can resist me when I'm wearing this getup."

He touched a strand of her hair, pushing it back from her face. "Those pajamas remind me of the pink cotton candy they sell at carnivals."

"The sugary sticky kind?" Krista asked.

"The sweet stuff I never could resist." He kissed her on the mouth, the thrilling contact over almost before it began.

Stepping back from her, he took off his jacket and stepped out of his boots. Now that she knew he wasn't here solely for sex, Krista couldn't help wishing he'd keep on stripping his clothes. She looked away from him, striving for composure. Her gaze fell on the bar across the room that her father had built himself when he refinished the basement.

"Would you like a nightcap?" she offered.

"I'm good," he said. "A few beers during the football game were plenty for me."

Penn State had lost the lead in the fourth quarter before regrouping in a come-from-behind victory that had thrilled Krista's family. They'd whooped and hollered. Charlie had even kissed Grandma on the mouth when the receiver snagged the winning pass in the end zone.

Before that, Krista had been under the impression Charlie was no bigger a football fan than she was. She wasn't convinced she had that wrong.

"It's best not to turn on the light beside the bar

anyway," Krista said. "I'd hate for it to shine under Rayna's door and wake her."

"You don't think she heard me arrive?"

"No," Krista said. "She was exhausted when she said good-night. I hear pregnancy can wear you out."

"I'm no pregnant woman, but I wouldn't mind sitting down myself," he said.

The downstairs furniture was old but functional. The sofa set had once been in the upstairs living room. Krista remembered her mother complaining the love seat was too small to comfortably seat two. When Alex sat down next to her and pulled her close with an arm across her shoulders, Krista considered the size to be perfect. That is, until Casper appeared from out of nowhere and perched on the arm of the love seat nearest Krista. After a moment, the cat relaxed and settled in for a stay.

"Hey," Alex said. "When did you make friends with Casper?"

"Just now, I think," Krista said. "Maybe she senses that Rayna and I are getting along better."

"Maybe," Alex said in a quiet voice. "I'm glad Rayna told you she was pregnant. I don't know how to help her."

"I'm not sure I do, either," Krista said. "Obviously she needs to tell Trey about the baby but she's not ready."

"I can see why," Alex said. "You've met Trey. He's a good guy. A hard worker, too. I'm not sure he's prepared to be a father, though."

"Or a husband," Krista added.

She leaned her head against Alex's shoulder. He felt solid, warm and stable. One day he'd make some woman a great husband and father. Krista ignored a pang of regret that the woman wouldn't be her.

"Let's hope we're wrong about Trey," Krista said.

"Yeah, he's young. But like you said, he is a good guy. He could surprise us."

"I hope he does," Alex said. "Good thing Rayna has your mother and grandmother. No matter what happens, they'll rally around her."

"She has me, too," Krista said.

"Yeah," Alex said, "but it will be tough for you to help Rayna from so far away if she becomes a single mother."

Krista's chest tightened, because every word he spoke was true. "Unfortunately there's nothing I can do about that."

"You can come home more often," Alex suggested. "And not only to help out Rayna. Everybody loves having you here."

As if to prove his point, Casper meowed.

"See?" Alex said. "Even Casper's warming up to you."

"Not everybody else is," Krista said under her breath.

Alex turned sharply. "Why do you say that?"

Krista hadn't spoken of the matter aloud in almost nine years. If she'd thought before opening her mouth, another nine years might have gone by. Except maybe the slip hadn't been accidental. Maybe it was time she talked to somebody about her father.

"Oh, come on. You must have noticed my father doesn't speak to me." Krista tried to adopt a light tone and failed miserably. "I'm not exactly his favorite person."

Alex frowned. "Joe doesn't say much to anybody unless it's during a football game."

"But especially not to me." Krista didn't enjoy sounding like she was sorry for herself. She had no right to feel that way. "Not that I blame him after what I did."

"What did you do?" Alex gazed at her intently, as if he really didn't know the answer. She cast her mind back through the years, recalling that he'd come into the nursery for the first time the winter after the accident. Could it be that nobody had ever told him the specifics of what happened?

"I thought you knew," she murmured, almost to herself. "I thought everybody did."

"Knew what?"

Krista swallowed what felt like jagged lumps in her throat and managed to croak out the damning truth. "That I put my father in a wheelchair. That he wouldn't be paralyzed if it wasn't for me."

"Whoa!" Alex took his arm from around her shoulders and turned more fully to face her. Casper jumped down from the arm of the love seat and disappeared in a flash. "Your father was paralyzed in a forklift accident."

"A forklift I was driving." Krista could tell that was news to Alex. She sighed, leaned her head back against the love-seat cushion and shut her eyes. She couldn't stand to see the censure that would be on his face after he heard the story. "For as long as I can remember, I'd do almost anything to get out of working at the nursery. I hated it that much. When I was in college, I stayed in Philly during the summers. But the July after my junior year, I came home for a visit and got roped into helping out."

Krista could her Alex's steady breaths and feel the warmth of his body but she still didn't open her eyes. The next part would be hardest to get through.

"A customer asked if someone could put the seven-foot blue spruce he'd bought into his truck," Krista said. "I hadn't driven the forklift in years. I should have gotten my father, but I wasn't speaking to him. I was too mad about being at the nursery."

She sucked in more air. In her mind's eye, she saw herself stalking over to the forklift, driving the bulky machine to the tree and getting in position to lift it.

"I put the forklift in Reverse gear by mistake," she said in a rush, eager to finish the story so she wouldn't have to speak of it again. "My father had just come out of the shed. I spotted him, but I was in a panic. I couldn't think what to do. He tried to get out of the way, but his legs were pinned between the forklift and the shed."

Alex didn't say anything for long, agonizing moments. "So it was an accident?"

Krista's eyes flew open. Alex was regarding her closely, not with censure, but with compassion. Hadn't he listened to the whole story?

"An accident I caused!" she said.

"An accident that could have happened to anybody." Alex took her right hand in his with a gentle grip. "Have you really been blaming yourself for this all these years?"

"I'm not the only one," Krista whispered. "My father blames me, too."

"He said that?"

"He doesn't need to say it," Krista said. "I can tell it's hard for him to have me home. He wants me gone."

Alex shook his head. "I don't believe that."

"It's true," Krista said. "He never once said he was glad I was here. Whenever my mom tries to get me to stay, he tells her to stop badgering me. You've heard him."

"You know something, Krista. One of the things I like about you is that you speak your mind. You need to talk to your dad about this."

"No!" Krista blurted, her pulse speeding up. "I can't."

"I told you about what happened with my mother," Alex said. "I'd give anything if I could apologize to her."

"It's not the same thing," she said. "You didn't know your mother would have an aneurysm."

"I missed her funeral."

"By accident," she pointed out.

"You put the forklift into Reverse by accident."

"Apples and oranges," she said. "If I'd been more careful, my father would be walking today. Even if you hadn't taken that trip to Canada, your mother would still be gone."

"She loved my father. She would have wanted me to be there for him," Alex said, then sighed heavily. "But this isn't about me. We're talking about you."

"It's a moot point," Krista said. "I probably won't have a chance to talk to my father alone before I leave tomorrow afternoon."

"That sounds like an excuse," he said. "What's the real reason?"

Alex was right, of course. She'd already passed up a half-dozen chances for a moment alone with her father. She shut her eyes and felt a tear seep out. "What if he doesn't forgive me?"

He brushed the tear from her cheek with the pad of

his thumb, then replaced his thumb with his lips, kissing her gently.

"That's a chance you've got to take," he said.

RAYNA WALKED QUICKLY through the lower level of the mall the next morning at a few minutes past ten, intent on reaching her destination before she changed her mind about what needed to be done.

A surprising number of shoppers populated the corridors taking into account the three feet of mostly fresh snow on the ground and the fact that the stores had just opened.

The dental practice where Rayna worked and her parents' Christmas Shoppe were closed for the second straight day, but at the mall it was business as usual.

Rayna released a shuddering sigh. At any other time, she'd enjoy coming to the mall. This trip, however, was completely unlike her usual visits.

She rounded a corner and there was the store, its name spelled out in all capital letters above the yawning entryway. Rayna placed one foot in front of the other until she was inside. The floor gleamed and lights in strategic positions showcased racks of the latest fashions for teens and young adults.

She spotted Trey talking to an exotic beauty with silky black hair and a willowy figure. No doubt she was one of the other salesclerks and a walking, breathing advertisement for the store's line of clothes.

Like Trey.

He looked away from the woman and spotted Rayna. A corner of his mouth kicked up, which in other circumstances would have done wonders for her confidence. Excusing himself, he headed straight for her.

She loved the way he moved, with his long gait and

fluid grace. He wore distressed jeans and an open-necked sweater that looked great on him. The identical items were hanging on racks at the front of the store.

"Hey, babe," Trey said with a wide smile. "What a cool surprise."

He appeared genuinely happy to see her, which deep down was what Rayna longed to believe. If they were alone, she'd let him touch her and kiss her and persuade her that was true. She'd arranged to speak to him in public to prevent exactly that. It was vital that she keep a clear head.

"Can you leave the store for a few minutes?" she asked. "I need to talk to you."

He cocked his head. "You sound so serious."

"Can you?"

"Well, sure." He gestured to the empty store. "We probably won't get many customers today. I'll ask Gia to cover for me."

Gia was leaning against the counter that held the cash register, openly watching them.

"Hey, Gia," Trey called. "I'll be back in ten."

"Take your time," she said, her voice as melodic as a bird's song.

"She's beautiful," Rayna remarked.

"I guess," Trey said, "but I prefer blondes."

Rayna couldn't allow comments like that, however welcome, to distract her. She needed to get this over with. "I saw a bench outside in the mall where we can have some privacy."

Rayna headed for it at a fast clip. With his long strides, Trey had no trouble keeping up. "You came to the mall just to see me?"

"Yes," she said.

"I could have stopped by your house after work," he said. "Would have saved you driving on the roads."

The main streets were in good shape and Alex had plowed a path through the neighborhood when the regular road crew had been slow in coming. Rayna could have told Trey that, but she wasn't in the mood for small talk.

They reached the bench, with its black wrought-iron legs and lacquered slats. Rayna sat down, keeping her back stiff and her legs together, amazed at how tired she felt.

Trey plopped down next to her.

"Before I forget," he said, "my brother invited us out to dinner tomorrow night. His treat."

She gaped at him. "I broke up with you, Trey! Remember?"

His brow furrowed. "I was kinda thinking that didn't stick."

"Because you watched half a football game at my house?"

"Yeah," he said, as though that made perfect sense. "And because you're here now."

"I didn't come because I want you back," she said.

He brushed a stray lock of hair from her face, gazing at her with soulful eyes. "Are you sure about that?"

She swatted his hand away, as angry with herself as she was with him. Of course she wanted him back.

"Why would I?" she countered. "You didn't even call and try to change my mind after I broke up with you."

He looked confused. "You wanted me to call?"

"I wanted you to want to call," she said. Because

that would have meant he valued their relationship as much as she did.

"I don't get it," he said.

Sadness descended on her, dark and bleak. Trey wasn't ready for a commitment—to anything. He had a job, not a career. Even the lease on the house he shared with his roommates was month-to-month.

"I know," she said.

"So if we're not back together," he asked, "what are you doing here?"

Now that they'd arrived at the pivotal moment, Rayna wasn't sure she had the courage to see it through.

It's better for you to tell him than for him to find out.

Rayna heard Krista's advice in her head, spurring her on.

You're stronger than you know.

"I came to tell you I'm pregnant," Rayna said.

"Whoa!" Trey's jaw went slack. "What?"

"I'm pregnant," she repeated, trying to keep a rein on her emotions. "It must have happened that time the condom broke because I'm about five weeks along."

"How long have you known?" he asked.

"Since before Christmas," she said.

"When were you going to tell me?"

"I'm telling you now," Rayna said woodenly.

He leaned forward and balanced his forearms on his thighs as though the weight of the world had been dumped on his shoulders. "This is wild."

Rayna choked back disappointment and tried to fulfill her sister's confidence in her.

"I'm having the baby," she said.

His eyes flew to hers. "I never thought you wouldn't."

"We'll have to work out some things." She ignored the ache in her chest as words like *custody* and *visitation* popped into her head. That was assuming Trey would care to be involved in raising the child at all. "But there's time."

"Okay." He sat up straight and reached for her hand, gazing at her with the his soft blue eyes. "Don't worry. You're going to be great at this."

You're going to be great, not *we're*.

"Will you be okay driving back?" he asked.

She nodded, afraid her voice might break if she spoke.

"Okay, then." He straightened and extended a hand to help her up, the smile that usually played about his lips absent. He held on to her hand a few seconds longer than necessary when she was on her feet. "We'll talk later."

"Later," she managed to say before she headed back through the mall the way she'd come.

Disappointment threatened to choke her. A part of her had held out hope that the pregnancy would spur Trey on to realize he loved her and wanted to be a family.

"Be strong," she said aloud, hanging on to Krista's words.

Rayna didn't have a choice now that she was going to become a single mother.

AT ABOUT THE SAME TIME Rayna was breaking news of her pregnancy to Trey, Krista was on the basement telephone to the airline.

"I'm sorry," the airline representative told her, "but your flight has been canceled."

Still gripping the receiver, Krista sank into the chair

beside the telephone, not sure what had caused her legs to give way.

Relief that she could spend more time with Alex and her family? Or dread that she couldn't use her imminent departure as an excuse not to talk to her father?

She'd called the airline almost as soon as she'd awakened, fully expecting to hear that the runways at Harrisburg International were clear and planes were taking off without incident. That was only true of the Harrisburg airport. In D.C., there were blizzard conditions.

"We're very sorry for the inconvenience." The airline's agent sounded apprehensive. Did she know this was the third time Krista's flight to Switzerland hadn't gotten off the ground? "Would you like me to check if I can get you to Switzerland today by another route?"

"That's an option?" Krista asked.

"Definitely," the agent said. "Dulles International isn't the only airport with flights to Switzerland. If you're willing to fly into Zurich instead of Geneva, there are even more possibilities."

As a veteran traveler, Krista should have known that. Zermatt, her destination in the Alps, was almost equidistant between the Swiss airports. Yet the two times before when her flights had been canceled, Krista hadn't inquired about alternate itineraries.

The first time, she'd even failed to ask why the airline couldn't put her on a plane leaving twenty-four hours later than her canceled flight rather than forty-eight.

"Shall I check for you?" the agent asked.

Krista did some quick mental calculations. If today's flight hadn't been scratched, she would have arrived at Zermatt in time to spend one full day on the slopes. The airline rep might still be able to make that happen, but it suddenly seemed like a lot of trouble for little return.

"No, thank you," Krista said. "I no longer want to go to Switzerland. I need to fly to Prague."

"I can handle that for you," the agent said. "Leaving today or tomorrow?"

Krista hesitated, not sure what she would say until the word was out of her mouth. "Tomorrow."

Aside from dread that she might have to face her father, there was no reason not to spend another day in Jarrell. Krista would still be back in Prague in time to fulfill her promise to Becca to help her with her New Year's Eve party. That is, if tomorrow's flight took off without incident.

Krista finalized the arrangements and hung up the phone. From the angle where she was sitting, she could see into Rayna's bedroom. The door stood open and no light shone from within.

Rayna must already be up and around, no surprise there. It was already a few minutes past ten, the latest Rayna had slept in years.

She'd tossed and turned after Alex left last night, thinking about what he'd said about her father, wondering why he hadn't talked about her leaving after that single mention.

He hadn't even kissed her when he'd left. Not properly, anyway. He'd brought his fingers to his lips, then gently laid them on hers.

He hadn't said goodbye, either.

She'd decided before falling asleep in the wee hours of dawn that she would track Alex down in the morning and say a final goodbye, if only to get closure.

Yet everything had changed with the cancellation of her flight.

She could hear the murmur of multiple voices upstairs and concluded her grandmother had decided to keep the store closed for another day.

That meant an increased possibility of running into her father. Even if he were sequestered in his office, he was bound to emerge at some point. Or if she were feeling brave, she could always knock on the door and ask to speak to him. Her stomach cramped, suggesting her courage was lacking.

The phone pealed, the loud jarring sound making her jump. She removed the handset from the cradle before it could ring a second time. "Hello."

"Ellie, Rick Mariani here." The man with the deep, raspy voice continued talking before Krista could tell him he'd mistaken her for her mother. "Great news. The purchase offer and the contract look solid so the sale can go through."

All thoughts of correcting the man about the mistaken identity flew from Krista's mind. "What sale?"

Mariani laughed. "The sale of Novaks' Nursery, of course."

Krista gasped loudly enough to be heard at the other end of the line. There was a long pause, then Rick Mariani's voice again. "This isn't Ellie, is it?"

"No." Krista tried to process the information that her parents were selling the nursery. Even after she'd found out her parents were struggling financially amid the formidable competition from the large CGC chain, it hadn't occurred to Krista they would sell. She became aware that Mariani was waiting for her to expand on her response. "It's her daughter Krista."

"Of course. The interpreter who lives in the Czech

Republic," Mariani said. "Weren't you with Alex Costas at Timeout the other night?"

His change of subjects threw Krista. "How did you know that?"

"Malt Green invited me and the wife to Timeout, too, but we couldn't make it," Mariani said. "When I talked to Malt yesterday, he said a good time was had by all."

Krista's mind was still whirling from the shock of hearing her parents were unloading the nursery but she managed to keep up a semblance of a conversation. "So you used to be friends with Alex in high school?"

"Alex and I are still friends," he said. "Hey, you should come with him to my New Year's Eve party. Consider yourself officially invited."

Too many gears were turning in Krista's mind to thank Mariani for the invitation or inform him she'd be in Prague to usher in the New Year. "Do you know my parents through Alex?"

"Sure do," Mariani answered. "I owe Alex for recommending me to them. Are either of your parents around, by any chance?"

The blood rushed to Krista's head and she swayed. From the conversation so far, she'd concluded that Rick Mariani was an attorney. If Alex had vouched for his friend, Alex must know her parents were selling the nursery.

Everybody must know—except Krista.

"Yes, they're here," Krista finally managed to answer. "I'll tell them you're on the phone."

She laid down the handset and rose, her legs feeling heavy as she trudged up the stairs in her stocking feet. With every step, the smell of brewed coffee got stronger.

Her mother stood in the kitchen beside the coffee-pot, pouring hot liquid into a mug. For once her father wasn't inside his office. He sat at the table, a full cup of coffee and a plate of her grandmother's homemade blueberry scones in front of him.

Her father spotted Krista before she could provide the reason for her appearance. "What are you doing in your pajamas?" he barked. "Your plane's leaving soon. You need to get dressed."

Krista winced even though she should be getting used to her father's attitude by now. "There are blizzard conditions in D.C. so I rescheduled the flight for tomorrow."

"Oh, happy day!" her mother cried. "That's three times your flight has been canceled. It's like a sign you shouldn't leave at all!"

"Stop it, Ellie," her father scolded. "You need to get it through your head the girl doesn't live here anymore."

"Don't tell me what I need to do," her mother shot back.

"Rick Mariani is on the phone," Krista announced before their sniping at one another escalated. "He'd like to speak to one of you."

Her parents instantly quieted and exchanged a meaningful look. "I'll talk to him," her father said.

Her mother lifted the receiver from the wall phone and handed it to her husband. He angled his body away from Krista as he greeted the attorney.

"You should change out of those pajamas, Krista." Her mother's tone held a quiet urgency.

"Later." Krista sat down at the table, making no attempt to hide the fact that she intended to openly listen to her father's end of the conversation.

Her mother leaned back against the kitchen counter, shifting from one foot to another. If she hadn't been holding a coffee cup, she probably would have wrung her hands.

Her father cast Krista a disapproving glance, but Krista didn't let it intimidate her into leaving the table. He mostly nodded and listened, telling Mariani in short sentences that everything sounded good to him.

"It'll be good to have this finalized," her father finally said. "Thanks for calling, Rick."

He hung up the phone. For long moments, the kitchen was completely silent except for the clink of the ice cubes generated by the automatic icemaker. Did her parents really think she hadn't figured out what was going on?

"You sold the nursery," she said bluntly. "Why would you do that?"

Her mother set down her coffee mug and folded her hands together. She looked at her husband, almost as though for permission to speak.

"We can't keep operating at a loss, Krista," her mother finally said. "It used to be that we had enough to carry us over during the off-season, but no more. We opened the Christmas Shoppe to bring in more revenue, but it's not enough. Start-up costs were higher than we expected."

"How long has the nursery been losing money?"

Her mother hesitated before answering. "Since a branch of the big chain opened a few years ago."

"Years?" Krista repeated. "If it's been years, why didn't you tell me the nursery was in trouble?"

Her mother hung her head and shifted her eyes. "I wanted to, but your father asked me not to."

Her father scowled, appearing not the least bit chastened. "Damn right I did. What were you going to do about it all the way over there in Europe?"

"I could have listened," Krista said. "I was a business major in college. Maybe I could even have helped you come up with a strategy to turn things around."

"It wasn't your concern," her father said.

"You don't think I'm concerned about what affects my family?" Krista couldn't hide the hurt that her father could believe such a thing of her. She tried to pull herself together. "What else don't I know? Are you selling the Christmas Shoppe, too?"

"We considered it," her mother said, "but it's becoming so popular your grandmother and I decided to try to keep it open year-round."

They hadn't mentioned that to Krista, either. If she hadn't been so upset, she would have put a verbal stamp of approval on the plan. A number of the customers she'd served had expressed disappointment that the store was seasonal. Krista could envision bolstering the shop by expanding the housewares section and selling craft items that could only be found at specialty stores.

"That hill where the nursery and shop are now gets too icy in the winter," her mother said. "Once the money from the sale of the nursery comes through, we're moving the shop to flatter ground. Alex found us a place where the rent is cheap."

Alex. His name kept cropping up. Although her parents' financial struggles were apparently none of Krista's concern, Alex was completely in the know.

And he hadn't told her about any of it, either.

Krista pushed her chair back from the table and stood up so abruptly that she banged her leg. She ignored the pain. It would be fleeting, unlike her anger.

"I'm going to get dressed." She turned away from her parents and hurried down the stairs to the basement.

Changing her clothes wasn't all she intended to do.

Once she was presentable, she was going to track down Alex and have it out with him once and for all.

CHAPTER FIFTEEN

MOUNDS OF DEEP SNOW bracketed the winding two-lane road that led out of Jarrell to the park located halfway up the mountain. A plow had taken a pass over the pavement, pushing the snow onto the shoulder and leaving a cleared swath Krista wasn't entirely sure was wide enough for two vehicles. Especially when one was her grandmother's generously sized Volvo.

It was probably a moot point.

She'd yet to spot another sign of life, human or otherwise, since she started the ascent.

The turn to the park entrance appeared so suddenly, she jerked the wheel to the right. The back end of the Volvo fishtailed. Heart hammering, Krista hung on tight to the steering wheel and managed to regain control.

She wouldn't be driving before the roads were fully passable if it weren't for Alex. Damn him.

Only a single lane of the park's meandering road had been plowed. The snow that had been displaced was packed high enough on both sides of the cleared pavement to make it seem like Krista was driving through a snow tunnel.

She didn't care. She'd tackle a blizzard in whiteout conditions in order to find Alex.

She heard the scraping sound of the snow plow before she spotted the Costas Landscaping truck in

the parking lot beside the visitors' center. She pressed
her foot down on the accelerator of the Volvo to reach
him more quickly. Too late, she realized he had yet to
plow the route she'd intended to take to the parking lot.

The tires hit the deep snow. Krista's body jerked
forward, then backward. The Volvo's engine shuddered
and died as the vehicle came to a jarring stop. She
heard something loud and ragged and noticed it was
her breathing.

This was Alex's fault, too.

Telling herself nothing could be gained by losing
her composure, she struggled to get herself back under
control. When her hands were no longer shaking, she
restarted the ignition and put the sturdy car in reverse.
The engine hummed and the tires spun, but the Volvo
didn't budge.

"Great," she grumbled. "Just great."

She turned off the engine and climbed out of the
car, where the air temperature had to be in the teens.
She stomped the short distance to the parking lot, glad
she'd thought to wear boots. Waving her arms like a
runway worker, she closed the distance between herself and the pickup truck.

Because of the glare from the snow, she couldn't see
the driver. She didn't take into consideration that he
might not be able to spot her. She kept advancing, the
truck getting closer by the second. It stopped abruptly,
brakes screeching. Alex got out, his palms uplifted, his
expression stunned. She picked up her pace.

"What were you doing?" His voice sounded about
an octave higher than usual. "Trying to get yourself
killed?"

She ignored his second question, unwilling to put

herself at a disadvantage especially because he had a valid point. "I came to see you, that's what!"

"Up a mountain after a snowstorm?"

"You're here."

"I wouldn't be if we didn't have a contract to clear snow for the park. And that's only because the astronomical society holds winter sky viewing parties up here." He looked behind her, eyes widening. "Is that your grandmother's Volvo against that snowbank?"

"So what if it is?" she retorted.

"She was okay with you taking it out in these conditions?" he asked.

"She knows where it is." After snatching the keys off the magnetic hook on the refrigerator, Krista left a note thanking her grandmother for the use of the vehicle.

Alex continued to stare at her as though a spaceship had deposited her in the parking lot. "How did you know where I was anyway?"

She'd repeatedly tried reaching him on his cell phone, to no avail. Either reception was poor in the mountains or he'd ignored her calls.

"Your dad told me you were here." Krista had had the good luck to notice Milo's truck pull into the Costas driveway when she was trying to figure out how to find Alex. "But never mind that. I found out, no thanks to you, that my parents are selling their nursery."

"That's what this is about?" He swiped a hand over his mouth, seeming to decide how to respond. "I'm glad Joe and Eleanor finally let you know what was going on."

"They didn't!" she said. "Your friend Rick Mariani did and only by mistake. I want to know why you didn't tell me!"

"It wasn't my place," he said.

"Oh, really?" She jabbed a finger at him and re-membered she'd forgotten to put on her gloves. The cold cut through her, chilling her so it seemed as though she'd never be warm again. "Let me see if I understand this. Getting my parents an attorney and helping them making decisions about the nursery, that is your place?"

"Joe and Eleanor are my friends," he said. "I care what happens to them."

"They're my parents! I should have known their business was in trouble!"

"Why do you think they didn't tell you?" Alex asked.

"You didn't tell me, either," she pointed out.

"Want to know what I think?" he asked, ignoring her valid observation. She shook her head no, but he didn't comply with that, either. "I think it's because you haven't kept in close enough touch with your family."

"You don't know that!"

"I know it took you eight years to come back and visit them," he said. "I know you let guilt over your father's accident keep you away from Jarrell."

"You're letting guilt keep you in Jarrell!" She didn't stop to think about what was going to come out of her mouth next. She just let the words flow. "That's the only reason you won't take that photography job."

"We're not talking about me," Alex said.

"You say that every time the subject comes up. You know what I think?" she asked, throwing his words back at him. "I think it's because you don't want to face the truth."

"Look who's talking," he said. "You didn't come all the way up here because you were angry at me."

Her muscles were tense and her heartbeat accelerated; her blood pressure felt like it was skyrocketing. "I feel pretty angry."

"You're angry at yourself," he accused. "Because being back in Jarrell has made you face the fact that you've been neglecting the people you love."

Now Krista's breathing was shallow, too. If there were a snowbank near enough to kick, she would give it a wallop. "What is this? More pop psychology?"

"Call it what you want, but I've watched you becoming part of your family again," he said. "I think you're afraid that when you leave, things will go back to the way they were."

Even through the red haze of anger, Krista believed his contention held a grain of truth. Krista hadn't been able to maintain close ties with her family from a distance. She hadn't been able to have a relationship with her sister at all. "You're wrong about that. I won't let them."

"Then why are you still here?" he asked. "Shouldn't you be on a plane back to Europe?"

"My flight was canceled again," she said. "You'd know that if you had bothered to stop by to say good-bye."

He gripped her by the front of her jacket, not violently but not gently, either. His skin was reddened from the cold, but his dark eyes were blazing. "I'll tell you why I didn't. Because I couldn't stand the thought of saying goodbye to you again."

The import of his words struck Krista. The anger,

so all-encompassing only moments before, seeped out of her. The quiet was absolute, with no wind blowing and no sign of any of the wildlife that lived in the park. Up on the mountain in this snowy parking lot, it felt to Krista that they were the only two people in the world.

"What are you saying?" she asked.

He let go of her jacket and grabbed one of her cold hands. His hand felt warm, but how could that be?

"I'm saying there's a reason we keep gravitating toward each other, and it's because of more than just pheromones," he said. "Maybe it's time to give what's between us a chance."

Even as a wild hope leaped inside her, she shook her head back and forth. "A long-distance relationship would never work. Prague is too far from Jarrell."

"Then move back to Jarrell," he said.

Her breath caught. The option had been lurking deep in her consciousness for days. Every time it tried to surface, she tamped it down. Now that he'd brought it out in the open, she was forced to consider its feasibility. Could she move back to Jarrell? Could she abandon the opportunities the Czech Republic afforded and restrict herself in the place she'd fled?

"Think about it. It makes a lot of sense. You said yourself your job in Prague wasn't challenging anymore. In Jarrell, you can help your mom and grandma run the shop while you decide what it is you want to do next. When the baby comes, you'll be around to help Rayna." Alex must have sensed that she was weakening, because his voice was getting stronger. He sounded very sure about what she should do with her future, reminding her of someone else in her life.

Krista snatched her hand back from his. "You're starting to sound like my mother, telling me what to do rather than letting me decide for myself. How would you like it if I told you to move to Prague?"

He let out a short laugh. "I'm not going to do that. And I can show you why not."

He started walking through the portion of parking lot that was clear of snow. Her choice was either to follow him or stand alone. She went with him.

"Where are we going?" she called.

"You'll see." He didn't stop until the snow was too deep to pass. He pointed off in the distance. "Do you recognize that view?"

From its vantage point along the ridge, the park offered a magnificent panoramic view of the valley below. Krista took in the beauty of the snowy farmland, the quaint town and ice-capped Susquehana River, a scene very similar to the one Alex had captured in her Christmas gift.

"You were right," he said. "I knew this was the place we first kissed. I took the photo eight years ago so you'd remember, too."

The admission hung between them, like breath that was visible in the frigid air. The past and the present intertwined, but Krista needed to separate them so she was sure she understood.

"Do you still want me to remember?" With the question, she felt as if she were opening a door that they could never again close. "Is that why you gave me the landscape for Christmas this year?"

"I think it must be," he said. "But it wasn't only because of the kiss. It's the view, too. Take a good look at it, Krista. Why move to Prague when nothing could be better than what's right here in front of our eyes?"

"Because I'd be there," she said softly.

"I'm not leaving Jarrell," Alex said, gazing away

from the view and directly into her eyes, "not even for the woman I love."

Joy burst inside Krista, in contrast to the stark white world around them. Alex Costas loved her. On the heels of that thought came another. If he truly cared for her, he wouldn't have so readily dismissed her suggestion that he move to Prague.

"You don't love me," Krista said, shaking her head to emphasize her words.

"I do. I didn't know what it was until recently. But if it wasn't love, it would have faded after eight years." Alex took both her hands in his. "Here's something else. I think you love me, too."

In the time Krista had known Alex, she'd never allowed the word *love* to creep into her mind. Deep down, she'd known how dangerous it would be to let things get serious between them. Alex wasn't a carefree bachelor, content to pick up and travel the world. He was a family man.

He brought his head down to hers and claimed her mouth, the immediate surge of excitement adding another layer to Krista's miasma of thoughts.

Could this passion that flared every time they touched be more than just sexual attraction? She had to admit that she loved the kindness in his eyes and gentleness in his expression. She loved the loyalty, however misguided, he showed his father. She even loved that he loved her.

But if she surrendered to her feelings, what did that mean for the rest of Krista's life? Would she be stuck here in Jarrell because Alex wouldn't leave?

Krista fought against the swell of emotions that threatened to make her agree to everything he was asking.

No matter how good a man he was, she couldn't love Alex. Loving him would be breaking the cardinal rule she'd set for herself when she ran into him again in her parents' kitchen.

She needed to protect her heart so she could return to the life she'd built for herself.

Krista anchored her hands against his chest, but couldn't bring herself to push him away and break off the kiss. He finally did that, lifting his head, bemusement on his face. "What's wrong?"

She took a breath before she answered. "I didn't tell you yet that my flight was rescheduled for tomorrow morning."

"So postpone it again and spend New Year's Eve with me," he said.

"I can't," she said. "I promised to help my friend Becca with her party."

He arranged his lips in a straight line, then said slowly, "Then go back for the party and say goodbye to your friends. While you're there, you can give notice at your job."

She'd been delaying the moment when she broke the inevitable news to him. She shook her head, and her heart seemed to shake, too.

"I'm not going to move back here, Alex," she said. "My home is in Prague."

"I get that living in Europe has been a good experience for you. But ask yourself this," Alex said. "Why are you relieved every time one of your flights is canceled? Hell, if you really wanted to get out of here, you would have gotten the airline to try different routes."

Krista had reached the same conclusion only that morning. She'd also figured out the reason she'd been content to stick around. "It's like you said, I needed more time to reconnect with my family."

"There's more to it than that. It's because you don't want to leave Jarrell at all." He paused before adding, "It's because you don't want to leave me."

"You're wrong," she whispered. He had to be.

Alex's eyes reminded her of an animal when it was wounded. He let her go abruptly, leaving her to stand on her own. A shutter dropped over his face, wiping out the pain.

"It seems like I've been wrong about a number of things." He turned his back on Krista and the scenic view and walked away. When there was a fair distance between them, he turned and called, "Let's get that Volvo out of the snow drift so you can get out of here."

Krista followed him across the parking lot in silence, trying to ignoring the heaviness settling over her heart.

Now that it was almost time to leave Jarrell and Alex for good, there was nothing more to say.

RAYNA SET DOWN THE crossword puzzle she'd been trying to do on the nightstand in her basement bedroom, stood up and pulled snow pants and her ski jacket from her closet.

She hadn't left the house since returning from the mall hours ago. If she were cooped up for another minute, she might scream. Or cry. With her hormones out of whack, sobbing was the more distinct possibility. The backs of her eyes had been burning since Trey's reaction to her pregnancy.

She fought the desire to cave in to despair, just as she had at the mall.

She. Would. Not. Cry.

The baby she was carrying would need a strong woman to raise her. It was about time Rayna started being that person.

She had it in her. She knew she did. So why did Rayna suddenly crave hearing her sister verify that?

Once she was dressed in her winter gear, Rayna climbed the stairs and ducked into the kitchen.

Her mother was bent at the waist in front of the open oven door, a padded mitt covering her right hand. The kitchen smelled of the chocolate chip cookies she was removing from the oven.

"Hey, Mom. Have you heard from Krista?" Rayna asked.

"Not since the note she left about Grandma's Volvo," Mom said without lifting her head. "I swear, I don't know what kind of daughters I raised, both of you taking off this morning like you did."

"You drove this morning, too," Rayna said.

"That was different." Mom set the hot tray down on the counter. "I had to take Milo to urgent care after he slipped on the ice."

"Grandma said he broke his arm," Rayna said.

"She's next door with him right now, although Milo's doing fine." Ellie reached for a spatula and began transferring the cookies to wax paper. "The doctor said it was a clean break."

"That's good," Rayna said.

"Getting back to what I was saying," her mother remarked as she scooped up another cookie, "sensible people give the work crews time to get the roads back to normal."

"You're right. I should be more sensible," Rayna said. "I'll make that one of my New Year's resolutions."

"Are you being sarcastic?" Her mom's attention was still on the cookies.

"No, I'm serious," Rayna said.

Mom lifted her head and looked at Rayna for the first time since she'd entered the kitchen. Her mother's expression crumbled. "Don't tell me you're going out again!"

"Only to the backyard," Rayna said.

"What are you going to do out there?" Ellie asked.

"I need some air," Rayna said.

She also needed the stamina to roll out three balls of snow, the first substantially bigger than the other two.

A little while later, she stood back and examined her handiwork. She'd solved the problem of the snow being too deep by picking a sheltered spot close to the house where the accumulation was substantially less.

Her second problem wasn't as easy to crack.

A sensible pregnant woman would not lift the second ball onto the first, no matter how much she wanted to build a snowman. So how could she get it up there?

The door to the porch banged open. Trey rushed down the three steps to the yard, slipping and catching himself on the hand rail. He had on the same clothes he'd worn at the mall and winter boots more suited for fashion than function.

"Don't pick up that ball of snow!" he shouted, lifting his feet as he navigated snow deeper than his boots.

Rayna found she wasn't in the mood to appease him. "Why shouldn't I?"

"You're pregnant!" he blurted. "If you want a snowman that bad, I'll build it for you."

"So now you want to do something for me?" She lashed out at him. "What makes you think I'll let you?"

He wrinkled his nose the way he did when something confused him, a mannerism she'd once found endearing. "Why wouldn't you let me?"

"I'm perfectly capable of doing things for myself," she said. "Not that I intend to let you off scot-free. You may not want to help me out with the day-to-day stuff but you're going to pay."

"We're not still talking about the snowman, are we?"

"Of course not," Rayna snapped. "We're talking about our baby, whom I expect you to help support."

"Well, yeah," Trey said, as if it were a given. "That's why I left work early."

It dawned on Rayna that Trey still had a few hours left on his shift at the clothing store. "How will working fewer hours at the store help you support our baby?"

"Working at the store won't cut it with a baby on the way," Trey said.

Rayna had known that, but she was surprised that Trey did. She made decent money at the dental practice, but it was a part-time job. She couldn't reach her earning potential as a dental hygienist until she finished school in another year.

She narrowed her eyes. "You're not going to quit your job, are you?"

"Not until I've got another one lined up," he said. "That's what I've been doing this afternoon, chasing down leads."

"You have leads?"

"I'm trying," he said. "I have a call in to Mr. Costas to see if he has anything full-time and I'm looking at online job sites. I'm still thinking about bartending school, too. If I could finish by the time the baby's born, maybe I could work two jobs."

Rayna didn't trust that she'd heard correctly. Trey had told her more than once that he only worked to fund his fun. "You couldn't play as much hockey with two jobs."

"Once the baby's here, I'll be too tired to play much," he said.

She needed to make sure she wasn't misunderstanding him. "Why?"

He was shivering. The snow was caked on the bottom of his jeans and his jacket wasn't warm enough for the cold temperature.

"I won't expect you to get up every time the baby cries," he said.

Rayna shook her head. "I can't live with you, Trey."

"Then we can get married," Trey said.

She swallowed a sob. "I can't marry you, either."

"Why not?" He seemed genuinely puzzled.

"Because the baby's not a good enough reason." She was going to have to spell it out, she realized. "I can't be with a man who doesn't love me."

"Who says I don't love you?" Trey asked.

"You told the guys at the hockey rink we weren't serious."

Trey looked taken aback. "Yeah, but I just meant neither of us take life too seriously."

"You never said you loved me."

His shoulders moved up and down. "I thought you knew."

Something bright surfaced in Rayna's chest but she kept it contained. Was it possible? Could she have been wrong about the way Trey felt about her? She needed him to spell it out so she had no more doubts.

"A girl likes to hear the words, you know," Rayna said.

Trey grinned, raised both arms to the sky and shouted, "I love you, Rayna Novak!"

She laughed, all the heartache and worry of the past few days disappearing as if it had never been.

"I love you, too, Trey Farina!" she yelled just as loudly, no longer trying to hold anything back.

"What are you waiting for?" someone shouted from the porch. It was Krista, holding one thumb up in the air and grinning widely. Rayna hadn't heard the porch door open, but she was glad of it. Krista would be back in Europe soon enough. This moment of pure happiness seemed even more joyous because her sister was witnessing it. "Kiss the guy!"

So Rayna did.

DAYS DIDN'T GET ANY LONGER than the one Alex had endured. While he'd plowed parking lot after parking lot of heavy snow, he didn't even have the luxury of looking forward to the night ahead.

How could he put his feet up and relax knowing the woman he loved was leaving tomorrow and there was nothing he could do about it?

He'd had to stop himself from going over to the Novaks' after he'd gotten out of his pickup. He'd already tried to change Krista's mind once and failed.

"Dad, I'm home," he called.

Alex hung up his jacket on the hook beside the door, stepped out of his boots and padded into the house.

The Christmas lights from the Novaks' display shone into one of the windows. Otherwise the front of the house was dark, the recliner where Alex usually found his father empty.

"Dad, where are you?" Alex called.

"In the kitchen," his father answered in a loud voice. "I'm making stir-fry."

Was that a joke? His father didn't cook, preferring to pop frozen meals in the microwave. Alex's dinner suggestion for tonight was going to be take-out pizza that showed up hot and ready to eat at their door.

The smell of teriyaki sauce and the sound of vegetables sizzling in the pan sure made it seem like his father knew what he was doing.

"Since when do you know how to cook?" Alex asked on the way into the kitchen. He stopped in his tracks at the sight of his father at the stove stirring the vegetables with his right hand. His left arm was in a sling.

"Leona was talking about Chinese food when she was here this afternoon," his father said in a conversational tone, "so I thought I'd give it a whirl."

"What happened to your arm?" Alex asked, his concern immediate, the dinner forgotten.

"Oh, that." His father glanced down at the offending limb. "It's broken."

"How?" Alex asked sharply.

"I stopped by the house today to get a heavier jacket. When I was going back out to the truck, I slipped on a patch of ice." Dad stirred the ingredients in the pan with vigor, chuckling aloud. "Can you believe it considering what we do for a living?"

Alex didn't appreciate the irony. "When did this happen?"

"Around eleven or eleven-thirty."

In other words, almost seven hours ago and Alex was only finding out about the accident now.

"Why didn't you call me?" Alex asked. "I could have taken you to the emergency room."

"You were working. There wasn't any need to bother you."

"It wouldn't have been a bother, Dad," Alex said. Surely his father knew he was more important to Alex than work.

"It wasn't necessary, with the Novaks next door," Dad said. "Ellie suggested one of those urgent care places. They fixed me up in a jiff."

"How bad is the break?"

"A hairline fracture," Dad said. "I've got to see an orthopedist tomorrow. But six weeks in a cast and I should be as good as new."

"I'll take you to the orthopedist," Alex stated forcefully.

Milo looked away from the pan to Alex. "What's going on, son? You're making an awfully big deal out of this."

Alex stroked his chin, not sure he could explain. "I'm just surprised you didn't call me."

"I'm only sixty-two years old," he said. "I can take care of myself, you know."

Alex flashed back to the time after his mother died, before his father had started taking the drugs for depression. Dad hadn't left the house in months. Some days he hadn't even showered.

"You do know that, right?" his father persisted.

"Well, sure." The conversation was getting too heavy. Alex figured it was time to change the subject. "Did you make enough stir-fry for two?"

"I did." Milo removed a pot of what smelled like rice from a burner, keeping the lid on. "But I hoped you wouldn't be around tonight."

"Gee, thanks," Alex said.

"I didn't mean it that way." His father reached into

an overhead cupboard and took down two plates, surprisingly competent even though he was using only one hand. "I thought you might be with Krista tonight."

"Nope," Alex said.

"Too bad. I like that girl."

"I like her, too, but she's leaving tomorrow."

"For good?" his father asked.

"For good," Alex confirmed.

Milo set the plates on the kitchen table. "You give any thought to going to Europe?"

"I'm not leaving Jarrell, Dad," Alex said. "My life's here. Our business is here."

His father nodded, seeming to understand there was nothing more to say. He'd already come as close to prying as he ever did.

"Speaking of business," Dad said, "there were some interesting messages on the answering machine when I got back home today."

"Oh, yeah?"

"One was from Trey Farina. He's in the market for a full-time job. Unless we can give him at least forty hours a week, we'll have to get someone else to help us out this spring and summer."

If Trey was thinking in terms of full-time work, Rayna must have told him about the pregnancy. It sounded as though he was taking impending fatherhood seriously, a very good sign. Too bad Costas Landscaping couldn't help him out.

"That's a loss." Alex went to a drawer and got out silverware. He took napkins from the holder on the counter. "Trey has a knack for landscaping."

"My thoughts exactly," Milo said. "I hate to let him go but I don't want the business to get any bigger."

During the busy months, Alex and his father hired

a part-timer but worked well the rest of the time as a two-man operation. They'd decided long ago to subcontract work rather than take on the expense of paying salaries and benefits to full-time employees.

"You said there were two messages," Alex said. "What about the other one?"

His father didn't answer until they were both seated at the table with plates of stir-fry. "It was for you. From Malt Green."

Alex could imagine the gist of the message. Despite Alex's repeated insistence that he didn't want the photography job, Malt kept offering.

"I hadn't heard that name in a long time," Dad continued. "I hardly remembered who he was until he mentioned photography."

"Malt has a business in Toronto," Alex said.

"I gathered that. Sounds like a pretty successful one, too." His father put down his fork. "Didn't you two used to talk about going into the business together?"

"I went into landscaping with you, Dad."

"But if your mother hadn't died, what would you have done?"

"She did die," Alex said.

"And you took over my contracts and kept my business going," Milo said. "I wasn't good for anything for at least a year."

His father's timing had been unfortunate. A few months before his wife died, he'd quit a solid job with another company to strike out on his own. He'd worked in landscaping for years and developed a solid reputation so it hadn't seemed like a risk. If Alex hadn't stepped in, however, his father's fledgling business would have collapsed.

"Your friend Malt started his business about that same time, didn't he?" Dad asked. He seemed to be hanging on Alex's response.

If Alex could have withheld his answer, he would have. "Yeah."

A sick look came over his father's face. "Oh, no," he said. "How could I not have seen this before?"

"Seen what?" Alex asked.

"I considered myself lucky that you liked landscaping work," Milo said.

"I do like it," Alex said.

"But not as much as photography."

Alex lowered his gaze. "What does it matter?"

"It matters," his father said. "You should have been a photographer."

"I am a photographer," Alex said. "I just don't do it professionally."

"Why not take that job your friend is offering?"

"That job would require me to travel," Alex said. "And I already told you I'm not leaving Jarrell."

"Because you're still looking out for me?" his father asked. Before Alex could open his mouth, Milo implored, "Be honest now."

"Yeah, okay," Alex admitted. "That's part of it. I'd like to be around if you need me."

"Is that why you made such a big deal out of my broken arm?" he asked.

"That's why."

Alex scooped some rice onto his plate, then poured some of the stir-fry over it. "This looks good, Dad."

His father shoveled a bite of food into his mouth and chewed thoughtfully. "Turns out I can cook."

"Pretty well, too," Alex said.

"I can do a lot of things for myself," Milo said, "including picking up a phone and calling my son when I need him, wherever he happens to be."

"What's that supposed to mean?"

"Think about it, Alex," his father said. "It'll come to you."

CHAPTER SIXTEEN

IT WAS SNOWING AGAIN.

Krista set down her packed suitcase in her parents' living room the next morning, hardly able to believe her eyes. She hadn't checked the status of her flight before showering and getting dressed because the skies had been clear.

Now they weren't.

She rummaged in her bag, searching for her original flight itinerary that included the number for the airline. At this rate, she should have programmed it into her phone.

She heard footsteps coming down the hall as she pulled out the sheet of paper. Her mother appeared, dressed for the day in black slacks and a dark sweater that made her look very pale.

Krista took a step toward her, concern shutting out all other thoughts. Although her mother hadn't been on death's door, as she'd insinuated, she was recovering from bleeding ulcers. "Are you okay, Mom?"

"I'm fine," she said. "Just sad that you're leaving today."

"I'm not so sure about that," Krista said. "Did you get a load of the snow? I was getting ready to call the airline to see if this flight is canceled, too."

"I already called about five minutes ago," her mother said. "Remember, you wrote down your flight number for me? Your plane's supposed to take off on time."

Krista imagined the snowflakes coating a runway, making travel less likely by the second.

"The flight status could change by the time we get to the airport," Krista said. "You might be stuck with me another day."

"Not this time." The corners of her mother's mouth dropped. "I checked the weather forecast. Isolated snow showers with less than an inch of accumulation in Harrisburg. It's not snowing to speak of anywhere else, either."

As if on cue, the snow stopped.

Krista felt her shoulders sag and air deflate from her lungs. She straightened and pasted on a smile to disprove Alex's theory about her being secretly glad whenever a flight was canceled. Anticipating how hard it would be to say goodbye to her family didn't translate to a desire to stay in Jarrell.

"It's just as well," Krista said. "It's about time I got back."

"I wish you'd never left," Ellie said.

"I know you do," Krista said.

Her mother blinked a few times. "I should apologize for the way I got you home, but I'm not sorry."

"I know that, too," Krista said. "And I forgive you, anyway."

Her mother let out a sound that was half laugh, half sob and wrapped Krista in a hug. She smelled of vanilla musk, the same scent she'd worn since Krista's childhood. Something else was familiar, too. The tenderness that swelled up in Krista's heart.

"It's so hard to let you go," Ellie said, still hanging

on. "I had such high hopes that you were falling in love with Alex."

Since yesterday on the mountain, Krista had shoved thoughts of Alex from her mind every time they encroached.

No good would come out of analyzing the gladness in her heart that he loved her. Or in questioning whether she'd told the truth when she claimed she didn't love him back.

"Even if I was head over heels for Alex," Krista said, hoping that wasn't the case, "it wouldn't mean I'd move back to Jarrell."

Her mother finally let her go and patted her cheek, the way she used to when Krista was a very young girl. "Maybe not, but I could hope. If you really love someone, you're willing to compromise. Look at your father and me."

"What compromise did you make?"

"I still love him even though he drives me crazy." Her mother smiled. "I'm going to eat some breakfast and then your dad and I will take you to the airport. Do you want me to make you anything?"

"No, thanks. I already had a granola bar. If I get hungry, I'll grab something in the terminal," Krista said. "Where are Grandma and Rayna?"

"They're getting ready to leave for work," her mother said. "Rayna's scheduled for a shift at the dentist today. Charlie's going to help your grandmother at the shop until I get there."

Krista wouldn't have minded giving a hand. She had ideas for helping the shop thrive as a year-round operation that she had yet to share. With time running short, she'd have to jot them down and put them in an email.

"I should say goodbye, then," Krista said.

She found Rayna in her basement bedroom, dressed in a pretty orange sweater that added vibrancy to her sister's complexion. Or maybe it had been Trey who caused that. Rayna had done a lot of smiling since yesterday when they'd gotten back together. Now she frowned.

"I can't believe you're going back today," Rayna said. "I haven't even told Mom, Dad and Grandma I'm pregnant yet."

"When is that happening?"

"Trey's coming over tonight so we can do it together," Rayna said. "I wish you were going to be here, too. You could help me calm down Mom when she freaks out."

"She won't be too bad," Krista predicted. "She'll get excited about becoming a grandma, just like I am an aunt."

Rayna gave Krista a sad smile and covered her still-flat abdomen with her right hand. "I wish you were going to be around to hear me complain about morning sickness and swelling up."

"Hey," Krista said. "You've got the man you love for that."

"I know," Rayna said, sniffling, "but it would be nice to have my big sister, too."

"You will," Krista said. "We'll get Skype on our computers and talk all the time."

"You promise?" Rayna asked.

Krista nodded. "I promise."

Then she was hugging Rayna and holding on as tightly as she had upstairs with her mother. Krista felt something rub against her leg. It was Casper. Krista realized she was going to miss the cat, too.

"Can I get in on that hug?"

Grandma entered Rayna's room and walked straight for them. Krista made room for her, hugging her grandmother with her right arm and her sister with her left while making sure not to step on Casper the no-longer-ghostly cat.

"I'm gonna miss you, honey," Grandma said. "I've loved having you home."

"I've loved being here," Krista said past a lump in her throat.

The lyrics of that favorite Christmas carol had it right.

There was no place like home for the holidays.

THE CLOSER THEIR wheelchair-accessible van got to the main terminal of the Harrisburg airport, the tighter Krista's chest became. By the time her mother shoe-horned the van into a parking space among the taxis, buses and cars clogging the passenger drop-off area, Krista felt as if she were in the grip of a vise.

"We can say goodbye here." Krista affixed a smile and turned around to look at her stern-faced father, who was sitting behind her. "It's too much trouble for you to come inside the terminal with me."

"I can manage it," her dad said, his voice gruff.

Oh, great. Krista had only minutes left to spend with her parents and she'd offended her father.

"I didn't mean to imply you couldn't," Krista said, backtracking as best she could. "It's just that with se-curity regulations the way they are nowadays, only passengers are allowed to go to the gate."

"I'm still going in the terminal," her father declared.

"I'll let you two off while I find a parking space." Her mother put the van in Park and operated the control that lowered the floor and deployed the ramp. "I won't be long."

Krista knew better than to offer to help her father get out of the van. She climbed out of the passenger seat, circumvented the ramp, lifted her suitcase from the trunk and met him at the sidewalk. Unsure what to do next, she positioned herself vaguely behind the wheelchair in case she was needed.

"I don't want you to push me," he said.

Krista had made yet another misstep in a visit that had been full of them. "Okay."

When they reached one of the terminal entrances, she had enough sense to wait for her father to push the button activating the automatic door. Once inside, she walked in silence beside him while he wheeled his chair over the hard floor until they reached her airline's check-in counter.

"I'll wait for you over there." Her dad indicated an out-of-the-way area with some empty chairs.

Krista was the fourth person in a line that went quickly, with an airline representative directing passengers to automated check-in machines. In almost no time, Krista had her seat assignment. She didn't need to check her bag because it was carry-on size.

If Krista had taken her grandmother's advice and boxed up her Christmas present from Alex, she could have checked that. A few days ago, that was exactly what she intended to do. After her encounter with Alex at the park, however, Krista had deliberately left the landscape photo behind. The memories that would surface whenever she looked at it would be too painful to endure.

Her father was exactly where he said he'd be, his wheelchair facing in her direction. After spotting no sign of her mother, Krista slowly headed in her father's direction.

Talk to him, Alex had advised. Here was Krista's chance, if only she were gutsy enough to take it.

"You all set?" he asked.

"All set." Krista lowered herself into an uncomfortable chair beside his wheelchair, feeling the tension building inside her.

Her father cleared his throat and watched the parade of people pass by. Some of them were in pairs, talking animatedly to one another as though trying to squeeze in as many words as possible before one of them boarded a flight. Yet Krista's father said nothing.

Suddenly Krista couldn't stand it anymore.

"I'm sorry my being home was hard on you." Krista blurted out the apology, surprised that she'd finally said the words aloud. She'd been thinking them since she arrived.

"What?" The terse question came out sounding like another growl.

Krista's stomach pitched and rolled. Clearing the air with her father no longer seemed like such a good idea. Now that she'd started the conversation, however, she needed to finish it. "It's okay. I understand. It's only natural that having me around would bring up bad memories."

Her father cleared his throat and narrowed his eyes. "What are you talking about?"

"The forklift," she said in a quiet voice.

"What about the forklift?"

Krista reminded herself that Alex admired her for speaking her mind. "We both know you wouldn't be in that chair if it weren't for me."

Her father gasped. "You think I blame you for the accident?"

"It was my fault," Krista said.

"It was an *accident*," he countered.

Krista shook her head back and forth, wondering why he'd try to convince her of something that was patently not true.

"You don't have to say that, Dad," she said. "I didn't want to be working at the nursery that day so I was careless. I know I was to blame."

A tortured look crossed his face. "What you said before, about believing it's hard on me to have you home. Is that why you stayed away so long?"

Krista had only recently admitted that was the reason to herself. "I wanted to make things easier for you."

"You think it's easy for me to have you thousands of miles away?" he cried. "You're my daughter, damn it!"

"But…but you told me to go to Prague," Krista said. "Mom was so against it. You were the one who encouraged me to take the job."

"Only because I learned life could be cut short at any time," he bellowed. "If there's something you're itching to do, you've got to do it."

Something Krista had never understood started to make sense. "Is that why Rayna's going to school to be a dental hygienist instead of going into business with you?"

"Hell, yes," her father said. "It's why I'm writing that children's book, too."

"What?" Krista couldn't believe she'd heard him correctly. "You're writing a book?"

"You didn't know?" He looked flabbergasted. "What do you think I'm doing in my office all day?"

"Writing a book," Krista said, wonder in her voice.

"That's what I just said."

Krista stared at her father, seeing him clearly for perhaps the first time. "What's your book about?"

"A boy in a wheelchair. He discovers he can do all sorts of things he never imagined were possible when he could walk."

Krista could barely speak past the lump in her throat. "Sounds inspiring."

"It's based on a true story." Her father was still snarling, but Krista detected an undercurrent of tenderness. "So we'll have no more of this nonsense about me blaming you."

Krista nodded, still unable to speak.

"And you'll visit more often than once every eight years." It sounded more like an order than a request. For once, Krista didn't mind.

"Okay," she managed to choke out.

He made a noise low in his throat that caused Krista to suspect the emotion of the moment might have gotten to him, too. He crossed his arms over his chest.

"Where's Alex, anyway?" he asked brusquely.

She'd believed the pain was gone, but it returned in an instant. "Why do you ask?" she ventured.

"I'm handicapped, not blind."

Krista bit her lip, thinking it was bizarre that she was having this conversation with her father, of all people. "We had, um, a bit of a disagreement."

"He didn't want you to leave," her dad guessed.

"Something like that," Krista said.

"I don't blame him," he said. "Neither do I."

A tear seeped out of the corner of Krista's eye. She

wiped it away but more tears fell when her mother joined them. All too quickly, it was time to say good-bye at the security checkpoint leading to the gate.

"Don't cry, sweet girl," her mother said. "Just come visit us more often."

"What do you know, your mother and I finally agree." Her father would have seemed like his own abrupt self if Krista hadn't noticed him blinking rapidly.

"You won't be able to keep me away," Krista said.

Krista wasn't fully in control of herself until she got through security and reached the gate. She chose a seat that had a vantage point of runways entirely cleared of snow. The skies were brighter than they'd been since she arrived in Jarrell eight days ago. So much had happened, it seemed incredible so little time had passed.

"Attention, passengers of flight 527," a voice over the loudspeaker said. "We have an important announcement."

Krista sat up straight, one possibility running through her mind. The quickest route to Prague when she'd rebooked her flight had been through Newark International. Krista hadn't heard a weather report, but it was entirely possible it was snowing in New Jersey. If so, her flight would be delayed or possibly canceled.

"We have a gate change. Flight 527 will now be leaving from Gate 12B," the tinny voice continued. "Please make your way to Gate 12B."

Everything inside Krista deflated, like an air balloon that had been popped with a needle. Alex was right, she realized. All along she'd been silently rooting for cancellations.

Because it was time to stop running.

That was what she'd done eight years ago when she

moved to Prague. With startling clarity, she realized that she'd allowed her involvement in her father's accident to shape her life.

She still wouldn't have stayed in Jarrell even if her father hadn't been paralyzed. She'd hated working at the nursery and had an innate wanderlust. But she never would have started to put down roots so far away from home.

She loved and missed her family too much to see them so seldom.

And now she was running again for no good reason except she'd fallen in love with a man who was determined to stay put.

Not only hadn't she admitted she loved Alex, she also hadn't tried hard enough to work out a compromise so they could be together.

"Did you catch that announcement about the gate change?" The young woman two chairs down from Krista was gathering her bags and standing up. Her long, straight blond hair reminded Krista of Rayna.

"I heard." Krista made no move to get up.

The woman beamed a friendly smile her way. "Don't wait too long. Our flight's about to board. I'll see you at the other gate, then."

"No," Krista said with conviction, "you won't."

The woman titled her head, bemusement evident on her fresh, open face. "Excuse me?"

"I'm not getting on the plane," Krista said. "I'm spending New Year's Eve right here."

"At the airport?" the blonde asked.

Krista laughed, feeling suddenly giddy. "No, in Jarrell. With Alex. He's the man I love."

"Good for you," the woman said. "The holidays are all about being with the people you love."

"Exactly." Krista scooped up her carry-on and hurried through the terminal, in the opposite direction of the gate. She walked so quickly she was nearly running, but that was okay. This time, she was running toward something.

Her steps slowed as a terrible thought occurred to her. This wasn't the first time she'd left Alex. It was the second.

Had Alex finally had enough in that snowy parking lot on the mountain when she'd thrown his gift of love back in his face? He knew what time she was leaving this morning, yet he hadn't dropped by the house.

Was she already too late to convince Alex that she finally understood that home truly was where the heart was?

She passed the security checkpoint at a much slower clip, plotting her next move, wondering how to convince Alex to give their relationship another chance.

"Krista!"

At the sound of her name, she raised her head. Alex was in the terminal heading straight toward her, looking tall and handsome and dear. Hope leaped in her heart.

"You came to say goodbye," she said.

He stopped steps from her and held up what looked suspiciously like a boarding pass.

"Not exactly," he said.

ALEX COULDN'T READ ANYTHING other than confusion in Krista's expression. He could identify with the feeling. Until everything had clicked into place this morning, that was exactly how he'd felt.

"I didn't intend to see you off at all," Alex said. "But

then I looked out the window and saw the van driving away with you in it. And that's when I knew."

"That you should have said goodbye?" she asked.

He was explaining this badly yet it was vital he get the words right. "I knew that the person I loved most would be in Prague on New Year's Eve while I was in Pennsylvania."

Krista gasped softly and brought a hand to her mouth. He couldn't decipher the meaning of her reaction so he kept on talking.

"I meant to give it another shot...convincing you to stay here for New Year's Eve," Alex said. "But I got to the airport too late. So I bought a ticket to Prague."

He could read her expression now. She seemed astounded.

"I want to spend the New Year's holiday with you, Krista," he said, "whether it's in Pennsylvania or the Czech Republic."

Her first hand joined her second so they both covered her mouth. Her eyes went wide.

"But I don't want us to be together only on the holiday," Alex said. "I want it to be all the time."

He was talking a lot, which seemed more evident because she wasn't speaking at all. It was time, however, that he laid it all on the line.

"I have a call into Malt Green to see how he'd feel about doing theme calendars of European landscapes," Alex said. "If that doesn't fly, I'll do freelance work."

The commotion of the airport was all around them, with people hurrying to catch their flights, regular announcements at the security checkpoint about items that couldn't be taken on a flight and the buzz of conversation. Krista still said nothing.

"For a woman who's usually so outspoken," he said, "you're awfully quiet."

Her hands dropped from her mouth. "Do you really mean you'd move to Prague for me? What about your father?"

"He convinced me he knew how to use a phone," Alex said. "He probably figured out I need you more than he needs me."

Krista was silent again, awe in her eyes. "I'm trying to wrap my mind around the fact that you still love me after what I said on that mountain."

"I've loved you for eight years," he said. "I'm not about to stop now."

"I think I've loved you that long, too. I should have told you so on the mountain. Can you forgive me?"

"I can forgive you anything."

She stepped toward him, and he wrapped her in his arms. Finally, he thought, he had her where he wanted her. He kissed her as thoroughly as he had that first time at the scenic overlook. A part of him must have known even then that this was the woman with whom he wanted to spend his life. Otherwise, he wouldn't have gone back up on the mountain and snapped that photo.

Except there was something even the sweetness of her kiss couldn't clear up. The flight board listing departures and arrivals had indicated her plane was boarding. He lifted his head but didn't let her go.

"Why aren't you at the gate?" he asked.

"Because I was praying for snow."

"Come again?"

"You were right about me not wanting to leave," Krista said. "I'll have to call Becca and apologize for not helping with her party. Because there's nowhere I'd rather spend New Year's Eve than in Jarrell with you."

"We can pay the change fees and fly to Prague after the New Year," Alex said, his brain working out scenarios. Hopefully that would be enough time to get his affairs in order. "We might even be able to travel there together."

Krista reached up and touched his cheek, smiling up at him. "Good. I'll call my boss tomorrow and give notice. Then you can help me pack."

He felt his brows crease. "Pack? Where are you going?"

She laughed. "I'm moving back to Jarrell."

"What?" He couldn't have been more shocked. "I thought Jarrell wasn't your kind of place."

"It's grown on me," Krista said. "I disliked the nursery but I enjoy the Christmas Shoppe. I think I can be a help Grandma and Mom. I have lots of ideas about how to make it profitable year-round. Imagine how much more business we could do if we put up a website and filled orders over the internet? I'd love to be in charge of that project."

"Would that be enough for you?"

"I can still do Czech translations on a freelance basis without physically being in the country. And I think it would be fun to start a geography club at the senior center."

"What about your dad?" he asked. "How do things stand between you and him?"

"I took your advice and talked to him," she said. "He doesn't blame me for the accident."

"That's great," Alex said. Still, he hardly dared get his hopes up. "But will you be happy in Jarrell?"

"Not if I live with my parents, I won't. I love my

family but I need my own space." She touched his cheek. "I'm planning to convince you to share it with me."

"It won't take much convincing." Alex planned to spend as much time with her as possible. "But to stay on your mom's good side, I won't move in with you. Not right away, anyhow."

"I'm okay with taking our time, but I should warn you that you were right about something else. I want a family." She smiled. "And I want it with you."

He pointed to his chest. "I'm a family man."

"But are you a traveling man?" she asked. "I'll go crazy if we never leave Jarrell."

"Not a problem," Alex said. "I have a job offer on the table that will solve that problem. If I take it, you can travel with me whenever you want."

"That job would be perfect for you!" She threw her arms around his neck, then drew back. "But what about Costas Landscaping?"

"Dad has someone else interested in becoming his new partner," Alex said.

"Who's that?" Krista asked.

"Trey Farina."

Krista's smile started slow, then widened. Not only would Krista have a happy ending, but it also looked like her sister would, too. "I've got a feeling we're all going to have a very happy New Year."

"You can bet on it," he said and kissed her again, the promise of their future together shining merry and bright.

EPILOGUE

Almost one year later

STRINGS OF MULTICOLORED LIGHTS, strands of glittery snowflake garland and an abundance of shiny ornaments covered the seven-foot artificial Christmas tree in the family room of Krista's rented house in Jarrell. The green of the branches was visible, but barely.

"What a beautiful tree!" Grandma exclaimed.

"Stunning!" Mom added.

"Sparkly," Milo said.

"Okay," Dad proclaimed.

"Interesting," Alex whispered close to Krista's ear, making her nerve endings tingle. But then almost everything Alex did had that effect on her. He was standing behind her, his arms loosely circling her from behind, as the group she'd invited over for dinner got their first look at her tree.

"I like the tree, but who decorated it?" Alex continued in an equally quiet voice. "Surely not the woman who thinks excess is tacky."

Krista was too used to Alex's teasing to go on the defensive. Besides, how could she when the outside of her house was plastered with lights and yard art that blinked on and off? Krista was especially partial to the dazzling snowman angel and the reindeer dancing on two legs.

"I have to be excessive," Krista whispered back. "Now I'm in the business of selling the stuff."

"You know, Krista, you could let the rest of us in on what you're talking about." Mom was back to her blustery self, complete with healthy color in her cheeks. It was as though last year's health scare with the bleeding ulcers had never occurred.

"Leave them alone, Ellie," Krista's father scolded. "Krista hasn't seen Alex all week."

Alex had been in South Dakota, photographing snowy images of Mount Rushmore for an upcoming calendar from Greenscapes Ltd. Krista traveled with him most of the time when he was on assignment, but not during the busy holiday season at Novaks' Christmas Shoppe. Their internet orders were already filled and shipped but they'd had more traffic inside the shop today than at any time of the year. Of course, it was only two days before Christmas.

"Krista sees him plenty," Mom retorted. "Alex is always over here."

Here was the cute brick Cape Cod Krista had been lucky enough to move into when she'd returned to Jarrell. Ironically the previous owner had rented out the house to Krista because he'd been transferred to Europe for his job. Alex still officially lived with his father, but it felt like the house was as much his as hers. He'd put in a handicap ramp so her father could visit and hired a friend to switch the carpet in the living areas to hardwood.

"Of course they're always together. They're in love. I wish I was." Grandma's romance with Charlie Crosby hadn't worked out, although they'd stayed friends. "I'm thinking of going back to the internet to find a beau."

Uh-oh, Krista thought. *Here we go again.*

The front door opened. Trey stepped over the threshold, toting a baby carrier with a blanket lightly draped over it, Rayna at his side. They were both dusted with white snowflakes.

"Merry Christmas!" Rayna called.

Krista knew better than to try to beat her mother and grandmother to the door. Mom reached the carrier first, turned back the blanket and reached inside. Lifting five-month-old Jake Farina from the carrier, she kissed him on his chubby cheek.

"I get to hold him next," Grandma cried.

Krista raised her hand. "I'm in line, too."

"Me, too," her father said gruffly. It turned out he had a soft spot for kids. He didn't have a publisher for his children's book but it was making the rounds through an agent at various houses.

"You're all going to spoil him," Rayna said. "Not that I blame you. How could you not?"

"I'm the worst," Trey said. "As soon as he whimpers, I pick him up."

"You're a great dad." Rayna stood on tiptoe and kissed Trey lingeringly on the lips. Once they'd shed their coats, she took her husband by the hand and led him to the family room.

"It started snowing. Pretty hard, too," Trey announced. "I'm glad I'm driving the company truck with the plow."

"Better you than me, buddy." Alex tightened his arms around Krista and dropped a kiss on her hair. "Although the snow's been good to me. Last year, it kept Krista from leaving."

The sight of the tree didn't faze Rayna, but then she'd helped Krista decorate it. Rayna's eyes danced as they met Krista's. "Well? Did you tell them yet?"

"Tell us what?" Mom looked over her grandson's head at Krista and Alex.

Krista exchanged a look with Alex over her shoulder. He nodded. All the most important people in their lives were present. There was no reason to wait.

"As of next week," Krista said, "I'll no longer be a renter. I'm buying the house."

"Oh, for goodness' sake, Krista!" her mother exclaimed. "I thought you and Alex were making things official."

"Give her a break, Ellie," Dad said. "Buying a house is a good investment."

"I think it's wonderful," Grandma said. "But how can you afford it, Krista?"

"*I* can't afford it. *We* can." Krista reached into the pocket of her slacks, slipped what was inside on her finger and held up her left hand to display a princess-cut ruby flanked by two smaller diamonds set in a white-gold engagement ring. "Alex and I are getting married this spring."

The room erupted with squeals, words of congratulations and praise for the Christmassy nature of the ring. Krista hadn't been hugged so much since last year when everyone thought she was returning to Prague.

"Have you given the destination wedding any more thought?" Rayna asked when the commotion died down. Her sister had known about the engagement because Krista had called her last night after Alex returned from his trip to South Dakota and gave her the ring.

"We decided to have a destination honeymoon instead. Alex is taking me to the Greek islands," Krista said. "We're getting married in Jarrell, somewhere Dad can walk me down the aisle."

"You'll be walking," her father said. "I'll be rolling."

Krista's mother gave her husband a penetrating look. "Joe, you haven't seemed very surprised by this engagement."

"I'm not," he said. "Alex called me from South Dakota and asked for my permission."

Krista gaped at Alex. "You did?"

"Sure did," he said. "I don't want to get on Joe's bad side. I know how much he loves you."

Krista felt her eyes tear up, aware she had Alex to thank for her improved relationship with her father. Behind Alex, hanging on a prominent spot on the wall, she caught a glimpse of the framed photograph he'd given her for Christmas last year.

She didn't need the view from the place where she and Alex had first kissed to remind her of how she felt about him. The love burned in her heart now and always, but perhaps even more so during the holiday season on snowy nights.

Something Alex had told her last year during one of the blizzards ran through her mind. She laughed, impulsively kissing him on the mouth and reveling in his immediate response.

When she let him go, she said, "Let it snow, let it snow, let it snow."

* * * * *

HEART & HOME

Heartwarming romances where love can
happen right when you least expect it.

COMING NEXT MONTH
AVAILABLE DECEMBER 6, 2011

#1746 THE COST OF SILENCE
Hometown U.S.A.
Kathleen O'Brien

#1747 THE TEXAN'S CHRISTMAS
The Hardin Boys
Linda Warren

#1748 BECAUSE OF THE LIST
Make Me a Match
Amy Knupp

#1749 THE BABY TRUCE
Too Many Cooks?
Jeannie Watt

#1750 A SOUTHERN REUNION
Going Back
Lenora Worth

#1751 A DELIBERATE FATHER
Suddenly a Parent
Kate Kelly

REQUEST YOUR FREE BOOKS!
2 FREE NOVELS PLUS 2 FREE GIFTS!

❧ Harlequin®

Super Romance®

Exciting, emotional, unexpected!

YES! Please send me 2 FREE Harlequin® Superromance® novels and my 2 FREE gifts (gifts are worth about $10). After receiving them, if I don't wish to receive any more books, I can return the shipping statement marked "cancel." If I don't cancel, I will receive 6 brand-new novels every month and be billed just $4.69 per book in the U.S. or $5.24 per book in Canada. That's a saving of at least 15% off the cover price! It's quite a bargain! Shipping and handling is just 50¢ per book in the U.S. and 75¢ per book in Canada.* I understand that accepting the 2 free books and gifts places me under no obligation to buy anything. I can always return a shipment and cancel at any time. Even if I never buy another book, the two free books and gifts are mine to keep forever.

135/336 HDN FC6T

Name	(PLEASE PRINT)	
Address		Apt. #
City	State/Prov.	Zip/Postal Code

Signature (if under 18, a parent or guardian must sign)

Mail to the **Reader Service:**
IN U.S.A.: P.O. Box 1867, Buffalo, NY 14240-1867
IN CANADA: P.O. Box 609, Fort Erie, Ontario L2A 5X3

Not valid for current subscribers to Harlequin Superromance books.
Are you a current subscriber to Harlequin Superromance books and want to receive the larger-print edition?
Call 1-800-873-8635 or visit www.ReaderService.com.

* Terms and prices subject to change without notice. Prices do not include applicable taxes. Sales tax applicable in N.Y. Canadian residents will be charged applicable taxes. Offer not valid in Quebec. This offer is limited to one order per household. All orders subject to credit approval. Credit or debit balances in a customer's account(s) may be offset by any other outstanding balance owed by or to the customer. Please allow 4 to 6 weeks for delivery. Offer available while quantities last.

Your Privacy—The Reader Service is committed to protecting your privacy. Our Privacy Policy is available online at www.ReaderService.com or upon request from the Reader Service.

We make a portion of our mailing list available to reputable third parties that offer products we believe may interest you. If you prefer that we not exchange your name with third parties, or if you wish to clarify or modify your communication preferences, please visit us at www.ReaderService.com/consumerchoice or write to us at Reader Service Preference Service, P.O. Box 9062, Buffalo, NY 14269. Include your complete name and address.

HSR11

Lucy Flemming and Ross Mitchell shared a magical, sexy Christmas weekend together six years ago. This Christmas, history may repeat itself when they find themselves stranded in a major snowstorm... and alone at last.

Read on for a sneak peek from
IT HAPPENED ONE CHRISTMAS
by Leslie Kelly.

Available December 2011, only from Harlequin® Blaze™.

EYEING THE GRAY, THICK SKY through the expansive wall of windows, Lucy began to pack up her photography gear. The Christmas party was winding down, only a dozen or so people remaining on this floor, which had been transformed from cubicles and meeting rooms to a holiday funland. She smiled at those nearest to her, then, seeing the glances at her silly elf hat, she reached up to tug it off her head.

Before she could do it, however, she heard a voice. A deep, male voice—smooth and sexy, and so not Santa's.

"I appreciate you filling in on such short notice. I've heard you do a terrific job."

Lucy didn't turn around, letting her brain process what she was hearing. Her whole body had stiffened, the hairs on the back of her neck standing up, her skin tightening into tiny goose bumps. Because that voice sounded so familiar. *Impossibly* familiar.

It can't be.

"It sounds like the kids had a great time."

Unable to stop herself, Lucy began to turn around, wondering if her ears—and all her other senses—were deceiving her. After all, six years was a long time, the mind could play tricks. What were the odds that she'd bump into *him*, here? And today of all days. December 23.

Six years exactly. Was that really possible?

One look—and the accompanying frantic thudding of her heart—and she knew her ears and brain were working just fine. Because it was *him*.

"Oh, my God," he whispered, shocked, frozen, staring as thoroughly as she was. "Lucy?"

She nodded slowly, not taking her eyes off him, wondering why the years had made him even more attractive than ever. It didn't seem fair. Not when she'd spent the past six years thinking he must have started losing that thick, golden-brown hair, or added a spare tire to that trim, muscular form.

No.

The man was gorgeous. Truly, without-a-doubt, mouthwateringly handsome, every bit as hot as he'd been the first time she'd laid eyes on him. She'd been twenty-two, he one year older.

They'd shared an amazing holiday season.

And had never seen one another again.

Until now.

Find out what happens in
IT HAPPENED ONE CHRISTMAS
by Leslie Kelly.
Available December 2011, only from Harlequin® Blaze™

LAURA MARIE ALTOM
brings you
another touching tale from

When family tragedy forces Wyatt Buckhorn to pair up
with his longtime secret crush, Natalie Poole, and care
for the Buckhorn clan's seven children, Wyatt worries
he's in over his head. Fearing his shameful secret will
be exposed, Wyatt tries to fight his growing attraction
to Natalie. As Natalie begins to open up to Wyatt,
he starts yearning for a family of his own—a family
with Natalie. But can Wyatt trust his heart enough
to reveal his secret?

A Baby in His Stocking

Available December
wherever books are sold!

SUSAN MEIER

**Experience the thrill of falling in love
this holiday season with**

Kisses on Her Christmas List

When Shannon Raleigh saw Rory Wallace staring at her
across her family's department store, she knew he would
be trouble…for her heart. Guarded, but unable to fight
her attraction, Shannon is drawn to Rory and his inquisitive
daughter. Now with only seven days to convince this
straitlaced businessman that what they feel for each other
is real, Shannon hopes for a Christmas miracle.

***Will the magic of Christmas be enough
to melt his heart?***

Available December 6, 2011.